THE CELTIC DECEPTION

IMBRIFEX
BOOKS

ALSO BY ANDREW VARGA

The Last Saxon King
A Jump in Time Novel, Book One

The
Celtic
Deception

A Jump in Time Novel
Book Two

Andrew Varga

IMBRIFEX BOOKS

IMBRIFEX BOOKS
8275 S. Eastern Avenue, Suite 200
Las Vegas, NV 89123
Imbrifex.com

IMBRIFEX.
BOOKS

THE CELTIC DECEPTION: A JUMP IN TIME NOVEL, BOOK TWO

Library of Congress Cataloging-in-Publication Data
Names: Varga, Andrew, 1969- author.
Title: The Celtic deception / Andrew Varga.
Description: Las Vegas : Imbrifex Books, [2023] | Series: A jump in time ; book 2 | Audience: Ages 12-19. | Audience: Grades 7-9. | Summary: In an attempt to block Victor Stahl's plot to take over the world, Dan and Sam jump to first-century Wales where they encounter druids, Celts, a Roman army intent on destroying everyone, and a fellow jumper stranded in time.
Identifiers: LCCN 2022044847 (print) | LCCN 2022044848 (ebook) | ISBN 9781945501869 (hardcover) | ISBN 9781945501890 (paperback) | ISBN 9781945501876 (epub) | ISBN 9781945501883
Subjects: CYAC: Time travel--Fiction. | Great Britain--History--Roman period, 55 B.C.-449 A.D--Fiction. | LCGFT: Historical fiction. | Novels. Classification: LCC PZ7.1.V39635 Ce 2023 (print) | LCC PZ7.1.V39635 (ebook) | DDC [Fic]--dc23
LC record available at https://lccn.loc.gov/2022044847
LC ebook record available at https://lccn.loc.gov/2022044848

Jacket design: Jason Heuer
Book design: Sue Campbell Book Design
Author photo: Andrew Johnson
Typeset in ITC Berkeley Oldstyle

Printed in the United States of America
Distributed by Publishers Group West
First Edition: September 2023

Once again for Pam, Leah,
Arawn, and Calvin

*Paulinus Suetonius obtinebat Britannos … igitur Monam insulam,
incolis validam et receptaculum perfugarum, adgredi parat … Stabat
pro litore diversa acies, densa armis virisque … Druidaeque circum,
preces diras sublatis ad caelum manibus fundentes*

Suetonius Paulinus ruled over the Britons …
He therefore prepared to attack the island of Mona, which had
a powerful population and was a shelter for refugees …
There stood along the shore hostile battle lines, thick with
arms and men … and druids all around, raising their hands to
heaven and pouring out dire prayers.

Publius Cornelius Tacitus
Annals
Book XIV, chapters 29 and 30
early second century

CHAPTER 1

My hand hovered over the doorknob to my condo. At the top corner of the door, almost invisible unless someone was intentionally looking for it, was the small piece of clear tape I had stuck across the door and the frame before I'd left for school. It was now split neatly in two—someone had broken into my place. Not that it surprised me. I'd always known Victor Stahl would come after me one day. Powerful men like him make sure to clean up all loose ends. And since I'd been the only person to witness him savagely stab my dad four months before, I was one big loose end.

If only I could call the cops. But the cops had been completely useless investigating the attack on my dad. I'd flat out told them that Victor was the guy who'd stabbed him, and they'd done nothing. They'd either been bought off to look the other way, or they didn't believe me because I was just some dumb seventeen-year-old with no evidence to back up my story, and he was a powerful congressman. No, the cops couldn't help—I'd have to handle this myself.

I took a deep breath and opened the door. Whistling to mask my nervousness, I tossed my backpack on the floor, hung up my coat, and headed for the living room. Even though I'd been expecting him, bile still rose to my throat when I spotted Victor sitting on my couch. He wore a dark blue pinstriped suit, and his neatly trimmed black hair was streaked with gray. He sat casually, like he owned the place, his right arm resting on the seat back.

He looked up at me with his dark, soulless eyes. "Master Renfrew, so good to see you again." He used a disgustingly friendly tone, as if his breaking into my house was a normal event and we'd just ignore the fact he'd left Dad in a coma and sit down to tea.

I glanced behind me, making sure my escape route was clear.

It wasn't.

Another man in a suit stepped out of the kitchen and crossed his arms over his chest, blocking my path to the door. This guy was built like a wrestler, with beefy arms, a thick neck, and an indifferent scowl that made me feel like a bug about to be squished. Somehow, none of my carefully thought-out plans had accounted for Victor bringing help.

"W-what are you doing here?" I stammered.

Victor shook his head in disappointment. "Now, Daniel, is that any way to treat a guest? I simply came to visit you and see how you are. It has been months since we last spoke."

Spoke? Was this guy freakin' serious?

The last time we "spoke," he'd just finished plunging a sword into Dad's chest. And the only speaking we'd done then was him barking orders at me. I curled my hands into fists to control the tremors of rage coursing through me. Every inch of me wanted to grab one of the medieval weapons displayed on the wall and ram it through his chest. I'd never make it, though. Victor was a great swordsman, and he'd brought muscle. I wasn't going to get out of this mess by fighting—I had to play it cool.

Victor waved toward one of the armchairs opposite the couch—as if it was his condo, not mine. "Please, sit. We have so much to talk about."

I perched on the edge of the chair, legs tensed, ready to bolt.

"So, Daniel, you left rather abruptly during our last meeting. Please tell me where you went."

"Why should I tell you anything? You tried to kill my dad."

"Ah, yes," Victor said, "a very unfortunate occurrence that I truly regret. How is your father? Has his condition improved? I send flowers every week."

I felt like puking. How dare he ask about my dad! "Call the hospital if you want to know how he is," I snapped. "Now can we skip the chitchat and get to the part where you tell me why you broke into my place?"

"Daniel, Daniel, Daniel," Victor sighed, like a disappointed schoolteacher. "I merely came here to have an amicable discussion about a few matters of importance. If your father had sat and listened to reason, he would not be in the hospital now. Unfortunately, he chose to cause problems." Victor leaned forward, his eyes narrowing. "Are *you* going to cause problems, Daniel?"

As if to emphasize the question, the guy in the suit cracked his knuckles. "No." I shook my head rapidly. "No problems."

"Good. Now if you answer a few questions to my satisfaction, I will be on my way." He steepled his fingers. "What happened while you were off in the past?"

"One minute I'm in my living room, watching you and Dad fighting … then Dad throws me some weird metal rod, I say this dumb rhyme that he'd taught me since I was a kid, there's a blinding flash of light, and, poof, I'm back in England in 1066. And amazingly I can speak and understand the language!"

Victor nodded. Clearly he was buying my story so far, which he should, since it was the truth. All my life I'd thought Dad was just some nerdy history professor. I had no clue that he belonged to a secret community of people who fixed glitches that appeared in the time stream and threatened to alter history. So when I'd accidentally teleported myself to medieval England, I stumbled around completely clueless for the first little while.

Now came the hard part—lying through my teeth about the rest of my time jump and hoping Victor didn't catch on. "I hid out in the village of Torp with a guy named Osmund," I continued. "I spent a few days there, picking cabbages and sleeping in the church … and then the rod suddenly warmed up and I could bring myself back home."

Victor stroked his chin thoughtfully, assessing my words. "Did you happen to encounter any other time travelers?"

You mean the two who got themselves killed while trying to kill me, or the one I can't stop thinking about?

"Don't think so," I said. "How would I know if I met one?"

Victor pointed to the tattoo on my right forearm—a black four-pointed star in a circle that I'd had for as long as I could remember. "All the community members bear that mark. Did you see anyone with this same tattoo?"

"No," I lied.

"Interesting," Victor responded, which he managed to make sound exactly like *I don't believe a word you're saying*. He gave a slight nod to the man by the door, and the huge goon walked over and stood behind my chair. I couldn't see him, and I couldn't hear him, but I could feel the menace radiating behind me. My hands began to tremble, and I gripped the armrests.

"Now, Daniel," Victor continued. "You have to forgive me if I do not have the utmost faith in everything you tell me. These are difficult times, and not everyone can be trusted." He leaned forward. "*Can I trust you?*"

I swallowed hard, and a trickle of sweat ran down my back. Victor didn't play games. This was a guy plotting to unleash a wave of global destruction that would kill billions, all so he and the other time jumpers allied with him could take over the world. I meant absolutely nothing to him. "Y-y-you can trust me."

He smiled, but his eyes remained cold, dark—reptilian. "Excellent! I hate it when people are dishonest. Nothing disappoints me more." He brushed the sleeve of his suit jacket, and his gold cuff links glinted in the light. "Now, Daniel, since it seems I can trust you, I want you to tell me what you feel about me."

This was a test, clearly, but what was the correct answer? Did he want me to say that I forgave him for stabbing Dad and that I hoped we could become the best of friends? Big nope. "I hate you," I said. "I hate your face. I hate your suits. I hate that you're in my house threatening me. I hope you get hit by a bus."

Victor clapped his hands and laughed. "See, Drake? I told you that young Daniel here was an honest boy. He would never lie to us."

"I still don't trust him," said the man behind me. "We should kill him."

"Wait!" I howled. "I'm telling you the truth!" I darted my head around, looking for a place to run. Drake had put the lock chain on my door, so even if I did get past him, there was no way I could get through the door before he caught me.

Victor tapped his lips with a finger. "That *would* be easier. But I am sure young Daniel here can be persuaded to be agreeable." He nodded at me. "Do you think we can come to an agreement, Daniel?"

"Yes!"

"Very good." He held out his hand to me. "Give me your time-travel device."

I wiped my hands on my pants, trying to remove the sheen of sweat that covered them. I couldn't give up my jump rod. Dad had taken a sword to the chest rather than surrender it to Victor. "Why do you want it?" I asked, trying to buy some time.

"For a simple reason. The members of our community should not be killing each other. There are so few of us left, and we perform such a vital task that it is sheer folly to continually shed blood among our ranks. However, I also believe that those who strive for greatness should not be hindered by those with small minds. The best way to stop you from causing any further problems is for me to take away your time-travel mechanism. If your father had only listened to this uncomplicated reasoning, he would not be in the hospital now." He waved his hand dismissively. "I do not believe in forcing people to do things. You can either bring me the mechanism willingly—and my associate and I will be on our way—or we will have to resort to measures that you will find much less palatable." He smiled at me. "I can assure you that no matter which path you choose, you will no longer be a threat to us and we will still have the device. The choice is yours." He leaned back and drummed his fingers on his knee, like he was waiting for a bus on a sunny day.

My heart pounded. Victor wanted the jump rod, and he was going to take it no matter what. Drake's meaty hands clamped down on my shoulders, keeping me firmly in my chair. His thick fingers were right beside my neck. All he had to do was squeeze. "I'll give you the rod," I said, my voice coming out as a squeak. "Just leave me alone."

"But of course," Victor soothed. "You will be free to lead a happy life. You can continue going to school, get a job, or do whatever other mundane things you had planned. Now go get me the mechanism."

Drake removed his hands from my shoulders and, for half a second, I thought about bolting, but I knew I'd never make it. I didn't trust Victor, and I definitely didn't trust Drake, but I'd always known this was the only way to get Victor off my back. I went over to the TV set. Underneath it sat a bin containing all the gear for my video games. I dug around in the pile of extra controllers, attachments, and cables, and pulled out a metallic rod about the size of a baton from a relay race. It was hexagonal, like a pencil, and divided into six segments. Strange glyphs were etched into each face.

"How very clever, Daniel," Victor said. "Hidden in plain sight. See, Drake, I told you the boy was smart. It would have taken us hours to find the device hidden there." He stood up from the couch and smoothed out the creases in his suit jacket before walking over to me and taking the rod from my hand. "Now, Master Renfrew, I do hope this concludes our business. You will find that I am a very fair man to those people I can call friends." He wrapped his hand around my wrist and slowly squeezed. I'd never felt such a tight grip; my bones felt like they were going to snap. I gasped and he yanked me even closer. "But never, *ever* go against me, Daniel."

He turned toward Drake. "Shall we leave now? I am sure young Daniel here has other plans for the evening." He picked up his overcoat from the arm of the couch and headed for the front door, with Drake following like an obedient dog.

I slammed the door behind them and locked it. With my back leaning against it, I took several slow deep breaths to try to calm myself but they did nothing to settle me. I just wanted to smash something. Victor had broken into my home and threatened to kill me. I felt so … violated. How could he just do whatever he wanted? I screamed as I pounded my fist against the wall. I wanted to kill him. I wanted to stop his insane plot. I wanted to make him pay for hurting my dad.

My shoulders slumped as my rage fizzled out of me. Who was I kidding? I'd never get to Victor. He was rich and powerful, and I was just some dumb kid who lived alone, barely surviving.

I sagged to the floor and pulled out my phone.

Vid call? I texted.

A few seconds later an answering text came back: OK when?

10 min

I couldn't stay here—the place reeked of Victor. What had he done while he was waiting for me to come home? Had he installed spy cameras? Bugged my rooms? I wasn't going to feel safe here for a very long time. At least not until I had ripped the place apart and made sure I wasn't being watched.

I took my phone and coat, applied a new piece of tape to the front door, and headed out into the street. Dusk had already started to fall, and the autumn wind had a chill to it. I turned a few corners and ended up at a coffee shop with free Wi-Fi. I got a doughnut and picked a small table near the back, where I could watch people but not be easily watched. I pulled out my phone. Within seconds the screen lit up, and Sam's mane of red hair and lightly freckled face appeared on screen.

"Hey," I said casually, as if the mere sight of her didn't take my breath away and twist my insides all up in knots.

"Hey. What's up?"

"Victor came to my house today."

Her green eyes widened. "You okay?"

"I've been better. He didn't hurt me, but he took the jump device."

She leaned closer to her screen, eyebrows raised in a question she didn't need to voice.

I shook my head. "I told him I never got out of the village I landed in. He asked me a few questions about his missing guys, but I played dumb. And he seems to still have no clue that you exist."

"Thanks." She smiled in relief. "Did you get any information out of him?"

"No. He asked all the questions; I could only answer. He brought muscle with him, too. I'm lucky they didn't kill me."

Sam's brow creased with concern. "You sure you're okay? You look pretty upset."

"Of course I'm upset! The guy broke into my place, pushed me around, and I couldn't do a thing. I felt so powerless."

Sam nodded sympathetically. "We'll get him."

"How? The guy can do anything he wants."

"You know how. Our only chance is to jump again."

An ache formed in my stomach. I hated time-jumping. On my first and only experience, I'd been stabbed, put on trial for murder, had my skull almost caved in with a war hammer, and fought on the front line of one of the most important battles of medieval history. Except for meeting Sam, time-jumping was just one nightmare after another.

But unfortunately, she was right: there was no other way to stop Victor. In our time, he was too strong, too protected. In the four months since we'd come back from England, Sam and I had done absolutely nothing against him. Things were different in history, though. In England we had taken out two of Victor's morons and even learned the first hazy details of his plot. Who knew what might happen on another time jump?

"All right," I grumbled. "So I guess we're stuck in a holding pattern until the next glitch pops up?"

"Yup. Could be next week—or next year. We just have to be ready to jump out whenever it comes."

"Yeah, yeah. I know," I muttered. It was killing me not to know when the next glitch would happen, but there was no way around it. Glitches were totally random. Trying to predict one was like trying to guess winning lottery numbers.

We talked for about half an hour, then I packed up and headed home. To my relief, the tape wasn't broken this time. I spent the next few hours ransacking my apartment, looking for any surveillance equipment Victor might have planted. I tossed books off shelves, ripped armor and weapons off the walls, and flung cushions to the floor but found nothing.

When I was finally satisfied that the place was clean, I went into the laundry room and pulled the large box of detergent off the shelf. With one hand I dug deep into the soapy powder like I was searching for the prize in a box of cereal. My fingers closed around a metal rod exactly like the one I had given Victor. A smile snuck across my face. No matter how much I hated time-jumping, I hated Victor even more. And with this other jump rod, I was ready to go back in history as soon as the next time glitch came around.

CHAPTER 2

Waiting for a new glitch to appear became a daily agony. I'd wake up, drag myself to school, and sit through one boring class after another, barely paying attention. Every time the bell rang I'd rush to my locker and check on the jump device to see if it had gone cold, signifying that somewhere in time a problem needed to be fixed. And every time, I was disappointed.

After school, I'd keep the rod close while I made dinner, watched TV, called the hospital to see if Dad's condition had changed, did my homework, and texted Sam. Then, while normal teenagers were hanging out, having fun, or just plain relaxing, I'd spend my night going through history book after history book, trying to pretty much memorize the entire freakin' span of human existence.

It was soul-crushing, but I had to do it. On my first time jump I'd been lucky and landed in Anglo-Saxon England—the history of which I knew fairly well—so I'd managed to figure out what the source of the glitch was. Even still, it took me forever to fix, and I almost died in the process. Next time I might not be so lucky. The thought of bumbling around somewhere in the past, even more clueless than I had been in England, scared the hell out of me. The only way to improve my chances of surviving and fixing the next glitch was to cram in as much history as possible.

As I flipped the page on the latest book that I'd pulled from Dad's collection, I shook my head. It was the first Friday night in November. All day at school, the only thing anyone had been talking about was the huge party that night at Jayden Patel's house, and here I was, reading. Not that I'd been invited, but it still sucked to know that everyone else my age was off having fun while I was studying. For about the millionth time I wished I'd paid more attention to Dad. He'd tried to teach me all this history stuff during my years of homeschooling, getting me to translate huge chunks of Latin texts, lecturing me for hours on famous battles and people, and making me memorize never-ending lists of dates and events. But since he'd never bothered to tell me anything at all about time-jumping, I always learned just enough to pass my tests. Now I was paying for that mistake.

I kept flipping through page after page until the words began to blur and my mind felt like it was going to liquefy and start dripping out my ears. At midnight I gave up and staggered off to bed, the jump rod clutched in my hand.

My side felt really cold, like I was sleeping on a wet washcloth.

What the … ?

Blearily I opened my eyes and rolled over to peer at my phone on the night stand: 3:27 a.m.

I flopped back on the bed, and my spine hit something cold and hard.

The rod! I jerked upright and grabbed my phone.

A text from Sam appeared: **U ready?**

5 min, I sent back.

I leaped out of bed, flicked on the bedroom light, and changed into the tunic and pants I had brought back from my Anglo-Saxon trip, a woolen cloak I'd bought at a medieval fair, and a pair of leather boots. Pausing for a second in front of the mirror, I nodded. Not bad. As long as I landed anywhere in Europe between Roman times and the Middle Ages, I'd probably fit in with only a few minor adjustments. That was a crucial part of time-jumping that I'd learned on my last trip—to always look like I belonged. Looking like an outsider only brought trouble.

In the living room, I considered my wall of weapons. Swords, axes, knives, and other medieval instruments of death stretched from floor to ceiling, the leftovers of my dad's career as a time jumper.

Swords were my preference. But what type? Every time period and region had its own style of sword and quality of steel. Showing up with too nice a weapon would draw attention to me, for sure.

Better play it safe.

I grabbed a wooden staff off the wall and headed into the kitchen, where I had prepacked a cloth backpack full of trail mix and two filled leather water skins.

Outfit? Check.

Weapon? Check.

Food? Check.

No use delaying any longer. I pulled out my phone, ready to text Sam that I was ready to jump, when a horrible realization hit me. In all the months of daily texting, we'd never once talked about how we'd find each other. On my first time jump I had just kind of landed close to her campsite, and she'd found me. But was that luck, or did the jump devices intentionally drop people close to each other? What if we weren't so lucky this time?

How will I find you? I texted.

For a few seconds Sam didn't respond, then she texted: We'll figure it out, followed a second later by: Just don't do what you did last time. 😜

Of course Sam would remind me of the first time we met. She still found it hilarious that I'd been shouting at the top of my lungs for help. How was I supposed to know that I had gone a thousand years back in time?

Funny, I texted. RU ready?

Leaving now.

I shut off my phone and buried it at the bottom of the overflowing garbage bin under the sink. If Victor broke in while I was gone, the last thing I wanted was him finding my phone and learning about Sam.

Then I gripped the rod and chanted the rhyme that Dad had made me memorize when I was a kid. *"Azkabaleth virros ku, haztri valent bhidri du!"*

The glyphs etched into the rod glowed with an intensity that bathed the room in white light, and I shut my eyes against the glare. A second later my body felt weightless, like I was floating in space. Up, down, left, right: all of it became meaningless. I wasn't sure whether I was moving or standing still. All I could feel was a bright light pressing against my eyes, forcing me to keep them shut.

As I floated through this shining void, my entire body trembled with excitement. Even though I'd done it before, the concept still blew my mind. Time travel shouldn't exist. Glitches in history shouldn't exist. And little rods that whisked me off through time and space just by mumbling some rhyme definitely shouldn't exist. But here I was, hurtling through time and space, about to land somewhere in history.

The brightness vanished and my feet hit solid ground. But something wasn't right—the ground felt sloped, as if I was standing on a hill. For half a second I fought to keep myself upright, then a wave of dizziness knocked me off my feet. I landed on my side and began rolling downhill, crashing through underbrush. I clutched my jump device and staff to prevent them from flying away as my body tumbled over roots, saplings, and rocks before finally coming to a stop in a shallow depression, in what felt like a grove of ferns.

I'd survived another time jump. Now to figure out what kind of mess I was in.

Panting heavily, and with my stomach still roiling from the after-effects of time travel, I blinked away the huge purple spots that blurred my vision. I was lying on a hill, staring up past the branches of pines and deciduous trees. The air felt warm but not hot, and the leaves on the trees were light green, like new growth. It looked like springtime in some northern part of the world.

First objective—don't get killed. My one-man avalanche had probably made enough noise to alert half the forest to my arrival. If anyone hostile was on their way to find me, my best chance of survival lay in seeing them before they spotted me.

I tucked the jump device into the back waist of my pants where it couldn't be seen and then belly crawled along the ground to slither under a large bush. From my hiding spot, I propped myself up on my elbows and scanned the forest for movement. Leaves waved lazily on their branches, birds flitted from tree to tree, and a few squirrels scurried between the trees. Everything looked normal so far, but I stayed rooted in my hiding spot. On my last time jump I'd been sloppy and overanxious to get the job done and go home—and I'd almost died twice because of it. Patience was my guiding principle now. I wouldn't leave this spot until I was positive no one hostile was out there. Only then would I try to find Sam.

About fifty steps away, a flicker of movement caught my eyes. I lowered my head to the ground and held my breath. A bead of sweat trickled down the back of my neck, and my fingers tightened on my staff.

A few seconds later a figure dressed in gray glided through the forest, soundless, and the tension eased from my body. Only one person I knew moved like that—Sam. She had on the same outfit she'd worn the first time we met: soft brown leather boots, baggy gray pants and tunic, and a drab-green cloak with its hood pulled up to hide her hair and face. In her hands she gripped a bow with an arrow nocked. Her head moved slowly from side to side, keeping watch as she crept forward.

I poked my head out from under the bush and waved her over. I knew I had a stupid grin on my face, but I didn't care. I was so glad she'd found me. I didn't think I could make it through this time jump alone.

She raised a finger to her lips and stalked closer until she crouched next to me. "Hi," she whispered. "Anyone else around?"

"I don't think so," I whispered back. "I just landed a few minutes ago."

"A few minutes?" Her brow furrowed. "Did you take a nap or something? I've been here for like an hour already, waiting for you to show."

"Right after I saw your text I hung up my phone, hid it, and then jumped straight out."

"Weird," Sam muttered. "I'll never understand how a few seconds at home can translate to hours in a jump. Anyway, at least you made it, and once again, you made it easy to find you." Sam smirked as she looked me up and down, taking in the dry leaves and dirt still clinging to my cloak from when I rolled downhill. "Any thoughts about where we are?"

I gestured to the trees. "The forest looks similar to what we had in England, so I'm guessing somewhere in northern Europe. Springtime, maybe? What year, I have no clue. You?"

She tilted her head to the side and gave me an are-you-kidding-me look. "They're trees, Dan. They look the same no matter what year it is."

"I know that," I said defensively. "But I thought you might have

seen something else while you were waiting for me. You know, a happy
villager or a big 'Welcome to the Sixteenth Century' sign?"

"No villagers, and definitely no signs." She looked over my shoulder
toward the lower part of the slope. "But if we head downhill, we should
find a river or a trail we can follow. At some point there's got to be a
village."

I got up from my hiding spot and brushed the forest muck off my
cloak and pants. "It's great to see you again, Sam."

"Yeah, yeah," she said dismissively, adjusting the jump rod she had
tucked into her archery bracer. "We can catch up later. Let's worry
about not dying first, okay?" She began heading downhill, picking her
way from tree to tree.

Great … Smooth move, Dan.

I'd been around Sam for two minutes and I'd already forgotten
that hostile locals or Victor's guys could be lurking anywhere, ready
to pounce. I followed her through the woods, constantly sweeping the
forest with my gaze. She practically floated across the ground, making less noise than a chipmunk. I muddled along after her, somehow
stomping on every dried leaf and fallen twig in the forest. A few times
she turned around and silently shushed me. All I could do was shrug.

As we neared the bottom of the hill, Sam waved her hand down.
I dropped to the ground, and she dived down beside me. Ahead of
us a wide dirt path cut through the forest. "Someone's coming," she
whispered.

All I could hear was the creaking of branches and the rustle of the
leaves. "I don't hear any—" Sam clapped her hand over my mouth.

Four tall blond men came striding along the path, each armed
with a long spear and holding an oblong shield that stretched from
shoulder to knee. None had armor. All wore pants and crude leather
shoes but went shirtless, revealing intricate designs painted in blue
on their bare chests and arms. They trod silently along the trail before

disappearing around the bend.

"I think they're Celts," I whispered. "Nobody else would have painted themselves blue like that."

"Geez … thanks, Dan," Sam replied sarcastically. "I thought the blue paint meant they were Smurfs." She rolled her eyes. "Can you maybe tell me something that isn't so obvious, like what tribe—or area—they're from?"

"You think I can figure that out just by some body paint?" It was my turn to give her a look of disbelief. "Celts lived everywhere from Ireland to the Middle East. Their civilization lasted over a thousand years. We could be pretty much anywhere, in any time."

We ducked low as the creak of wagons and the thump of feet came from down the road and a procession that must have been at least a hundred people long began to trudge past. Men pulled small two-wheeled carts piled high with wooden furniture, linens, and hand tools. Women carried wicker bushels filled with food and utensils. Even the children worked, herding sheep and goats, or carrying live chickens upside down by their feet. It was like an entire village had packed up their lives and decided to move. They didn't look thrilled about it, either. The adults all shared the same hunted look, and every few seconds someone would glance over their shoulder in the direction they'd just come from.

"Looks like they're running from something," I whispered to Sam.

She chewed her lip and her brow creased with concern. "Yeah … But what? Only something really—"

A rustle of underbrush warned of someone behind us.

Sam and I sprang to our feet, ready to fight, but then froze. Three men with their upper bodies covered in blue swirls stood steps away, their spears leveled at me and Sam.

CHAPTER 3

The lead Celt towered over us, his spear raised so its sharp point hovered just in front of my nose. His long blond mustache reached past his chin, and his hair was smeared with white goop so it stood up in spikes. "Where are the rest of the Romans?" he spat. His words came out in whatever Celtic dialect he spoke, but through the power of the jump rod pressed against my lower back, I understood everything as if I'd been speaking his language since birth.

With slow deliberate movements, Sam raised her hands above her head and then pulled back her hood, letting her red hair fall in shimmering waves around her shoulders. "Do I look like a Roman to you?" she asked, her words matching the man's dialect.

The Celt's eyes widened. He looked Sam up and down and then nodded appreciatively. "A maiden with fiery hair like the great Queen Boudicca herself." He winked at her. "Nay, you look nothing like one of those foul Romans. You look like a woman I would like to see more of." He lowered his spear point and gave her a huge smile. "I am called Atto, O pretty one. How are you called?"

Sam smiled back at him. "Genovefa."

"Such a beautiful name." Atto did a short bow. "Well, Genovefa, I am at your service. Are you well? Did this Roman—?"

"I'm not a Roman!" I snapped.

"Quiet, Roman!" Atto said. "We will let the chief decide on this matter."

Sam nodded in my direction, a slight smirk on her lips. "He isn't a Roman. He's with me."

Atto sidled up next to Sam and smoothly put his arm around her shoulder. "Although no false words could possibly pass your beautiful lips, I still must take you both to see the chief. The decision rests in his hands."

He nodded to his two men, and they pushed me toward the main track. The creep made sure to escort Sam himself. So while I got spear points leveled at me, she walked arm in arm with Atto. He was probably about twenty, muscular, and had a mouth that never shut. He kept up a constant chatter, talking about his prowess with the spear or in wrestling or about how many Romans he'd killed, all while piling on compliment after compliment to Sam. And she seemed to just suck it up. She clung to his every word, smiling back at him and asking him all sorts of lame questions that kept him babbling on.

As we picked our way downhill, I tried to think of a suitable backstory to explain who Sam and I were, and how we got here. The key to surviving in history was to not seem out of place, and these guys were already suspicious. Unfortunately, my knowledge of Celts was pretty limited. Except for some coins and a few scribbles on pottery or curse tablets, the only surviving records about the Celts were from Roman or Greek sources, and a lot of those were biased, so historians didn't have much to go on. I knew some general points about Celts, but nothing specific enough to help me pick out a name for myself or explain what we were doing here.

And it really didn't help that Sam and Atto kept distracting me by carrying on like they were on a first date. I'd known Sam for five months, and no matter how hard I tried to make things more serious between us, she still thought of me as a friend, or worse, a brother. But now some shirtless douchebag with a cheesy mustache pays her a few compliments and she's all smiles and chuckles? Please.

Thankfully, when we reached the road, Atto shut up. A few travelers glanced with disinterested expressions toward us, but just as quickly continued on their way. Wherever the group was headed was more important to them than Sam and I were. The only person who seemed remotely interested in us was a short, stocky man dressed in a fur-trimmed green cloak held in place by a large gold pin. He separated himself from the middle of the crowd and met us at the road's edge. He had long blond hair like the rest of the Celts, but it was thinner and going gray in places. He wore red-and-black-plaid pants, a silver-colored tunic belted at the waist, and around his neck glittered a thick ring of twisted gold. "Who are these sprites you found in the forest, Atto?"

Atto thumped his chest with his fist. "Lord Trenus, I found these two spying on you." He pointed at me. "His clothes make me believe he is a Roman. No man of the Ordovices would garb himself in that manner."

Ordovices? Probably a tribe name, but totally useless for helping me figure out what year it was. My knowledge of Celtic tribes was up there with my knowledge of high fashion—nonexistent. All I knew was that there were tons of them, and they spent as much time fighting each other as they spent fighting the Romans. If these guys pressed me for any sort of details about who Sam and I were, we'd be screwed.

Trenus walked in a slow circle around me, looking me up and down and feeling the fabric of my cloak and tunic. I tried not to fidget as he carried out his examination—even though he made me feel like a bug under a microscope. "Has your mind gone for a wander, Atto?"

Trenus finally asked. "This man is no Roman. Look at his hair and eyes—both are fair like yours and mine. And look at his weapon. He carries only a stick! No Roman would dare enter our lands so armed." He turned to me. "You, how are you called?"

"Umm ... Asterix!" I blurted, saying the first Celtic-sounding name that came to mind.

"Well, Asterix, which tribe do you belong to?"

Crap ... "Um ... well ... you probably never heard of our tribe. It's ... um ..."

"We're Iceni," Sam interrupted.

Iceni? Was that a real tribe, or had she just made something up and hoped no one would call her bluff? I glanced at her, trying to get an answer, but her face remained expressionless.

"You have traveled a long way from Iceni lands." Trenus nodded and stroked his long mustache. "If you are fleeing the Romans as well, then you are welcome to join us on our journey to the Island of the Druids. No one should ever be left to suffer at Roman hands."

Druids? My ears perked up. Now *they* were something I actually knew about. Druids were the law givers, historians, priests, teachers, and wise men of the Celts—basically the Jedi knights of Celtic times, except without the cool light sabers. But one question remained: between the druids and the Romans, which one of them was the time glitch? Only one way to find out.

I nodded almost imperceptibly to Sam, and she turned to Trenus. "We would be honored to join you."

Atto beamed at her. "My heart rejoices that you will stay with us." He grabbed her hand and placed it over his heart. "I look forward to seeing more of you, Genovefa. But, for now, I and my men must continue guarding the way." He kissed her hand and then released it, before he and his men faded back into the forest.

Oh no ... Atto's leaving ... how horrible.

"We thank you for your hospitality," I said to Trenus. "Do you know how far away the Romans are?"

Trenus waved his hand in the same direction his people had come from. "The vile Romans will be upon us within two days—maybe less. Before we left our village, they had already destroyed a village two valleys over and killed or enslaved everyone who lived there." He spat a long stream of spittle into the dirt. "But they will find no satisfaction when they reach our village. We have already burned our houses and fields, so their greedy hearts will find only ruin."

Damn ... Two days.

The frightened looks on the faces of the people passing by made sense now. These people had destroyed everything they owned just to keep it out of the hands of the Romans, and now they were fleeing for their lives.

"Do not fear," Trenus added. "The druids have promised safety to all who flee the Romans. We will reach their island long before the Romans find us." He motioned to the tail end of the refugee column that was just disappearing down the path. "Shall we join the rest of my village now?"

"You go," Sam urged. "We'll catch up."

Trenus nodded and left me and Sam alone by the roadside.

"Asterix?" Sam asked. "What type of name is that?"

"It's the only one I could think of." I shrugged. "It's from a comic book series about Celts fighting Romans. How did you come up with Genovefa?"

"It's an older form of Guinevere ... you know, the queen from the King Arthur tales? I'm pretty sure we're somewhere in England in the first century, so I figured it would work."

"England again?" I threw back my head in disbelief and stared up at the sky.

"Afraid so," Sam said.

"How can you be sure?"

Sam nonchalantly flipped her hair off her shoulder, apparently proud that she had figured out something historical that I hadn't. "Atto said my hair looked like Queen Boudicca's. She ruled a Celtic tribe called the Iceni and led them in a huge rebellion against the Romans. She even burned London and a few other cities before she was defeated. She died around the year 60 or 61."

I blinked in astonishment. "How do you know all this?"

"In English class last year we had to write an essay about someone who inspired us, and I picked Boudicca." Her eyes sparkled. "What's not to love about a redheaded queen who burns cities?"

"So do you think the time glitch has something to do with her?"

"I doubt it. You heard Trenus—we're far away from Iceni territory. It has to be something else. Something more local."

Island of the Druids ... Romans ... first-century England. I had a vague memory of some long-forgotten history lesson that my dad had tried to teach me, but nothing concrete. "Any ideas?" I asked Sam.

She shook her head.

"Maybe you could ask your new boyfriend," I muttered.

Sam chortled. "Are you jealous, Dan? Of Atto?"

"Of course I am. The guy was hanging all over you. And I didn't see you pushing him away like you do with me."

"Hold it!" Sam stuck her hand out so her palm was directly facing me. "I like you, and I think you're a great guy. You taking me to the homecoming dance was, without a doubt, the most romantic thing a guy's ever done for me. But let's get one thing straight—I may have kissed you in the heat of the moment that night, but we're never going to be more than friends. I made that clear the last time we were here. Or did you forget already?"

"No, I remember," I muttered.

"I was only being nice to Atto to help us," Sam continued. "Did you forget those spears pointed at us? If saving my life means batting my eyelashes and laughing at some guy's lame stories, you can bet your ass that's *exactly* what I'm going to do. Or should I let you have a go at trying to talk your way out of the next bad situation?"

"No," I said, avoiding her chastising glare.

She crossed her arms over her chest. "Are we done here?"

I nodded.

"Good. Then let's catch up with Trenus and his people, and try to figure out why the jump rods brought us here."

For the next few hours we trudged with the Celts through winding tree-covered hillsides. Gradually the land flattened out, and the road stretched downhill toward the coast. Ahead of us lay only a flat plain that ended at the sea. And in the distance, across a narrow tidal strait, lay a huge island. Thousands of Celtic refugees already stood on the near shore, waiting for boats to take them across.

The villagers gathered around Trenus. "Soon we will board the boats that will carry us to our new home on the Island of the Druids," the chief announced, "where I pray that the gods will finally grant us protection and peace from the endless savagery of the Romans."

While the villagers cheered, I tried to penetrate the fog hazing my memories. Something about this island bugged me. I distinctly remembered sitting at the kitchen table while Dad lectured on and on about the Roman conquest of Britain. There had definitely been something in there about an island off the coast of England.

Wait ... not England ... Wales.

Craaaaaaaaap ...

The blood drained from my face and I suddenly felt cold. With a horrible certainty I knew where we were. We were on the Welsh coast in year 60 of the common era. And in the distance was the island of Anglesey, where the druids had established their college. From there they spread their knowledge and wisdom throughout the

Celtic world—until the Romans came and savagely killed or enslaved every last person they found.

CHAPTER 4

S am paled as I told her the news of the impending massacre. "You mean all these innocent people are going to die?"

"Unfortunately." My gaze swept along the channel separating Anglesey from the rest of Wales. Small boats and rafts skimmed across the water, ferrying Celtic refugees to the island. These poor people assumed they were heading somewhere safe—with no idea that when the Romans arrived, the island would become their cage. They'd be trapped.

"Is there any chance you could be wrong?" Sam looked over her shoulder as if expecting the Roman legions to appear suddenly on the road behind us.

"Maybe. The history books are really vague on the timing of the attack. They can't even agree on the year. So the Romans currently heading this way might not be the invasion force; they might be a raiding party, or even just scouts."

"And how do we find out?"

I exhaled slowly as I racked my brain, desperately trying to remember what Dad had taught me. But there were so many gaps. "We might be able to tell if we know how many troops the Romans are sending. They sent multiple legions for their attack on Anglesey. So if any of the Celtic scouts actually happened to see and count the Romans, then we'd know."

"So what are we doing standing here? Let's go get some answers." Sam turned and headed over to where Atto, Trenus, and a group of Ordovices stood in discussion. I had no choice but to go chasing after her.

Atto waved a greeting as Sam approached. "Genovefa!" He beamed. "The sun shines warmer upon me whenever you are near. How can I be of service to you and your little Roman friend?"

She sidled up next to him and put her hand on his arm. "Have any of your scouts actually seen the Roman army? Do they know how big it is?" she asked.

The smile faded from Atto's face for a second. When it returned it didn't have the same intensity as before, and the men with him shifted uneasily. "They sent two legions—with my own eyes I counted their standards."

Two legions!

"Are you sure?" I asked.

"Atto speaks the truth," Trenus said somberly. "Rumors come to us that the Romans march to destroy the druids. They think that once our wise men are gone, our will to fight will be gone as well."

Grimly I nodded to Sam. I wasn't wrong—we were in Wales during the destruction of the druids. And we only had two days to find and fix the time glitch before the Romans arrived.

Atto thumped his painted chest with his fist. "I will not let myself be vanquished so easily!"

"Nor I!" yelled another man.

"We will make these Romans pay!" shouted another Celt.

They spoke bravely, but only Atto and a few others were properly dressed for war or had designs painted on their skin. The rest looked more like farmers or merchants or craftsmen. Most of them had weapons, and could probably tell good stories about the fights they had been in, but they weren't warriors. I saw it in the way they stood and the way they held their weapons. They were brave, but that wouldn't be enough. The Romans were going to wipe them out.

"How many fighting men have you got?" I asked.

"When it comes to defending our lands, all of us will fight!" Atto said. "It is in our blood. So do not fear, there are plenty of us here to protect you."

"I don't want your protection!" I snapped. "I can defend myself."

"Of course you can." Atto winked and nodded toward my staff. "You look like a man who is quite skilled at holding his stick. I am sure many men have learned to fear it."

My ears burned as Trenus and the other Celts chuckled along with Atto. The annoying Celt wouldn't be laughing so loud if I grabbed his ugly mustache with both hands and ripped it off his stupid face.

"Atto, do not make fun of our guest," Trenus admonished, but he didn't stop smiling. "We have extended our hospitality to him, so we must treat him with honor."

"I only jest." Atto placed an arm around my shoulder and gave me a friendly squeeze. "My words have not caused ill feeling, I hope."

"Nope," I muttered through gritted teeth.

"Excellent," Atto said, as if this was the best news he heard all day. "So what about you, Little Roman? Will you fight alongside us?"

Fat chance. I planned to be long gone before the legions arrived. I'd never experienced a massacre before, and I was quite happy skipping this one.

"Of course I'll fight," I lied.

"That is the spirit!" Atto clapped me on the back. "Let us show these dogs that we are free people. Tell me, how many men have you killed?"

"Seven," I declared without thinking. Each shocked and pained face was permanently etched in my memory. One time jumper I stabbed in the throat, and six Normans I had killed during the Battle of Hastings.

"Seven, eh? That must be one mighty stick you carry."

He clearly didn't believe me, but I didn't care. I knew how to fight; along with all the lessons in history, my dad had been teaching me martial arts and how to use swords, axes, knives and a slew of other medieval weapons almost since the day I could walk.

"Stop cackling like a bunch of hens," Trenus said. "The time has come for us to leave this shore." He pointed to the strait, where a large boat, rowed by at least thirty men, had left the island and was now nearing the beach. Behind it, like ducklings following their mother, came a string of empty boats, all tied to the lead one by lengths of rope. Trenus clapped his hands, and his fellow villagers stopped what they were doing and turned to listen. "We cross now for the Island of the Druids," he announced, his voice carrying to all. "Your carts must stay behind, I fear. Bring only food and those small items that are absolutely needed."

A loud chorus of grumbling followed this announcement. "I cannot leave my tools behind," yelled a man standing next to a cart laden with an anvil, hammers, tongs, chisels, bellows, and scrap metal.

Trenus held up his hands for silence. "There is only enough room in the boats to take people, Esico. Would you leave a family on the shore just so that your tools could have their place?"

Esico thrust his chest out. "Of course I would never allow a family to be left behind. But what of my tools? We will need them on the island."

Trenus pointed to the broken carts, furnishings, baskets, and tools left by others who had sought refuge on the island. "We leave our goods for now and, if time allows, we will come back for them. That is the best I can offer you."

"So be it," Esico grumbled as he reached into his cart and pulled out a heavy hammer. "But this I keep for smashing Roman skulls." He tucked the hammer into his wide leather belt, then hefted two baskets of food off the cart. With his family beside him, he boarded one of the boats. The rest of the villagers followed his lead, packing themselves into the remaining crafts.

Sam and I stayed onshore, not sure where to go. "Genovefa! Little Roman! Come, there is room for you here."

Him again.

I scanned the other boats, searching for empty spots, but every one was packed with passengers and riding dangerously low in the water.

Sam nudged me and smiled. "Looks like we're hitching a ride with your new best friend."

I scowled and grudgingly took my place in Atto's boat, making sure Sam got the seat farthest away from him. Unfortunately that meant I ended up in the seat right behind him. Which also meant that I was stuck paddling, since I was at the side and not in the middle.

"Away!" yelled someone on shore, and a group of men pushed us off the beach and into deeper water. Those with paddles dug hard, trying to propel our craft against the heavy current. With so many people weighing down the boat, it took all our strength to keep the vessel on course.

Atto nodded toward the water as he paddled. "This is what the sea is like when it favors us, but most times it is much worse. The foul Romans will never be able to send their army across the waves when the sea grows angry."

I shook my head and continued paddling. Atto had no clue how tough the Romans were. Their armies had conquered the entire Mediterranean. This little stretch of water would be like a puddle to them.

After about half an hour of muscle-breaking paddling, we reached the island. Hundreds of Celts armed with swords and shields stood on the shore waiting for us. And not waiting in the welcome-to-our-island sense with hula dancers and leis; they stood armed and alert, closely watching everyone. As each boat landed, a squad of eight to ten Celts would approach with weapons drawn, and they'd order the men from the boat to strip to the waist, raise their arms above their head, and turn around.

I knew absolutely nothing about Celtic customs, but this didn't feel right. "What are they looking for?" I whispered to Atto.

"I do not know," he shrugged. "Roman spies? Disease?"

With a loud crunch, our boat grounded itself on the pebble beach. As the rowers pulled in their paddles, a squad of ten armed Celts approached our craft.

"All women and children are free to disembark," one of the Celts said. "All men, take off your cloaks and tunics, and raise your arms."

"What manner of welcome is this?" Atto shouted, raising his fist.

The Celt shrugged. "The druids command and I obey. If you do not like our welcome, go complain to the Romans—they will be here soon."

Atto's lips curled in distaste, but he didn't say anything. Instead, he splashed ashore, took off his traveling cloak to reveal his shirtless upper body, then he raised his arms and turned around. One of the Celts nodded and waved him through.

"You worried?" Sam whispered to me.

"Nah, I'll be fine. If Atto can make it through, I sure as hell can. You go ahead and I'll catch up."

"Okay." Sam grabbed her bow and backpack and joined the rest of the women and children from our boat as they began hopping into the shallow water and heading to shore, their belongings clutched in their hands.

I confidently splashed toward the waiting guards. I was just about to take off my cloak and tunic when I remembered that I still had the jump device jammed into the back of my pants.

Damn … How do I do this without them seeing the jump device?

I dropped my staff and backpack on the ground and untied my cloak. As I swung it off my shoulders in an attention-diverting flourish, I pushed down on the jump rod hidden at my waist and prayed as it slid down my pant leg that it would land inside my boot. Somehow it did, and I took off my tunic, raised my arms overhead, and waited to be waved through like Atto.

The eyes of the Celt watching me widened as if I had sprouted fangs and a second head. "I have him! I have him!" he yelled as he leveled his spear at me. "Tell the druid!"

Other warriors swarmed around me, their swords and spears dangerously close to my skin. Their eyes kept drifting to my hands raised above my head and the tattoo on the inside of my right forearm.

"I'm innocent!" I yelled frantically. "I haven't done anything!"

My eyes darted left and right, and I realized the warriors surrounding me weren't advancing. They were only penning me in, making sure I couldn't escape. But why? Was my tattoo freaking them out?

"What is the meaning of this?" demanded Trenus as he pushed himself through the ring of armed men to stand beside me.

"Get out of the way," one of them ordered. "This does not concern you."

Trenus crossed his arms over his chest and pulled himself to his full height. "I am Trenus, chief of my village, and I demand to know what your grievance is with this man."

The warrior nearest me arrogantly waved his sword at Trenus. "You may be a chief, but we act on the orders of Cenacus the Druid. Now stand aside."

Trenus raised his fist, and the men of his village brandished their weapons and closed in. "We found this man by the road," Trenus explained. "We gave him our hospitality. When you attack our guest, you attack all of us."

"And what hospitality are you providing here?" Atto called out. "You invite us to your island, offering us safety, then you attack us—your guests? That is not the way of our people. That is a Roman thing to do."

Men from the other villages gathered around us, nodding and shouting in anger. "Aye!" yelled a man. "Our laws demand the safety of guests. How dare you break these laws!"

The Celt confronting Trenus lowered his sword and looked nervously around. He and his fellow warriors were now surrounded by hundreds of farmers and villagers, all holding weapons and shouting complaints about the poor treatment they'd received.

This was getting ugly fast. One wrong move and this standoff could escalate into an all-out brawl. I lowered my arms slowly and grabbed my walking stick. If the crap hit the fan, I wasn't going down without a fight.

"Quiet!" a voice boomed.

Heads turned in the direction of the shout and a hush settled over the crowd. People bowed their heads and moved aside to reveal a stern-faced man with long brown hair peppered with gray and a short beard. He leaned heavily on a thick gnarled staff as he approached, his left leg dragging behind him. Unlike the vibrant clothes that the rest of the Celts chose, he wore a simple gray tunic and pants with a light gray cloak over his shoulders. "Who bears the mark?" he called out.

The Celt who had been arguing with Trenus jabbed a finger at me. "He does, O wise Cenacus."

The man stopped in front of me. He looked about my dad's age, his blue eyes clear and sharp. He stroked his beard with one hand as he looked me up and down, scrutinizing my clothes, my boots, and the staff I carried. Around us the crowd pressed in, watching intently but saying nothing. Even Atto was silent for once.

I kept clenching and unclenching my fists to stop my hands from shaking. *What the hell was going on?*

With a speed I didn't think possible from a guy his age, he grabbed my wrist. His fingers felt thin and bony against my skin, like death itself gripping me. I desperately wanted to pull away but knew that would only cause more problems. He raised my arm so that my tattoo was at his eye level. He studied it for a few seconds and then let go of my wrist. "Welcome to Wales, time jumper," he said.

I jerked back, stunned. He'd spoken English—not Celtic. I stared intently into his blue eyes. "Who are you?"

He smiled and pulled back the sleeve on his right arm, revealing the same tattoo. "We have much to speak about," Cenacus said, shifting back to Celtic. He turned and addressed the crowd surrounding us. "Did he come here with anyone else?"

Trenus stepped forward, his eyes lowered as if he, the chief of a village, wasn't worthy to look at the druid directly. "Aye, he was with a woman. We found them together in the woods."

"Where is she now?" Cenacus asked.

Trenus pointed to where Sam and the rest of the women had gathered to wait after the boats had landed. "The one with flame-red hair who carries a bow."

Cenacus turned to look in the direction Trenus pointed. As if by magic, any people obscuring his view stepped aside, creating a clear path to Sam.

Cenacus raised a finger and wordlessly beckoned for her to come over.

For a second Sam remained motionless, eyes darting around to find an escape route. But where could she run to on an island totally filled with Celts? She shook her head and walked slowly to my side like a prisoner heading to her execution.

Cenacus held out his hand to her. "Give me your bow and arrows."

Without a word, Sam handed them over.

The druid pulled one of the arrows out of the quiver and examined it. "Very nice," he said as he returned it to the quiver. He then turned the bow over in his hands. "A beautiful bow—recurved like the Scythians use … and reinforced with horn as well. Too bad neither the Celts nor the Romans use bows like this." He returned the bow to Sam and looked her up and down, his brows raised and with a finger tapping his lips. "Amazing," he said in English, so softly that only Sam and I could hear him. "A female time jumper. I never knew they existed. Do you have the tattoo?"

Sam shook her head but said nothing.

"I want you *both* to come with me. We have so much to talk about." He clapped his hands together loudly three times. "Continue examining all who come to the island," he announced to the warriors who had been guarding the beach. "If any more arrive, notify me immediately." With that, he started to limp away from the shore, the crowd reverently parting for him.

There was no choice but for us to follow him, so I slipped my tunic and cloak back on, picked up my staff and headed after him, Sam falling into step beside me. She raised an eyebrow toward me, as if asking what was going on, and I shrugged back. Was Cenacus one of Victor's guys? How had he become so powerful here? What did he want with us? And, if he was here, why wasn't the time glitch already fixed?

CHAPTER 5

Cenacus led us to a small wooden-framed cart pulled by a single horse. With aching slowness he pulled himself up into the cart seat. "I can't walk far because of my leg," he explained through gritted teeth. "So this is how I get around the island. You two should hop in the back. It's a bit of a ride."

Sam and I locked eyes for a moment and exchanged nods before hopping into the back of the cart and onto a thin padding of loose straw. Cenacus snapped the reins and the cart lurched forward.

We passed through a large open field where tents, lean-tos, and small huts made of turf or wood crowded on top of each other. Chickens and geese ran between the ramshackle buildings, pecking for food, while everywhere Celts were hard at work, tending to small gardens or making their shelters more secure against the elements. I'd never seen so many people crammed into such a small space—it was as if half the Celts in Wales had been packed into this little area. Despite the crowding, and the fact that all these people had abandoned their homes, leaving everything behind, everyone laughed and chatted with their neighbors as they worked. The Roman threat seemed to be the furthest thing from their minds.

"Why isn't anyone worried?" I shouted to Cenacus over the clacking of the wooden wheels, trying to start a conversation. I wasn't normally the chatty type, but my life depended on figuring out which side he was on.

"Because they're Celts," Cenacus snorted. "They always think they'll win, no matter how bad the odds. But we know differently, don't we? And that's why we must work together to get off this island before the Romans arrive."

My ears perked up at his answer. He wanted to get off the island? That was a good sign. "Do you know what's wrong with the time stream?"

"Patience." He raised a hand. "All will be answered."

He began driving us away from the refugee camp toward a rise in the distance. The cart trundled along a narrow track, passing vast fields of grain, still green. As the cart began its slow climb uphill, a waist-high wall of turf came into view. The wall extended in a square about the length of a football field around a cluster of circular huts with thatched roofs. Compared to the refugee encampment we had just left, this place seemed almost empty. I was about to ask why, but then I noticed the cloaked, gray-haired men and women who tended gardens or simply sat outside the huts. This was obviously where the druids lived.

The cart passed through a gate in the low wall and then lurched to a halt in front of one of the huts, where Cenacus gingerly lowered himself from his seat and led us inside. There were no windows. The only light came through the open doorway and from the dying embers in the central fire pit. "It should be safe to talk here," Cenacus explained, switching back to English. He leaned down and blew on the embers of the fire, sparking them to new life. The addition of a few small branches got the flames going and sent smoke rising lazily to the ceiling, where it seeped into the thatch. The firelight now showed a small room with a bed, a simple wooden table, chairs, and a leather-bound chest. Straw covered the packed-earth floor, providing additional warmth.

Cenacus sat down at the table and gestured for us to take the seats facing him. "First, allow me to introduce myself. Here, I go by the name Cenacus, but at one point in time people called me William Anderson." He winced as if pained by the memory. "But I haven't heard that name spoken in a long time. What are your names?"

"Dan," I answered, instantly biting my lip to stop myself from yelping. Sam had kicked me under the table.

"Genovefa," she said quietly.

Cenacus smirked. "Not the trusting type, are you, Genovefa?"

"Nope," she answered, her voice lacking warmth.

"Smart move." He nodded. "If only I had been less trusting, I wouldn't have been stuck here for the last seventeen years."

Seventeen years! I tried to contain my surprise; after all, he could be making up a story to trick us. Beside me Sam looked at Cenacus through slitted eyes, not masking her disbelief.

"That's a long time," I said. "What happened?"

"If I'm going to tell you the full story, we might as well get comfortable." Using the table for support, Cenacus pulled himself to his feet and limped to one corner of his hut, where a clay pitcher stood. He grabbed it, returned to the table, and poured us each a mug of fruity-scented wine.

Sam nudged me with her foot under the table to get my attention. She stared at me and then at her cup, and shook her head slightly in warning. I flicked up my right thumb in response.

Cenacus didn't notice our mistrust. He drained his cup, then refilled it before starting on his story. "So, like I said, I've been here seventeen years, although probably only about two and a half, maybe three years have passed in modern time since I jumped out. I landed here in 43 CE, when the Romans first invaded England. I was young then, just turned thirty-five, and it should have been an easy trip. Go in, find the problem, fix it, then leave—like I'd done tons of times before. I never expected my own partner to attack me. We'd been time traveling together for years, so I would have trusted him with my life." He stared down at his worn and wrinkled hands. "Anyway, we landed, fixed the time anomaly, and then, just before we were about to travel back home, he starts asking me all these questions, like what did I think about the direction our own world was heading, and wouldn't it be better if us time travelers took over. Well, he must not—"

"Wait a second," I interrupted. "Can you rewind to that part about the questions? Did he tell you *why* he was asking them? Did he tell you what their plan is?"

"He didn't go into details, but I'd been hearing rumblings in the traveler community for years that some guy named Victor Stahl was planning something big. At first, they sounded like the typical conspiracy-theory garbage. You know—wild, apocalyptic claims that he planned to 'cleanse humanity' and put time travelers in charge. The sort of stuff you laugh at and ask 'Who would actually be dumb enough to believe something like that?' Even when Victor was elected to Congress, I didn't worry—every time traveler needs a day job, and what better job than politician? Sit around all day, do nothing, get paid—sounds perfect to me." He chuckled, but the laughter faded from his face and his brow grew heavy. "Then I started hearing about the disappearances and murders in the traveler community. Everywhere—Africa, Asia, South America, Europe—they were all being hit. There were rumors that Victor and his allies were taking out any time jumper who wasn't willing to toe their line."

"But why? What is their plan?"

"I don't know. My partner never bothered giving me the full recruiting speech. He asked me his questions. I gave him my answers. And the next thing I know, he's stabbing me. I end up lying in a pool of my own blood, and he grabs my time-travel device and leaves me for dead."

"I'm so sorry," I said. "The same thing almost happened to me on my last jump. A guy had a knife to my throat and was about to kill me. I was saved in the nick of time."

"You're lucky, then, kid. I wasn't nearly as fortunate. My partner left me in bad shape. A druid found me and managed to stitch me up well enough that I survived, although he couldn't do much about my leg. He brought me here to this island and, over time, I healed. Since I didn't have my device translating for me anymore, I had to learn the language. I actually started to like living on this island. So I relaxed for a few years, learned everything I could from the druids, and eventually became one of them." He ran his thumb around the rim of his mug. "Things were going great. I felt like my life finally had a meaning that was missing in our modern world. I could have lived here happily until I grew old and died. But now the Romans are coming, and I don't want to be part of this massacre ... so I created a glitch."

"Wait, *you* created the glitch?" I asked. "How?"

"Let me tell ya, it wasn't easy. From what I've seen in my past trips to history, most glitches occur when an event happens that shouldn't. You know, a king decides to battle his opponent in the swamp instead of on the high ground like history recorded, and his army ends up losing instead of winning. Or an archer makes a shot that he shouldn't have made and now some general is dead." He snorted. "But I'm some middle-aged guy with a bad leg who's stuck in Celtic Wales. There are no kings around here. The closest thing we have are the damn Romans, but I sure as hell wasn't ever going to get close to them—they kill druids on sight. So I was stuck for the longest time, trying to figure out how to mess up history enough to get a pair of you guys here, but still not mess it up so much that there'd be permanent damage to the time stream." Cenacus tapped a finger against his temple. "Then I hit on an idea. What if I didn't worry so much about creating an event that messes up history, and instead tried to create an object? You know, something that was so obviously out of place in history that it would completely piss off the time stream?" He looked at us both expectantly, as if waiting for some sort of acknowledgment of his genius.

My exposure to glitches was severely limited, so a lot of what he said flew right over my head. I decided it was better to come clean about my ignorance than to blindly nod along and get even more confused. "I have no clue what you're talking about."

"Think about it this way," Cenacus said. "What would happen if I somehow managed to create an assault rifle with a few thousand rounds of ammo and then gave it to one of my Celtic friends just before the Romans arrived?"

A vision flashed through my head of a wild blue-painted Celt standing on a hill and mowing down hundreds of Roman soldiers. "Oh … I got it now. So what did you create?"

He sat a bit straighter in his chair, clearly pleased with himself. "Over the years I managed to save up a small hoard of gold coins. I melted these down and turned them into a golden tablet listing all the rulers of Britain from Roman times until modern times."

"A tablet? That's it? How does that create a glitch?"

"Don't you get it, kid? In the wrong hands, that information would completely alter the course of history! Any ruler would know who'd succeed him, so this tablet would lead to assassinations or battles never happening. We're talking about the complete rewriting of the Roman line of emperors … or the English succession of kings. This tablet is the biggest time glitch ever!"

It still didn't sound as history-altering as an assault rifle, but I wasn't going to argue. "Well, I guess it worked, because we're here now," I said. "So now you want us to bring you home?"

"Damn right!" He clapped his hands together. "The seventeen years

I spent here were some of the best I've ever had, but I'm not ready to die yet. I want to watch a football game again. I want to eat French fries. I want to visit South America. There's still a lot of life left in these bones."

"Great story." Sam crossed her arms and leaned back in her chair. "But how can you go home without a jump rod?"

Cenacus nodded toward me. "I'll travel out of here with him. Your clothes and equipment can travel through time with you, so why not a person? He can piggyback me."

"Have you tried this before?" I asked. "Does it actually work?"

Cenacus shrugged. "I've never heard of anyone trying it before. But in theory ..."

He had told his story with so much sincerity that I had no choice but to believe him. And with that belief came an overwhelming sense of pity. Seventeen years stuck in history—it was like a prison sentence. Cut off from friends, family, and the world he'd known. "All right," I said. "If you're willing to try it, so am I."

Sam gaped as if I'd lost my mind, but I wasn't worried about jumping with Cenacus. After all, I'd still get home. He was the one risking his life.

"Thank you! Thank you!" Cenacus's eyes lit up.

"No problem," I said. "Now go get that tablet so we can destroy it and all go home."

Cenacus shook his head. "Me? I can't. I don't even know where it is."

"What? You created it."

"I've been trying for two years to get this stupid tablet to become a glitch," Cenacus sighed. "At first I thought all I had to do was create the thing and—poof!—instant glitch." He shook his head in disappointment. "That sure as hell didn't happen. I waited months for one of you guys to show up, and no one ever came. That got me to thinking. There's going to be a ton of Romans swarming this place soon, so the likelihood of one guy finding it by himself is pretty slim. And a group of illiterate soldiers isn't going to stop to figure out what's written on the tablet—they're just going to hack it into pieces so everyone gets a share of the gold. I needed to hide it someplace where it would be found by one or two people at most, so that they wouldn't destroy it and it could survive to mess up history." He took another sip of his wine. "I tried burying it locally, but that never seemed to work, and I only ended up wasting more months waiting for someone to show up. Finally, I got desperate. Because of my leg, I can only travel by cart, and even then only for a short time. So I had two Celts bury it somewhere in the north, far away from where the Romans will attack." He leaned back in his chair and raised his mug triumphantly toward us. "And obviously that worked, because here you are. But that's also why I don't know where it is."

"Well, go get those two Celts to dig it up, then," I said, stating the obvious.

"I can't. They left for the mainland to keep tabs on the Romans. They won't be back for days. That's *if* they make it back."

I gaped at him in disbelief as an ache settled in my chest. "So you're saying we're all stuck here?"

Cenacus's brow furrowed. "No. Just use the rod to find the glitch."

"What are you talking about?" I almost yelled.

"You know … you just use the 'find time glitch' setting."

I cut my eyes at Sam, who looked just as confused as I felt.

"Umm … we don't know how to do that," Sam said.

Cenacus slapped the table with his palm, shaking our mugs. "How do you *not* know?"

"We don't know any settings," I admitted. "We just know how to jump into history and then jump out when the glitch is fixed."

Cenacus's jaw dropped. "You mean you two have traveled through time without even knowing how to *find* the glitches? What have you survived on … dumb luck?"

I shrugged. "Pretty much."

Shaking his head, Cenacus held out his hand. "Give me your rod and I'll show you."

I pulled up my pant leg and grasped the jump rod tucked into my boot. Cenacus watched my movements, his eyes alive, like a kid at Christmas waiting to open the biggest present. Something about the way he was watching me creeped me out, and I paused.

"Sorry." Cenacus pulled his hand away. "It would be stupid of you to just hand it over." He limped toward the fireplace, grabbed a piece of charcoal, and returned with it to his chair. On the table top he sketched six symbols in a row. "Twist the sections to match these."

Sam and I both began twisting our rods to line up the symbols. As soon as the last one clicked into place, the metal beneath my fingers developed a strong pulling sensation, like I was holding a magnet over metal. No matter where I pointed the rod, it tugged toward the far wall of Cenacus's hut.

I felt giddy—I'd actually learned a rod command!

"Do you feel it?" Cenacus asked. "The stronger the pull, the closer you are." He drew some more symbols on the table. "Try this one."

We did, and now my rod pulled in Sam's direction, and hers was pointing at me.

"That's how you find other time-travel devices," Cenacus said. "Do you feel anything other than your two rods?"

"No." Both Sam and I answered at the same time.

Cenacus nodded. "Almost all travelers go in pairs. It's safer. But if they arrive somewhere in history and sense other time travelers nearby, they usually leave—no sense in crowding things and drawing attention. Not to mention all the troubles that have been going on. It got really hard to trust ..." His voice trailed off.

I held the jump device out at arm's length as a horrific thought entered my mind. "Is this how Victor's been hunting down people back home? Does he just twist the sections and then find other jumpers, no matter where they're hidden?"

"Don't worry yourself. Except for the command to jump out, none of the other rod commands work in our time, only in history."

Sam leaned forward eagerly, her hostility gone. "I know my dad once jumped out of the past even though he hadn't fixed the time glitch. Do you know that setting?"

Cenacus stroked his chin and stared at the symbols he had drawn. He drew a few others, then erased those and drew some more. With an angry swipe of his sleeve he erased these as well. "I can't remember," he said, shaking his head. "I never used it that much. The main commands are get in, find any other travelers, find the problem, and get out. If you're smart and careful, you never need to leave early."

"What about the rods?" I asked. "Do you know who made them? Do you know how they work? Do you know why time glitches happen?"

"Easy, kid. Slow down," Cenacus said. "I'll tell you everything I know about these things, which unfortunately is not much. Every time jumper has asked these questions before, and no one's ever found the answer. Sure, people have their theories—all of them crazy yet plausible at the same time—but nothing's ever been proven. I can't even—"

The blaring of a trumpet interrupted him. Another trumpet sounded from a different direction, echoing the first. Then another and another until it sounded like a thousand trumpets were going off.

Cenacus's face paled. "That doesn't sound good." Grunting, he pulled himself to his feet and hobbled to the open door.

Sam and I followed him to stand just outside his hut. From our vantage point on the hill, we had a good view over the refugee camp and across the strait. Large fires burned on the mountain peaks of the Welsh mainland, their orange flames bright against the dusky sky.

"Signal fires," Cenacus declared somberly. "The Romans are coming. They'll probably be here tomorrow."

Dread settled over me. It was like standing on a beach knowing a tsunami was coming. I felt small, insignificant, powerless. "Do you think we can find the tablet before the fighting starts?"

"I don't think so." Cenacus's fingers drummed nervously on his walking stick, and he gazed out at the signal fires for a few seconds, as if searching for wisdom in their flames. "You two need to split up," he finally said.

"Split up?" Sam snorted. "What for?

"Because the Romans are right on our damn doorstep!" Cenacus snapped. "There won't be enough time for both of you to ride across the island, destroy the tablet, and then come back for me. The only way we can pull this off is if one of you goes and smashes that sucker while the other one stays here to jump out with me."

"You have a cart," Sam said. "Why don't you just ride along with us?"

"Have you seen my horse?" Cenacus grunted. "The thing's about a hundred years old. It even gets tired pulling my wagon *downhill*. There's no way it will be able to haul me wherever we need to go, especially if we have to travel off the trails. And I sure as hell can't walk it. So I'm stuck here … unless you two want to carry me?"

Sam's lips curled in annoyance. "Yeah, not happening. And neither is us splitting up. There has to be a better way to do this."

Cenacus stamped his walking stick on the ground. "There is no better way! If you two had shown up weeks ago, or even days ago, we'd have plenty of time. But not anymore. Now our only chance is for one of you to go for the tablet while the other stays with me."

Damn it. The guy did have a point. "Can you give us a minute?" I asked him.

"Yeah, sure."

Sam and I retreated about twenty steps and then we bent our heads close so Cenacus couldn't hear us. "You're not seriously thinking about splitting up, are you?" Sam whispered.

"I am. You've seen him move around; he's slower than a turtle. It makes sense for you to go destroy the tablet while I stay here with him. As soon as the rod turns warm, I'll know you succeeded, and then we both jump out."

"Why do you even care?" Sam asked. "Some random guy who got himself stuck in the past is *not* our problem. We're just here to save history."

"I can't just leave him here. Do you remember how helpless we felt when we thought we were trapped in Anglo-Saxon England? Well, this guy's been here seventeen years! We have to help him—it's the right thing to do."

"It's the dumb thing to do," Sam scoffed.

"But look at what he's taught us already," I countered. "What if, once we get him back home to our time, he can tell us even more stuff? He might even be an ally in our fight against Victor."

Sam shook her head and exhaled loudly. "Fine. If you're dead set on helping him, I'll go along with it. After all, you're the one staying back." She jabbed a finger at my chest. "I'm telling you now, though. I hate this plan."

I raised my hands. "Duly noted. But come on, how bad can it be?"

Sam glanced toward Cenacus, who was watching us from the doorway of his hut. "I don't know. There's something about him that I just don't like."

That didn't surprise me—trust was definitely not one of Sam's strong suits. I didn't say anything, though, and together we walked back to Cenacus, who looked at us expectantly, clearly waiting for our decision. "I'm staying," I said. "Genovefa will be going to find the tablet."

"Excellent!" Cenacus practically jumped at the news. "Now, the sun's going to be setting in about another hour, so it's too late for her to start out today. But if she leaves at the crack of dawn, she could hopefully reach the tablet by tomorrow evening and destroy it. As soon as that happens, I'll leave with you."

"Tomorrow evening?" I said. "Isn't that cutting it kind of close? What if the Romans attack before she finds the tablet? Do you have a backup plan?"

"I have one," Cenacus replied, "but I don't think you're going to like it. You ever fight in a battle? A big one?"

"Yeah," I said hesitantly, "at Hastings. Why?"

"Really? Hastings?" His eyebrow raised in surprise. "Which side?"

"With the Anglo-Saxons. In the shield wall."

Cenacus stared intently again for a few seconds at the signal fires in the distance. "This just might work," he said, more to himself than to me. He then pointed to the mass of Celts milling around in the large camp below us. "Do you know what the Celts need more than anything else?"

I shrugged. "Flamethrowers? Tanks?"

"Leadership. They're going to lose this fight because they're too disorganized. They need someone to show them how to fight as a group—and how to fight defensively. They need *you*."

"That's your backup plan?" I took a step back and waved my hands in front of me. "Uh-uh. You're crazy. I can't lead the Celts. I'm only seventeen. They'll never listen to me."

"They'll follow you if the druids tell them to."

"Okay, how about none of them will listen to me because I'm not going to do it?" The idea of getting men like Atto to listen to me for even five seconds seemed impossible.

Cenacus turned toward me, a pained expression in his eyes. "I know you don't like the idea, and believe me, I understand your doubts. I've lived with the Celts for almost twenty years, and they are some of the most obstinate people you'll ever find. But understand this—you're now the only hope most of these people have. None of them have the large-scale battle experience that you have. You know how to fight at close quarters. You know how to deal with troop formations. They need your help."

"But won't that just mess up history? I know the time stream can repair itself from minor issues, but me helping the Celts kick ass doesn't sound minor to me."

"Trust me, kid. You're not going to win here. History won't change. All I'm asking you to do is to help the Celts kill a few extra Romans to slow them down a bit. Give your partner some extra time to find the damn tablet. And if that isn't enough to convince you, then do it for all the innocent women and children who are going to die or be sold into slavery if the Celts don't put up a better defense."

Cheap shot. I bowed my head, not willing to look at the refugee camp below. Unfortunately, the cheap shot was working. Even though all these people lived almost two thousand years in my past, the thought of so many of them dying made me sick to my stomach. The Celts had been fighting the Romans for over four hundred years, and these were the last few free Celtic tribes left. All the rest had been conquered, with millions dead or enslaved. The Romans still had to win here to keep history flowing properly, but if I could save a few lives by helping the Celts fight better, then I'd have to do it. "Fine," I said grudgingly.

"Excellent!" Cenacus pulled the hood of his cloak up. "I'll go tell the other druids the plan. They'll need to agree with it before I can make it happen."

"Agree to it? You mean this isn't a done deal?"

"Definitely not. I'm one of many druids. All of us have to agree for this to happen."

"And how likely is that?"

Cenacus shrugged. "I don't know. The druids always try to take the path of wisdom. But sometimes there are many paths leading to the same destination."

"You know, that was probably the most useless answer I've heard in ages."

The corners of his mouth curled into a smile. "Now you know what it is like to deal with druids: a lot of words, not many answers. But I'll do my best to convince them of this path." He motioned once again to the teeming mass crowded in the fields below. "While I'm busy with the druids, you should use this time to spread your name among the Celts. They're a strong-willed people, reluctant to be led by anyone, especially outsiders. To get them to follow you, you must prove your courage to them."

This half-baked plan of his was getting worse by the minute. "What am I supposed to do," I asked sarcastically, "pick fights with everyone?"

Cenacus paused for a second and stroked his beard. "That might work. And also brag about any battles you've been in. The Celts love tales of fighting."

"Are you serious? I thought whatever the druids say goes."

He shook his head. "Druids are held in great esteem, but we only offer advice. I can get the Celts to *listen* to you. Your task will be to convince them to *follow* you." He stamped his staff on the ground. "But we're wasting time here. We both have work to do." He limped away from the hut, moving off slowly along the path.

Sam and I stood just outside his doorway, watching as he headed toward another druid hut.

"What do you think about this guy?" I asked Sam.

She glanced around to make sure no one was within listening distance. "I still don't trust him. Sure, he taught us some rod commands, but what do we actually know about him?"

"Nothing, really," I admitted. "Though I can't find any holes in his story. The ancient historians said it took about twenty years of training to become a druid. If the druids here accept him as one of their own, he's definitely been here a long time. And the rod commands he taught us work, so he wasn't lying about being a time jumper. Do you think he's hiding something?"

"I don't know. I just don't like having to trust people."

"I know," I chuckled. "It took you forever to trust me."

"And I'm still regretting it," she replied, her green eyes sparkling with mischief and her lips curled into a slight smile. She didn't smile much—there was rarely anything to smile about on time jumps—but when she did, it made her whole face light up.

Too bad I had to ruin this moment. "Whether you trust him or not," I said, "I don't think we have much choice."

Sam nodded reluctantly. "Yeah, you need to stay with the Celts and whip them into shape. From what I've seen, they don't have the battle experience to hold off the Romans for long." She twisted a strand of hair around a finger and chewed on the end. "Are you worried?"

My stomach was doing backflips just thinking about trying to act like I had some authority over these people. Since my dad was not a fan of organized sports, I'd never been part of any team. My knowledge of how to motivate, or even get along with others, was severely lacking. Hell, we didn't even have a family dog that I could order to sit or go fetch. But I did know warfare, Dad had seen to that, so I knew exactly how the Romans would attack and what the Celts needed to do to defend themselves.

"If they listen, I might be able to save some of them," I said. "There's no way we can win this battle, though. According to history, the Romans sent in two full legions for the assault."

Sam rested her hand on my shoulder, unwittingly making my heart beat faster. "You can do this. You just need to get your ideas out, and the Celts will see that they make sense."

"I wish it was that simple. You've seen how Atto looks at me—he thinks I'm a joke. If I really want the Celts to listen to me, I'll need to prove my courage. Maybe I should punch Atto out—that might make a bunch of people happy." I smirked.

"No punching Atto out!"

"Just a suggestion."

She smiled again and grabbed my hand. "Come on. Let's go make you some friends."

CHAPTER 6

Trenus's villagers had made a place for themselves on the outskirts of the refugee camp. A few lean-tos and tents had already sprung up on the grassy plain, while some people had spread out blankets in preparation for sleeping under the stars. Fires dotted the field, and the smells of cooking food wafted through the air. Despite the fact that the Romans were on their way, everyone seemed festive. People laughed, sang, and boasted of how they were going to destroy the invaders the moment they set foot on the island.

As Sam and I approached the camp, the chatter tapered off and everyone began whispering to each other, while going through extreme efforts to stare at the fires, the grass, the sky—basically anything that wasn't us.

Sam gripped my hand and pulled herself closer. "Something's wrong."

"Ya think?" The Celts were acting as if Sam and I were about to trigger the zombie apocalypse.

Trenus motioned for us to stay where we were, then came sidling over. He didn't move with his usual confidence. His shoulders were hunched, and he seemed almost hesitant to approach us. "Is all well, Asterix?" he asked as he nervously rubbed his knuckles. "Have the druids taken offense?"

Oh … Trenus and his group were worried that we had brought dishonor upon them. "No, everything's good," I said. "Cenacus just asked me for some help."

Trenus startled back. "The druid asked for your help?"

"Maybe. He's not sure. He's now talking with the other druids. It might be nothing."

The village chief drew himself to his full height and clapped me on the back. "Find yourself a warm spot by one of the fires, friend of the druids," he said loudly so all the villagers could hear. "Our plight is yours. You will honor my village if you stay with us this evening."

His announcement brought a remarkable change to the attitude of the surrounding villagers. Suddenly men and women were calling us over, asking us to join them as they made space by their fires. But one irritating voice rose above the rest. "Genovefa! Little Roman! Come dine with us!"

Sam waved enthusiastically. "It's Atto," she said, as if I could have forgotten that voice. "Let's go sit with him."

That sounded about as much fun as having Victor in my living room again. "There are plenty of other Celts offering to share their fire."

"But he's not a farmer like everyone else. He's a warrior. You'll need his support." Sam grabbed my arm and steered me in Atto's direction. "So be nice."

"I'll be nice," I whispered to her through gritted teeth, "when he stops being a jerk."

Half dragging me, Sam led the way to Atto's fire pit. He stood, still shirtless of course, with his arm around a tall, slender woman with a smiling face and striking eyes. She wore a simple knee-length dress fastened at the shoulders with two gold brooches. Her long golden hair cascaded down the front of her light blue dress, ending just above her waist. She was beautiful—almost as beautiful as Sam. *What is a babe like her doing with a clown like him?*

"Atto, who are your friends?" the woman asked, her tone curious but inviting at the same time.

He motioned to Sam. "This is Genovefa. And the one behind her is Asterix. They are of the Iceni. They joined our group as we passed through the hills."

The woman pulled away from Atto and approached us. Without warning, she took Sam's hands in her own and then planted a kiss right on Sam's lips.

Sam's eyes widened and her body stiffened, while I choked back a laugh. Very little surprised Sam, so it was funny to see her thrown. As I tried to think of something witty to say, the woman released Sam's hands and kissed me the same way.

Wow! If this was how Celtic women said hello, I could really get used to this time period.

"Any person Atto calls friend, I call friend as well," the woman said warmly.

Atto draped his arm around the woman's shoulder again and beamed a huge smile. "This is Senna, the light in my sky, the fire in my heart—my wife."

"You're married?" I blurted. "To her?"

"Aye. Senna and I joined our hands together five summers ago. Our children are around here somewhere." He swung his head from side to side, as if searching. "Vata! Cario! Where have you two wood sprites hidden?"

Married with kids? Atto?

A grinning girl of about four and a slightly younger boy came running up to him. Atto scooped them both up in his arms at the same time. "Have you been getting into mischief, little piglets?" he asked.

"No," said the girl, her eyes wide.

"What?" Atto spun them around in a circle, making them squeal with delight. "My little princess and warrior have been behaving? What child of mine does not get into mischief?"

Vata and Cario laughed, and Atto did a few more spins before putting them down. He turned to his wife. "Senna, my love, hunger gnaws at my belly. Let us eat."

He motioned to an open patch of ground by the fire. "Genovefa, Little Roman, come dine with us. We have food to spare. The people of the island have stored much grain for the coming attack, and they have fish as well." A small iron cauldron hung over the flames, half filled with a mush of boiled grain and a few tiny pieces of fish. I thought the food in Anglo-Saxon England had been bad. This stuff looked like lumpy glue and smelled vile. Sadly, it wasn't much for four people, and even less if Sam and I joined them. Atto and Senna had probably left behind or destroyed most of their food stores when they fled their village.

"Do you have a bowl?" I asked.

Senna reached into a wicker basket and handed me a carved wooden bowl. "Aye, do with it what you will."

I pulled my backpack off my shoulder, carefully undid all the ties, then dipped the bowl into my pack.

Sam crouched next to me. "What are you doing?" she asked, dropping her voice so Senna and Atto couldn't hear.

"Contributing to dinner," I whispered back. "I can't take food from these people. Look at how little they have. If any of them survive the massacre, they're going to be starving within a few days. They'll need everything they can get."

"So what's in your backpack?"

"Trail mix."

"What else?"

"Nothing. Just trail mix."

"Are you serious?" Sam hissed. "You jumped through time and all you brought with you was a backpack full of trail mix?"

"Yeah," I shrugged. "I hated those breakfasts in Anglo-Saxon England. All that barley porridge made me nauseous. Do you know how many times I wanted a snack, and all they had was smoked mutton or raw leeks? I lost ten pounds on that jump. I wasn't going to starve again." I pulled out the bowl heaped with nuts, raisins, and seeds. "Don't worry; I didn't get the kind with M&M's. Plus, I toasted it in the oven to stop germination, so even if we drop any of it, we won't mess up the time stream by planting non-native crops."

Sam looked toward the sky and shook her head.

"And what did you bring?" I asked.

She started counting off on her fingers. "Extra cloth for bandages, a sewing kit, ibuprofen, water-purification tablets, flint and steel, and"— she dropped her voice to the barest of whispers—"two chocolate bars."

"Aha!" I said, pointing a finger at her.

"Hey, I like chocolate," she said defensively. "And it's not like I filled my backpack with it."

"But I knew *you'd* bring all the smart stuff. That's why I brought trail mix. And of all the things we packed, which one are we using right now?"

She laughed and helped me reseal my backpack. "Okay, I'll give you this one. It was a good idea."

We joined Atto, Senna, and their kids by the fire, and each of us received a small bowl of stew that we topped with trail mix. Surprisingly, the fish mush didn't taste as wretched as it smelled— although I still preferred the trail mix.

"Are you two joined by marriage?" Senna asked, as we ate.

Sam coughed hard, nearly choking on her stew. "No!" she said, her cheeks turning red. "I'm only seventeen."

"And?" Senna asked. "Atto and I agreed to our marriage contract in my fourteenth summer, as do most women in my village. Seventeen summers is much too old to be still alone. Are you waiting for Asterix to gain more wealth and fame before you agree to the contract?"

"I'm not ready for marriage," Sam said firmly. She turned to me and mouthed the words *Help me.*

There was no hope in hell I was going to wade into this conversation. The last thing I wanted was Atto and Senna to start directing their nosy personal questions my way. Besides, it was fun watching Sam squirm.

"Not ready?" Atto snorted. "Half your life is over already. My own mother saw only thirty summers before she passed on, and her mother saw thirty-six."

Senna nodded and stroked Sam's hair. "You are too pretty to remain unwed. If this one"—she jerked a thumb at me—"has not the wealth you seek as a bride price, I am sure that there are many men here who would be willing to swear to a contract with your family."

Sam shifted uneasily and stared intently at her fish stew, letting her hair fall forward over her face.

"So," Senna persisted, "shall I find a husband for you?"

An odd strangled sound came from Sam.

"Is that a yes?" Senna asked.

A long, clear blast from a horn rang out, saving Sam from any further embarrassment. All heads turned together to discover the source of the sound. In the darkness, a line of torches could now be seen snaking down the hill from the druid compound. An expectant hush spread through the camp as the druids descended, their light gray cloaks making them look like ghosts in the darkness.

"What's happening?" I asked.

Senna stood up and stared toward the figures. "A meeting of great importance, clearly. We must follow." She took Cario in her arms.

Atto grabbed Vata by the hand and turned to me and Sam. "Coming?"

"Yes," I said, and stood. I couldn't believe this was happening. Twelve hours ago I'd been at home asleep in my bed, and now the druids were gathering. This had to be where I was going to be made leader of the Celts. The thought sent little chills of terror through me. What if no one listened to me? Or worse, what if they listened too well and then they defeated the Romans?

I barely paid any attention to our surroundings as we trudged deep inland, passing fields of grain and isolated stands of trees. My mind was preoccupied with everything I'd have to do. First I'd have to get them to learn how to fight in formation, as they were more used to fighting as a mob than a unit. And then I'd have to teach them how to form a shield wall. Those two little things would probably save thousands of lives. And of course I'd also have to teach them some tactics to use against cavalry. There was so much they'd need to learn … and so little time.

Suddenly our little group stopped walking. We were standing in a field at the back of a large crowd of Celts. There were thousands of them jammed together, all staring silently toward a grove of oak trees atop a low hill. A small stone altar stood just before the grove, and beside it a large stack of wood seemed ready for a bonfire. The druids stood in a perfectly spaced circle around the altar, their torches held out in front of them with both hands. A single druid stood behind the altar. His hood was pulled up, keeping his face in shadow, but a huge gold medallion hanging around his neck glinted in the torchlight.

Raising his arms skyward, the chief druid began to chant in a deep powerful voice, his words ringing out over the assembled Celts. He chanted faster and faster, his words coming out at a feverous pitch … and then he stopped.

On this cue the other druids in the circle threw their torches onto the pile. The flames licked at the dry timber, and soon a huge fire lit up the darkness. The chief druid clapped his hands once. "The time for war is upon us," he announced. "The Romans approach and will be here soon. At this time we must choose a leader to guide us into battle. Who would lead our people?"

This had to be my cue. Wiping my sweaty hands on my pants, I raised my hand. "I will—"

"Let me lead," a man shouted, cutting me off, "and I will push the Romans all the way back to Rome!"

Wait … What … ?

A burly man pushed his way through the crowd until he also stood on the low hill, next to the chief druid. He had shoulder-length hair and a large shaggy mustache reaching to his chin. He was older than most of the others—and wore a blue cloak trimmed with fur and held in place with a huge gold clasp.

"I vote for Prasto!" yelled someone from the crowd.

"Prasto is a fool!" another man shouted. He bulled his way past everyone and stood facing Prasto. "I will lead us to victory!" he shouted. "An entire Roman legion fell before my might! My men slaughtered—"

"A Roman legion?" yelled a third man. "Even your own men do not believe such lies. Where now is the standard that they carried into battle? Let us have proof of your deeds!" This man stepped forward, to more cheers. "I will lead our people!"

Four more men climbed up the hillside, making seven in total. All were older with shoulder-length hair and sweeping mustaches, their arms and necks glittering with gold bands and rings and medallions. They reeked of confidence, and each man had a large section of the crowd cheering for him.

I stood rooted to the spot. I couldn't get up on that hill—people would laugh at me.

"Come on," Sam urged. "Get in there."

"Look at those guys," I said. "They're *real* leaders—the people love them. There's no way I can persuade people to follow me when those guys are up there."

Sam put her hands on my shoulders and turned me around to face her. "You have to. As much as I don't trust Cenacus, he was right about one thing: the Celts are going to get slaughtered here—you said it yourself. So I know you're scared, but you still have to get in there. Only you can give these people a fighting chance. Now go save them."

The seven men vying for leadership all looked so kingly, dressed in their vibrant tunics and gold ornaments. And me? I had only my ratty cloak and a wooden staff. I looked like some kid in a bad Halloween costume.

The chief druid raised both hands. "Does anyone else believe he has the skill to lead our people?" He turned around slowly, making sure he did not miss any last-minute challengers.

I swallowed the lump forming in my throat and raised a hand. "I will lead the people," I shouted.

CHAPTER 7

With a chorus of laughter and insults ringing in my ears, I pushed my way out of the crowd and entered the circle of firelight.

The druid chief tapped his staff firmly on the ground. At this signal, everyone fell silent. He looked around at the eight of us and then motioned to the first man. "State your claim," he said.

With his chest thrust out, the first man addressed the massed Celts. "I am Prasto of the Cornovii," he bellowed. "My war bands have killed hundreds of Romans. So many of the foul invaders lie dead that they now fear to pass into the lands beyond the Frost Peak Mountains. We pillaged from them, we killed them in their homes, and we burned down their towns. The name Prasto is dreaded by all Romans." He stroked his luxuriant mustache. "The Romans who come here shall never leave these shores! We will let them land, and then we shall bring all our numbers to bear against them, driving them back into the water. Women in Rome will weep and men will rue the day the Romans chose to challenge us here!"

He clapped his hands, and a tall man in a multicolored cloak came to stand beside him. The guy pulled a small harp from the leather satchel hanging by his side and began to strum a tune and sing.

Prasto the Bold, the Romans did fight, along the riverside.

He charged their lines, and smashed their shields ...

His song went on for what felt like half an hour, just one outrageous lie after another, all put in verse and accompanied by the plinking of the harp. And the worst thing was that Prasto's bard wasn't the only one there. Each of the guys vying for leadership had brought their own. So I was stuck there for ages listening to a bunch of idiots spouting endless drivel about how awesome they'd be in battle and how many victories they'd already achieved. Yet none of these would-be leaders had anything inspiring to offer. They all seemed to believe that one massive charge would knock the Romans back into the water—as if the Roman army was made up of cowards and weaklings who'd run away at the first sight of a few Celts waving swords.

Because I was the youngest, and also the least known, I spoke last. But that at least gave me a chance to think up something to say. I watched the faces of the people in the audience who were listening to all these unbelievable lies and boasts. The warriors clearly had blood-lust in their eyes; they hung on every word of every song, cheering at the bloody parts. They didn't care who led them; they just wanted a chance to kill Romans. But the women and the ordinary working men didn't look so confident. They held back, conversing in hushed voices whenever any of the Celts spoke of simply flinging the Romans back into the strait.

Finally, after another unbelievable song and another round of cheering, it was my turn. I took up position next to the chief druid, and he raised his hands for silence. For about the thousandth time, I wiped my hands on my pants to get the sweat off them. I really hated public speaking. The crowd had already laughed at me before; what if they started laughing at me as I spoke? Luckily the huge bonfire had ruined my night vision, so I could only see the people nearest to me—the rest were hidden in the darkness.

I took a deep breath to calm myself. "Great speeches from every man here," I announced. "Unfortunately, I don't have a bard to sing my praises. And I don't have tales of hundreds of battles where thousands of Romans died."

"Then what do you have?" someone shouted to a chorus of laughter.

"I have the truth," I yelled. "Listen to the tales these men have told you. They say they killed thousands of Romans and burned countless cities. But then why are they all here? Why are we huddled together on this island, waiting for the Romans to attack us, if these men have told you the truth?" I pointed to Prasto. "He claims to have burned Roman villages." I pointed to the next man. "He claims to have destroyed a legion." I proceeded to point to each man in turn and retell his most exaggerated claim. "If you believe these men, they have all killed so many Romans that Rome itself should be quaking behind their walls in fear of their approach." I slammed the end of my staff into the ground. "But they're not. The Romans are coming here to kill us."

This got the crowd muttering. I didn't know whether they were angry at me for challenging the stories they'd just been told or angry at their leaders for making up those stories, but I had to press on now. I needed to get these Celts to see the truth. "These men all tell you stories of great battles, and then have exactly the same vision of how to defeat the Romans. They want to charge at the Romans and send them back into the water. But how many of you own armor?" Very few of the crowd grunted in response. "The Romans have armor ... and they know how to fight together. If we want to win, we need to start fighting like Romans."

"I will not hear any more of this!" Prasto yelled. "The boy wants us to fight like Romans! Who is he to talk to me like this?"

"I am Asterix of the Iceni. And I'm trying to save your stupid skin from certain death."

"Bah! I am not a scared boy like you." Prasto thumped his fist against his chest. "I do not fear death. When I die, the gods will take me to the lands of the undying, and I will live a life of eternal happiness there."

I pointed with my staff toward the crowd—to the men and women who stood huddled together with hunched shoulders and fear etched across their faces. "You may not fear death," I said. "But what of the men and women who are not warriors, who have come here for peace and safety, and to flee the Romans? I want to save *them*."

"And the men who follow me will give them peace!" Prasto yelled back at me. "By killing every Roman who sets foot on this island."

"Two legions are on their way," I said. "That is ten thousand professional Roman soldiers. And they will have auxiliary troops as well, probably bringing their numbers closer to fifteen thousand. You think you can kill all those men with a single charge?"

"We will!" Prasto shouted defiantly.

"No. You won't."

Prasto clenched his fists. "I have led my village for years, bringing them peace, prosperity, and victories against the Romans. Who have you led? What have you done?"

"You don't know me, but I know how to fight. I know how to kill. And I know how to defend this island against the Romans so that thousands don't have to die."

"And what would you do? Have us run away?" Prasto scoffed. "You are a long way from Iceni lands. Did you run all that distance?"

"I'd build defenses," I said. "We could put walls along the beaches to block their attack. We could build siege weapons like the Romans do, so that we could destroy their boats before they land."

Prasto waved his hand dismissively at me. "Walls? How do you know where the Romans will land? How will you protect this entire island? Your plan has no merit. Courage and honor are what will bring us victory."

"Courage and honor?" I snorted. "That's going to get you killed. Do the Romans fight with either?"

"So you want us to fight like them?" Prasto spat on the fire so that his spittle hissed in the flames. "I will not fight in their manner. They fight like cowards, hiding behind shields and throwing their spears. That is not the way for a man to fight."

"You'll die quickly, then," I said.

"Do you doubt my courage?" He puffed out his chest again and glared at me.

"No. I doubt your ability to survive." I raised my voice so everyone could hear me. "All of you are brave," I said, "but the Romans are not. They hide behind shields and use catapults and ballistae to attack you from far away. While you stand there on the field, yelling your battle cries and proving your courage, they will kill you. So you have a choice: you can either die with bravery, or you can follow me and I will show you how to live!"

A loud murmur rose from the masses in the field, and I basked in the tumult. I'd aced the speech. I'd never felt so calm under pressure before. I'd blown everyone else's arguments away.

The lead druid raised his hands for silence. "Have you finished?"

"Yes," I said.

"Time to vote!" he yelled.

Celts are morons.

After all the screaming, the shouting, the raising of hands, did I win their vote? Hell, no. Did Prasto the loud, obnoxious braggart win? Hell, yes. I didn't even come close. A few older men and some of the women voted for me, but that's it. In the Celtic world, if you wanted to get ahead, you clearly needed some guy with a harp and a strong voice to spread lies about you.

With the foul taste of defeat in my mouth, I stormed off in search of Cenacus, finally finding him back near the main path, heading toward his rickety cart. "I thought you were going to make me the leader of the battle," I snapped. "What the hell happened?"

He cast a furtive glance around, then grabbed my sleeve to pull me closer. "I tried," he whispered. "But the chief druid changed his mind and decided to put it to a vote. It's the Celtic way." He shook his head. "I'm sorry. I did all I could."

I'd told Cenacus his plan was insane, but he had somehow persuaded me to believe in it. And it wasn't even the embarrassment of losing that had me so angry, it was the fact that thousands of Celts would die because Prasto was clearly an idiot. "So what happens now?"

"Your friend still leaves at first light to dig up and destroy the tablet. And we need to figure out a way to buy her as much time as possible."

"That's *it?*" I snapped, not bothering to hide my disappointment. "That's your druid wisdom?"

Cenacus bowed his head. "I'm sorry," he mumbled. "I did all I could."

"Whatever." I stormed off, though I was in no rush to get back to the group. The later I returned, the less likely I'd see Atto again; I was sure he'd have plenty to say about my failed leadership bid.

By the time I got back to the camp, most of the fires had burned down, but a few people were still up and about. And, of course, one of those people was Atto. He leaped up as I approached, a stupid grin on his face.

"So, Little Roman," he chuckled, "you wanted to lead us into battle?"

"Yup," I said, my voice a monotone. "But that's not going to happen now."

"Your words carried much strength. Soon we will get to see if your arm has strength as well."

I didn't know whether he was making fun of me—and right now I didn't care. I needed time to figure out how to slow down the Romans, and his blathering was just distracting me.

A wall would help, but what can one guy do?

I pinched the bridge of my nose and sighed. *If we could get the Romans while they were still crossing, that would be best. But to do that we'd need ...*

Wait a second ...

"Atto!" I blurted. "Do you know where I can find some axes, a few shovels, a thick leather cloak, and about a thousand paces' length of rope?"

Atto gave me an amused grin. "That's a lot of rope. Are you planning on making a net, Little Roman?"

"Just tell me! Can you get me this stuff?"

"Aye, it should not be hard. What do you plan?"

"I'm going to try to stop the Romans."

Atto clapped his hands together and laughed. "First you want to lead us into battle: now you want to beat the Romans with rope and a cloak. The gods have touched you, Little Roman." He tapped his temple with a finger. "No matter. Stay here and do not worry. I will get your goods. I look ahead with joy to seeing what you create." He began to walk away, chuckling to himself.

Atto was receding into the darkness when Sam and Senna appeared, as if they had been waiting for him to leave. "Where have you been all night?" I asked.

"I might have found you some help," Sam said. "Tell him, Senna."

"I listened to the words you spoke at the druid grove," Senna began. "And many of the other women listened as well. We are not fools like our husbands. We know that most men speak only to hear the sound of their own voices. But you speak with thought behind your words, so we would help you if we can."

A faint spark of hope ignited in my chest. "How many are you?"

"Not many. A few of the wives—and some of the older men and children as well."

A bunch of women, kids, and old men. Not much of a fighting force but, for what I planned, I didn't need fighters. "Can they follow orders?"

"For the lives of our children, we will do anything."

I nodded. "Meet me at first light with everyone you can gather. We'll see what we can do to stop the Romans," I said before walking off into the darkness.

"And where do you go?" Senna called after me.

"I have to find Atto. We're going to need more rope."

CHAPTER 8

A flash of pain jarred me awake. I sat up instantly, my heart pounding and my ankle throbbing. Senna stood a few feet away, a wooden bucket in each hand.

"Apologies, Asterix," she said. "I stumbled over your foot in the darkness."

No danger.

I relaxed and rubbed the sleep out of my eyes with the heel of my hand. Dawn hadn't come yet, so the camp lay shrouded in a misty cloak of gray. Sam had slept curled up next to me to share warmth, while Atto and his kids lay bundled in woolen blankets next to the smoldering embers of the fire.

"You're up early," I said to Senna.

"Aye, chores must be done, and before dawn is the best time to do them." Senna offered me one of the wooden buckets. "Will you walk with me?"

I shrugged out of my blankets and shook off the chill. "Where are we going?" I asked quietly, grabbing the bucket.

She put her hand on my arm and steered me toward a group of

trees a few hundred paces away. "A small pool lies amidst the trees. I want to fetch fresh water before it gets stirred up by all the others."

We threaded our way through the field full of sleeping people. Not even the animals were up yet, so we proceeded in ghostly silence. My mind raced as I thought of all the things I'd need to do to get my plan into action before the Romans arrived. *How many people did Senna have? And would they be of any use?*

Her hand trailed down my arm and grabbed my hand. "You have a warrior's hand," she observed. "You have fought before."

"Yeah, a few times."

I wondered whether we had enough rope. I might need to get hold of some more axes as well if Senna had recruited enough people.

"Do you have any stories of great battles? I would like to hear of them."

"Sorry. The only battle I was in was pretty fierce. I lost some good friends there and I almost died. I'd rather not talk about it."

I'll probably need more shovels too. Those should be easier to find.

We entered the woods and stopped at a small spring flowing out from a jumble of mossy rocks. The water splashed over the stones to collect in a shallow pool. Senna took the buckets, filled them, then set them by the edge of the pool. "Come wash yourself, Asterix," she suggested.

I was a bit grimy after all that paddling the day before. I dipped the edge of my cloak into the pool and used it to scrub my face and hands.

Senna watched me with an amused smile on her face. "You are a funny one." She grabbed the gold shoulder clasps that secured her dress and, with a gentle tug, pulled them off. The light blue cloth fluttered down, gathering at the waist, but leaving her naked from the waist up.

Whoa …

"Come, let me help you off with your cloak," Senna said, reaching toward me. "I will wash you."

"I'm good!" I yelped, raising my hands. What was she doing? Atto would kick my ass if he saw this. I looked over my shoulder to check if anyone was watching.

"Is something wrong?" Senna asked. "You turn away from me. Does that mean you do not find me pleasing?"

I hung my head and stared at the ground. "No! I mean, yes! I mean ..."

She lifted my chin up with a finger. "Look at me. Tell me what you see."

She was tall like most Celts, with piercing blue eyes and straw-colored hair that flowed over her shoulders and down across her chest, covering her breasts and ending just above her waist. A lifetime of hard work in the sun had given her a tanned, lean, muscular build. "You're beautiful," I said. "But this isn't right."

Senna knelt by the pool and leaned forward. Her hair dangled close to the water, so she held it aside with one hand, revealing small round breasts. She splashed a few handfuls of water across her body and then washed her arms and neck. "And why is this not right?"

"You're topless."

"Of course. It is very hard to wash one's body while wearing clothes." She shook her head at me. "Why does the sight of me distress you so much?"

"You're married," I said, trying to keep my eyes off her semi-nakedness but failing miserably.

"And? Atto and I agreed to a marriage contract, but he does not own me. I am a free woman, and I can do as I wish." She stood up and put her hand on my arm, sending shivers of excitement through me. "And right now I wish to show you how much I like you." She leaned forward and kissed me.

I knew I should push her away, but I couldn't resist the softness of her lips—couldn't bring myself to move at all. As my blood pounded in my ears, her hands slid under my tunic and caressed my back.

My entire body was on fire for this gorgeous woman, but my brain kept screaming that this wasn't right—her husband and kids were sleeping only a few hundred paces away. They could wake up and catch us at any moment. And what about Sam? Even though we weren't a couple, she was the only one I wanted. This could ruin any chance I'd ever have with her.

With a burst of willpower, I pulled myself away from Senna. "Why are you doing this?" I panted.

A look of disappointment crossed her face, but it instantly faded, replaced with a knowing smile. "I was right about you," she said. "You are not like other men."

She sat down by the pool and dipped her toes in the water. "Come sit with me," she said, patting the ground next to her. "I will not press further if you do not wish it."

The smart thing would have been to run. But from what? A beautiful woman? A calm woodland pond? Two dangerous-looking buckets? With tentative steps I sat down next to her, making sure to leave a healthy gap between us.

She cupped some water from the pool and continued washing her feet and legs. "The Romans are coming soon," she said, "and in the battle many men will die. My husband is the bravest and kindest man I know and will no doubt be one of the first to charge the Romans. But, even if the gods grant us victory, I doubt I will have a husband when the day is over." She bit her lip and gazed across the pool toward the far side. "If that comes to pass, my children and I will face a winter of hardship. Our kin are all gone, we have lost our livestock, and our home is a smoking ruin. We have nothing. We will most likely die without the aid of a strong man to hunt for us and build us a shelter."

She turned to me, her blue eyes piercing mine. "And that is why I sit with you, Asterix. You have shown strength and wisdom—you will not rush foolishly into the jaws of Roman steel. I have no doubt you will survive this fight. If Atto falls, I will need a husband. And I want that man to be you."

"*What?*"

Senna caressed my cheek with her hand. "I do not have much wealth to bring to our marriage, but neither do you. So ours will be a marriage of equals."

"Why me?" I asked as I leaned away from her. "You're young. You're beautiful. You could have your pick of men."

Senna's eyes narrowed hungrily. "You have the hands and scars of a warrior, yet the words and wisdom of a druid. You will achieve great things, and I want to be by your side, providing you with strong sons."

Marriage? Sons? This conversation had turned into a train wreck. I didn't know why she thought I was marriage material, but I needed her to change her mind quickly. "You don't even know me," I said. "I'd make a terrible husband. I'm young. I'm irresponsible. I'm broke."

"I have watched you, Asterix. A mother must always be careful of those who come near her children. And I see that you are a good man. You have shared your food, and you try to stop the men from killing themselves. That is enough for me." She put her hand on my shoulder. "Will you protect me if Atto falls?"

"But—"

"If you think of Genovefa, have no fear. I am content to share you and be a second wife, or even a third wife. Many women will be seeking new husbands after this battle, so I realize you may end up taking many wives."

Why couldn't I have normal teenage problems? Marriage? To multiple women? It might have been normal in Celtic times, but it was not happening for me. All I wanted was to get out of here as fast as I could. "You don't need me," I said, "because Atto will survive."

"And if he does not? You were the one who warned us of the might of the Roman army. You stood before us all and told us our doom was coming. Do you take back those words?"

I exhaled slowly. "No."

"So what will become of my children? Will they starve? Or will you join with me?"

What she wanted was impossible, but I had no words to explain why I couldn't help her. This would be so much easier if she wasn't also half naked. "I just … can't."

"We are clearly of the same wealth, I have agreed to allow you multiple wives, and I can see by your eyes that you desire me." She grabbed my hand and placed it on her bare chest just over her heart. "Give me one reason why you cannot agree to this, and I will not press my suit any longer."

Because you're from two thousand years in my past.

Because I'm time-jumping out of here as soon as I can.

I had no reason to offer that she would understand or believe, and all I could think of now was her soft skin and the beating of her heart beneath my hand.

Senna leaned over and kissed me again. "Consider our bargain sealed then, Asterix of the Iceni." Smiling, she got up and fastened the dress back up onto her shoulders. "I must go now, as Vata and Cario will wake soon and start crying for me." She nodded toward the buckets. "Can you carry those?"

I got to my feet and reached for the buckets but stopped. Instead, I stood next to the pond and watched Senna head back toward camp, her hair shimmering gold in the rising sun. *What had I gotten myself into?* If only I'd stayed asleep this morning, none of this would have happened.

I slapped my forehead with my palm. She hadn't woken me accidentally—she had set the whole thing up!

I'd always worried about the men attacking me, but it had never occurred to me to worry about the women. After seeing Senna in action, though, I realized that the women were the dangerous ones in the Celtic world. The men were all bluster and showmanship, easy to figure out. But the women? They were cunning, with a survive-at-all-costs attitude. Definitely the ones to watch out for.

I slunk after Senna, moving slowly so as not to spill the water. I hoped Sam was still sleeping—this was one conversation I didn't want to have. *Hey, Sam, want to hear a funny story? I went to fetch water with Senna. She showed me her boobs, and now she thinks we're engaged.* Yeah, I was going to keep this little story to myself. I just hoped Senna would do the same.

By the time I made it back to camp, Sam and Atto were both awake and standing with Senna by the fire. I looked at the three of them and tried to figure out whether Senna had revealed anything. Atto wasn't reaching for his sword, and Sam wasn't scowling at me, so I guessed I was still safe.

I kept my head bowed and placed the buckets beside the fire. "I brought some water," I said, cringing at how painfully obvious this statement was.

"You are a good man to help Senna." Atto threw his arm around my shoulder and gave me a friendly squeeze.

"Yes, he is a very good man," Senna agreed, her eyes lingering over me. She then turned to Atto, threw her arms around him, and kissed him. "Did you sleep well, husband?"

Atto crushed her in his embrace. "Aye. I dreamed of you."

I turned away from their display of affection and noticed Sam watching me. I took a step toward her, then stopped. I wanted to hold her and kiss her like Atto held Senna, but I knew we didn't have that sort of relationship. But did we at least hug occasionally? Or were we the kind of friends who stood awkwardly next to a fire pit, looking at each other but not saying or doing anything?

"So, when are you leaving?" I asked Sam, trying to break the weirdness of the moment. I regretted the question as soon as it left my mouth. There were so many friendlier and less awkward things I could have said.

Sam bit her lip and turned away from me to bend down and roll up her blanket before tying it to her backpack. "I'm going to stock up on food and then set off," she said, not meeting my eyes.

"You are leaving, Genovefa?" Atto asked. "Where are you going?"

"The druid needs me to head north," she said as she stood up and tossed the backpack over her shoulders.

Atto grasped her wrist and gently stroked her hand. "Will you be gone long?"

"I hope not."

"Well, may your feet have wings upon the trail," he said. "My heart waits for the day we can meet again." He leaned in and kissed her.

Instead of slugging him, Sam blushed but didn't pull away.

"Excuse me!" I said loudly, before Sam enjoyed herself too much. I knew I had no right to protest after what had gone on between Senna and me in the forest, but I still felt jealous. The man had a way about him that everyone liked, especially women.

As Atto stepped away from Sam, I reached over and shifted a strand of hair away from her face. "Be careful."

Sam smiled weakly. "I'm just going for a hike across the island. You're the one about to face the Roman army." She traced the scar across my forehead with her fingertips—a memento of when I had charged the Norman lines. "Don't be a hero, Dan. You don't have to win this one."

"I know." I pulled her tightly to me. "Just hurry," I whispered.

"I'll do my best. As soon as the jump rod goes warm, get yourself out of here."

"I will."

She kissed me lightly on the cheek and then broke off our embrace.

"I'd better go now." She slung the quiver of arrows on her back and grabbed her bow. Without another look back, she began heading off northward.

I felt hollow inside. As soon as she succeeded in destroying Cenacus's tablet, we'd both jump out of Celtic times and be back in our own time—in our separate homes, hours away from each other, where our only contact was texting or the odd video call.

Atto clapped me on the shoulder, breaking my train of thought. "So, Little Roman, what are you planning to do with all that rope?"

I looked over at the pile of items Atto had brought me the night before. A few coils of rope, three leather cloaks, two axes, and a shovel. Now all I needed was manpower. "Senna, where are the people you told me would help?"

"What?" Atto turned to Senna, a surprised look on his face. "You are part of this?"

"You know I love you, husband, but I cannot just stand by and watch you die. I believe Asterix has a way to stop the Romans, and therefore I will do as he says."

"Look at him, Senna." Atto gestured with his hand from my feet to my head. "He is not a warrior. He does not even carry a sword. What does he know of war?"

"Atto," Senna said calmly, as if talking to a child. "Asterix speaks the truth. Our people have won many fights against the Romans, but we are losing the war. We cannot stand against them like we have always done—that only leads to death." She placed her palm tenderly on his cheek. "I will not allow myself to die in a doomed charge against the Romans. I will try *his* way."

Atto grabbed her hand off his cheek and kissed it. "All right, my love. I had hoped to have you at my side during battle, but if you wish to stand at the rear with the Little Roman, I will not stop you. At least Cario and Vata will be safe with you."

"You could join us, husband, and be at our side."

He shook his head. "You know I cannot. I must be with my war band at the front, hurling the Romans back into the sea."

Senna bowed her head and pulled away from him. "Come, Asterix," she urged, her voice cracking. "The others wait for us on the beach."

Senna snatched up the axes and shovel while I piled the rope in among the cloaks and slung them all over my shoulder. What was I going to do with all this? Last night I had visions of making onagers— Roman catapults that could fling small stones a few hundred feet. But onagers needed lots of twisted rope to power the throwing arm, and the stuff that Atto brought me was total crap. It was dry and loose, with no springiness at all. It just wasn't going to cut it. *C'mon, Dan, think. What can you do with this stuff?*

I trudged mutely after Senna, my mind working feverishly to figure out something that I could construct instead. We arrived at the beach, where about thirty people waited—mostly women, some kids who looked just shy of their teenage years, and a few older men. One or two faces I recognized from our crossing yesterday, but most were unknown to me. Everyone looked expectantly at me, as if hoping I'd provide a miracle to save them from the Romans.

I turned and looked along the beach, hoping for inspiration. Thick, dark clouds hung low in the sky, threatening rain, and the wind whipping over the water brought the smell of the sea and the taste of salt to my lips. *Where would the Romans land?* The strait that separated our island from the mainland was long and narrow, maybe only five hundred paces across at its thinnest point. They could land just about anywhere.

How hard would it be for the Romans to paddle their boats against the current as they came across? The water flowed strongly to the north, and the waves were tipped with whitecaps as they passed over hidden rocks and shoals.

Hold it …

Was I going crazy? "Wasn't the water flowing the other way yesterday?" I asked.

A man with tanned skin and a worn, crease-lined face chuckled. "Aye, these are no easy shores. I have fished the waters around this island all my life, and no passage is more treacherous. Two sea gods fight constantly over this channel. For half the day one brother is stronger, and he pushes the water that way." He pointed north. "But then his strength fails him and his brother overpowers him, and pushes the water the other way. Only for two short spans each day does the water lie still, as the two sea gods rest from their fight."

During our crossing yesterday the water had been calm compared to now, and even then my arms had ached from hauling on the paddle. There was no way the Romans would be stupid enough to try to cross at any time other than when the tide was calm. "Where's the best place to cross with an entire army?" I asked.

The fisherman rubbed his stubbled jaw and squinted out over the water. "The strait does not have many good places for crossing. At the wider part the water flows slower, but hidden rocks and quicksand can foul a boat or make one wrong step a man's last. And in the narrows the water flows treacherously fast, even when both sea gods grow tired and little water enters the channel." He motioned to a beach a few hundred paces north of us. "If I were to bring a fleet of boats across, I would do it there. The water is no better or worse than elsewhere, but the landing would be easier."

The beach he was pointing to did look like a good place to land an army. It started off as a long sandy stretch and then sloped gradually up before merging into a grassy field. About a hundred paces back from the beach, and off to one side, a wooded rise looked out over the water. If I set up there, I'd have a good view over the channel and would also be away from the main fighting.

"Come on," I urged my group of helpers before tossing my supplies over my shoulder and heading for the hill. I had a location I could defend; now I had to figure out what to build there. A wall would be useless, and onagers required stronger rope.

No matter how hard I tried to think of something else, there was only one weapon that I knew of that could be built with my meager supplies and tools. But it wasn't Roman—it was from the Middle Ages. Building it would probably create a glitch just as bad as Cenacus's tablet—maybe even worse. I had to think of something better.

I reached the top of the hill and dropped my supplies. The breeze was stronger here, pushing my hair into my eyes. I brushed the annoying strands away and surveyed the beach below.

"So what are we going to do?" Senna asked.

Good question. My one idea might save thousands of innocent lives, but it might end up giving the Roman army a super weapon that could change history forever.

With the tips of my fingers, I massaged my temples, trying to fight off the ache building up behind my eyes. *What should I do?*

As if sensing my dilemma, Senna put her hands on my shoulders and nodded encouragingly. "Be the leader I know you are, Asterix. Save us."

Save us.

How much suffering had this poor woman endured if she was willing to put her life, and the lives of her children, into the hands of some kid she just met yesterday? And it would only get worse for her and the rest of the Celts if I didn't do something.

"Okay, this is the plan." I leaned over and started drawing with a stick in the dirt, the people huddling around me. "We need to chop down at least ten thick trees, trim off their branches, and then join them together like this." I scratched the outline of two triangular prisms. "We'll also need to build a large wicker basket—about two paces long on each side, and three paces high. It has to be strong enough to carry at least ten men. And we need rocks, lots of rocks, of all sizes."

"Are we building a tower?" one woman asked.

"No. We're building something that will destroy Roman boats before they can reach the shore." At least, that's what I hoped we were building. There was also an excellent chance we were building a huge monument to futility.

"How will this destroy boats? I do not understand," a man said.

"Enough!" Senna stood up straight and clapped her hands loudly. "We are here because we trust Asterix—we should not question everything. Totia, you take the wee ones and get them fetching stones. Dump them there." She pointed to a spot on the top of the hill. "Duro, you take the men and start chopping down trees and stripping them bare. Just make sure to choose ones with straight trunks—and no dead wood." She turned to a lady in a green dress. "Ria, you gather the women and begin weaving the basket."

Without another word, the men and women rushed to do Senna's bidding. With all the extra people, we had a shortage of proper tools, but some of the older kids were sent back to camp and returned with knives, spears, and swords—anything that could cut wood. Soon the hill echoed with the meaty thunks of steel biting into timber.

It was slow and tedious work. Give me a chainsaw, a power drill, a hammer, and a wheelbarrow, and we could have whipped up these frames and piled all the rocks within an hour. Instead, we did everything by hand. With each load of rocks that I carried up from the beach and with each tree trunk that I helped drag into position, my palms became more raw and the ache in my back grew. The pain was made worse by our unwanted audience. Warriors from the camp, attracted by the noise, started coming to watch us. They sat on the grass, guzzling from clay jugs and laughing at our efforts. With so little to do on this island, we were the only entertainment around—and it looked like we were a comedy.

"They build a tower to hide in," one man joked.

"No, no. They weave a huge basket to hide *under*," another responded.

"You could help us instead of just sitting there," I snapped.

"We are helping," the first warrior answered. "We are making your work area smell better." He stood up, turned around so his butt faced in my direction, and cracked a loud fart. The warriors howled with laughter and raised their jugs in salute.

And that was exactly why the Celts were going to lose this battle—they just couldn't take the Roman threat seriously enough to work together. Gritting my teeth, I ignored the idiot and continued lugging another rock to the top of the hill. The Celts would end up losing—I couldn't change that. But I was still going to make sure that the Romans paid a price for their victory.

CHAPTER 9

B y noon the two frames had been fully constructed and a long pole had been mounted on a crosspiece between them. The next step was to attach the wicker container to one end of the pole, but the women were still working on weaving the giant basket.

I sat down and wiped the sweat off my brow with the edge of my sleeve. The frame looked sturdy, even though the only thing holding the wooden beams together was Atto's crappy rope.

This might actually work.

A patter of footsteps warned me of Senna's approach. She sat down on the grass beside me, adjusted the skirt around her legs, then passed me a clay pitcher. "Drink. You have worked hard today."

"Thanks." I tilted the jug back, expecting water, but instead tasted the sweet honey flavor of mead.

She motioned toward the almost finished siege weapon. "Will this stop the Romans?" she asked.

I exhaled slowly, trying to pick my words carefully. I couldn't give her false hopes—they'd just be crushed when the Romans arrived. "No. It won't," I finally said. "But, if it works, it will slow them down.

If only we had a hundred of them."

She clasped her hands beneath her chin and stared out at the churning water. "What will become of us if the Romans win?"

Oh, geez …

This was even worse than the last question. I wished I could tell her that she and her family were going to live long happy lives under the Romans, but history said otherwise. "Sorry, but I only see slavery or death."

Her face paled and she swallowed hard. "And how do we avoid this fate?"

"Run. Get as far away from the battle as possible. Take your kids. Take Atto. Take anyone who will listen."

Her head snapped up and she turned to face me. "Where, Asterix?" she cried, her voice quivering with anger and fear. "We have already run! We left our village and traveled to the farthest ends of the land. But even that was not far enough, so we came to this island." She clenched her fists and beat them against her thighs. "Where else can we run? There is only water left."

I put my arm around her shoulders and she buried her face in my chest, her body heaving as she sobbed. "I'll do my best to stop the Romans," I assured her, stroking her hair. "We just need …"

A faint rhythmic thudding cut off my response and sent shivers through me. I knew that sound too well—it still came to me in my nightmares. I whipped my head around, trying to locate the source of it. My group of workers had heard it too. With curious eyes they scanned the mainland.

The thudding sound became clearer—the distinctive stomping of hundreds of horses moving together. A group of horsemen wearing chain mail and helmets and armed with spears appeared through a gap in the trees, riding along the road on the other side of the strait. With their long blond hair and bushy mustaches, they looked nothing like

Romans, but more like Celts. Except, where the Celts favored bright blues and reds, these men were dressed in gray or brown cloaks and pants.

The bunch of lazy hecklers got up from the grass, all laughter gone now. They gripped their weapons and watched the approaching horsemen, as if sizing them up.

"Batavians," spat one bald warrior contemptuously. "The dogs of Rome. Attacking wherever their masters order them to."

"Except dogs have more honor," another warrior added.

The squad of horsemen veered off the road and headed toward a wide flat space about two hundred paces down shore from us on the other bank. There one of the riders called twice on his horn. A second later came an answering call. Soon more squads of horsemen converged in the same spot.

The sight of the Batavians spurred on my little work crew. The women hurriedly finished weaving the large basket, then the men raised it up and lashed it to the central pole of the trebuchet before filling it from the pile of rocks. On the opposite shore, the parade of Batavian cavalry ended, and the Roman legions came into view, the synchronized beat of their marching feet echoing across the water. Thousands of men marched five abreast down the Celtic road, each carrying a short sword, two spears, a large rectangular shield, and wearing matching armor and helmet. A man on a white horse led them, his golden breastplate and the horsehair plume on his helmet clearly marking his importance.

"And there is the master of the dogs," a man said bitterly. "I thought the bastard would have stayed in his villa, not come here and risk getting his fine clothes dirty."

A warrior snorted. "Look at his armor. We will not see him amid the fighting. He will be at the back, the first to run and the loudest to boast."

On an order from the horseman, the Romans veered off the road and began hacking down trees and clearing space for a camp. The old fisherman had guessed correctly: the Romans were going to cross close to our position.

"Their numbers are endless!" Senna gasped.

I could only stare across the water as more and more Romans appeared. With a discipline and order that the Celts could never match, the Roman soldiers began digging a large defensive ditch and piling up the dirt into a short rectangular wall around the clearing. Others carved stakes and embedded them upright in the ditch.

A feeling of helplessness settled over me like a shroud. How was my one crappy little siege weapon going to slow down *that* many troops? And would it even work?

My little work crew and the Celtic warriors were all watching me, probably asking themselves the same thing. By now the basket had been filled with rocks, the throwing arm pulled into position. It was ready to fire.

I rolled a head-sized stone into the sling we'd created from a leather cloak, then looked around to make sure no one was in the way, in case the contraption collapsed. "Stand back, everyone," I yelled.

I licked my lips and took a deep breath. *Moment of truth.* So many people had put their faith in me; I hoped I wouldn't disappoint them. With a quick kick, I knocked the blocking piece of wood aside, and the wicker basket filled with rocks plunged downward, whipping the throwing arm and sling upward.

My mouth hung open as fifty pounds of rock sailed through the air and splashed into the middle of channel.

"Yes!" I pumped my fist into the air, and around me the Celts cheered and shouted.

The warriors, who had spent the day drinking and heckling us, stood staring in amazement.

"We must build more!" the bald warrior shouted. He turned toward me. "What do you call that device?"

"It's called a trebuchet." I stood watching the ripples in the water disappear rapidly among the churning waves. *And if I'm lucky, I didn't just royally mess up history.*

Warriors went running back to camp to get more men, and soon I had hundreds of people clamoring to help. Even Atto showed up, although his contribution seemed to consist mainly of making sure his mead jug was never empty. With so many people around to cut trees and collect rocks, the biggest problem became a shortage of rope to lash everything together. We had only enough to create four more trebuchets.

As my army of volunteers worked, I left Senna in charge and headed off into the trees to see whether I'd just created a new time glitch. Once out of everyone else's view, I pulled out the jump rod and spun the sections to form the pattern Cenacus had shown me. I turned in a slow circle, the rod held out in front of me like a flashlight. As expected, it pulled weakly to the north, where Sam was heading, but also much strongly toward my lone trebuchet.

Crap ...

I tucked the rod back into my pants, hidden from sight by the length of my tunic, then returned to the crowd and clapped my hands for attention. "We need to hide these weapons from Roman sight," I announced. "So I want dry branches piled up around them as high as possible."

"Why use dry branches, Little Roman?" Atto asked me. "Will not green branches hide them better?"

"They would—but dry branches burn better. And, when I say so, we're going to destroy these weapons. They can't be allowed to fall into Roman hands."

No one argued with that logic. These people had burned down

their homes and farms rather than let the Romans get them. They now rushed about, gathering dry sticks and branches and piling them up nearly to the top of the frames. Others smeared the trebuchet beams with animal fat so the fire would spread quicker when the time came to destroy them. By the end of the day, with our supply of rope exhausted, we had completed and disguised five trebuchets. They stood there on the hill: history's ugliest siege weapons.

Atto clapped me on the back as he admired their bulky shapes silhouetted against the darkening sky. "You did well, Little Roman." He thrust a clay jug into my hands. "Come drink with me. You may not be a warrior, but these weapons will kill many Romans."

I looked across the strait to where torches marked the boundaries of the Roman camp. They had finished building their defensive wall, and thousands of tents now covered the enclosed field. Unfortunately, Atto's scouting report was dead on. The Romans had brought two full legions and hundreds of Batavian cavalry—over ten thousand men in total. Hardly anyone was moving around now—only the guards on the walls and the workers stuck with unloading hundreds of flat-bottomed boats along the shore. Tonight the Romans would recover from their march, but tomorrow they'd be coming for us.

"I hope you're right," I said.

He grabbed the jug back from me and upended it so mead splashed out across his face. He then wiped his mouth with the back of his hand and grinned at me. "We shall find out tomorrow—but tonight we celebrate!" He threw his arm around my shoulders and led me back toward the camp.

The sounds of singing and music rang out as we neared, and the smells of woodsmoke and seared meat carried on the air. In the clearing, a huge bonfire burned, lighting up the encroaching night with its flames. Around it, five spits held roasting sheep and pigs. Two musicians played a simple melody on a flute and drum, while all the people from Trenus's village clapped and stomped enthusiastically as they danced around the blaze.

"They have started without us," Atto yelled over the din. He spotted Senna near the fire, grabbed her by both hands, and twirled her toward the dancers and the bonfire.

Senna pulled herself out of his grasp and rushed over to me, her cheeks flushed with excitement. "Come dance with us, Asterix."

She grabbed my hand and pulled me into the circle of villagers. The dance was easy to figure out, and since most of the participants were drunk already, I wasn't the worst dancer. I spun several pretty women in circles, and everyone clapped and laughed. The beer and mead flowed freely, and roast meat was there for the taking. It was easy to forget about the day to come.

I danced to a few songs and then went to sit by a smaller fire, away from the main celebration. My insides felt all knotted up with anger and hopelessness. I knew the Romans had conquered many nations in becoming such a great empire, but I had never fully under-stood what it meant to be one of these people trampled by the great Roman war machine. The Celts dancing around me in the firelight didn't deserve such a fate. They were just ordinary families. Farmers. Women. Children. In the distance, Vata and Cario danced with Atto and Senna, their tiny arms outstretched as Atto twirled them around. They laughed and pranced joyously, not realizing that this could be the last night of their life.

From the corner of my eye I saw Cenacus, decked out in his usual druidic gray, hobbling around between the campfires. Everywhere he passed, people greeted him and offered him drinks or food. He seemed happy now, smiling and laughing with them, or giving a comforting pat on the shoulder.

I waved to him and he nodded back at me, changing his course to come over.

He lowered himself gently to the ground next to my little fire, wincing at the obvious pain from his leg. "Just the man I wanted to see," he said, as he reached into his cloak and pulled out a leather wineskin. He took a swig and passed it to me. "Wine?"

I waved it aside. "I've been celebrating too much already."

He chuckled. "Yeah, these Celts sure know how to throw a party."

"You wanted to see me?" I asked.

Cenacus's face turned serious. "Your friend is still in this time zone, right? She didn't jump out, did she?"

I shook my head. "Nope. The rod is still cold. She hasn't found the tablet yet."

Cenacus sighed, dragging his bony fingers through his gray hair. "I've never heard of a female time jumper. Is she any good? Does she actually know what she's doing? We're not going to die waiting for her, are we?"

"I trust her with my life," I snapped back. I wouldn't have survived my first time jump if it hadn't been for her. "If she hasn't found it yet, then *you* probably forgot to tell her something important."

"Easy." The druid raised his hands. "I meant no disrespect. I'm just getting antsy. I want to get out of here. She took a shovel with her, right?"

"Yes, she took a shovel." I shouldn't have snapped at him. Cenacus was just asking what I was too chicken to admit. Sam should have been done by now; what was taking her so long?

I jabbed a stick at the fire, stirring up a flurry of sparks. "Any idea when the Romans will attack?"

"They should hit two hours after dawn, when it's at the lowest tide. They'll have about an hour to cross then before the water starts rising again." He raised his face to the night sky. "We'd better be out of here by then. Your little trebuchets might hold off the Romans for a while, but …"

"I know. The strait's long and wide, and the accuracy on those things is terrible. But even a few lucky hits might buy us some time."

"Asterix! Wise one!" Senna called out. "Come dance with us." She stood halfway between the circle of villagers and our fire, waving us over, her cheeks flushed from dancing. In the firelight her hair shimmered around her like a halo.

"Later," I yelled back.

She smiled at me. "I will hold you to that promise," she shouted, then headed back to join the dancers.

Cenacus watched her walk away and nodded appreciatively. "She likes you."

"Yeah, I know. Too much."

Cenacus tilted back his wineskin and drained the rest of its contents. "I've lived with the Celts for seventeen years now, and it's nights like this that are always the toughest. These are the nights when they say goodbye to life. They dance, they sing, they drink all their beer and mead, eat as much as they can, and spend the night in the arms of someone who puts a twinkle in their eyes." He motioned to the crowd of villagers dancing around the fire. "Take my advice, kid, and don't get too attached to these people. Otherwise, you'll start to think you're one of them—and then you'll never be able to leave."

"Is that what happened to you?"

"Yup, I forgot my own rule—I made too many friends. And tomorrow they're all going to die." He stood up and leaned heavily on his walking stick, although I wasn't sure whether this was because of his sore leg or the amount of wine he'd drunk. "Well, kid, I'm off to say a few more goodbyes. I'll meet you tomorrow morning. I just hope your friend hurries so we can get the hell out of here."

I watched him skulk off into the darkness, then returned my attention to the Celts as they celebrated. Cenacus had warned me not to get attached to them. Too late for that. How could I not feel something for a people whose only crime was wanting to be left alone? And for that simple reason, the Romans were going to crush them. Tomorrow, a few hours after dawn, thousands of their troops would come across the strait, bringing death and destruction.

My thoughts drifted to Sam. Where was she? Was she okay? She could have broken her leg or been attacked by wolves. While I sat here by a warm fire, my belly full of mead and food, was she shivering in the dark somewhere, scared and hungry?

My fingers drummed nervously on my thigh.

Please be all right, Sam.

If she wasn't, I was in for one hell of a battle tomorrow.

CHAPTER 10

"I have never met a more stubborn man!" Senna yelled. "Goats have more sense than you!"

"You do not understand," Atto soothed. "I must do this."

Cracking open my eyes, I propped myself up on my elbows. It wasn't even dawn yet; the camp lay shrouded in dim gray light. But, other than the children, I was the only person still in their blankets. Everyone else was busily sharpening weapons, strapping on armor, or packing up camp. The Roman attack was just hours away, and the rod still pressed coldly against my lower back.

Come on, Sam, get me out of here.

A light rain fell, each drop hissing as it hit the huge fire blazing close by. Atto sat cross-legged by the flames, the fresh wash of lime in his hair making it stand up all white and spiky. His sword lay across his lap, and he scraped a stone along the blade. The rain didn't seem to bother him, but that was probably because he was completely naked. No shirt, no shoes, no pants. Just a determined look on his face as he continued sharpening his sword.

Ugh ... Never gonna unsee that. I cringed and tried to wipe the image from my mind.

"Little Roman, you are awake!"

"Uh … yeah." I stood up and stretched to get rid of the kinks in my back, while trying not to look at him. Instead I focused on Senna, who sat beside Atto with her back toward me. Her blond hair was gathered in two long braids, and her dress clung to her skin from the rain. She dipped her hand into a small clay pot resting near her knee, and her fingers came out covered in blue gunk. She then drew a long, sinuous design across Atto's arm with the blue paste, matching the ones that already covered his chest and legs.

"Please, Atto," she said. "I beg of you again, do not do this."

He cupped her face in his hands. "Senna, I fight in this manner for you and our children. My entire war band will be fighting in the old style. When the Romans see us charging them naked, they will know we do not fear them or death. The Romans lack bravery, so they will turn from us and run. And then we will kill them all."

She lowered her head and stopped drawing. "Is there no way for you to see sense? There are just too many Romans, Atto. You will die."

He kissed her softly. "Do not fear, my love. I will come back to you. And if I do not, then we shall meet in the glorious afterlife, in the fields of the undying." He stood and stretched his arms out in front of himself to admire her designs. "You have done well. No matter what happens, men will remember my bravery today." He bent and kissed the sleeping forms of his children. "Be well, little ones." He picked up his sword and spear, and kissed Senna one more time. "I must go now. Keep the children safe."

He turned and left our fire to join the warriors heading for the beach. Some carried shields or wore chain-mail armor, but those were the minority. Most went to battle wearing only pants and maybe a pair of leather arm guards. Then there were the men like Atto, either super brave or incredibly stupid, heading to battle fully naked.

Senna wiped her cheeks with the heel of her palm to brush away the tears. "Asterix," she said, her eyes following Atto's retreating figure. "Please try to save my fool husband from himself."

I stood there unsure what to say as the rain drummed its sodden rhythm on my head. "I'll try," I finally mumbled.

She ignored my weak response and knelt over the still sleeping forms of Vata and Cario. "Time to wake," she urged, stroking the tops of their heads. They opened their eyes, and Senna hugged them tightly, burying her face in their hair. "I will meet you at the hill, Asterix," she said, still not looking at me.

I didn't have to be a genius to realize Senna wanted to be left alone. I grabbed my backpack and snacked on some trail mix as I headed for the hilltop, my mind filled with worries about the coming battle. Without armor, and with little in the way of battle tactics, the Celts were going to get slaughtered. The trebuchets might help slow the Roman attack, but how much help was *too* much? Cenacus had told me not to worry, that nothing I did here would change the overall course of history, but was he right?

For the millionth time I wished that Dad had taught me anything at all about time-jumping.

An ache formed in my stomach. I hadn't thought once about Dad since I'd jumped back into Celtic times. Had he come out of his coma? Was he wondering where I was?

I miss you, Dad.

I reached the top of the hill and looked out over the strait. The sun had risen but remained hidden behind the clouds, leaving the shores shrouded in gray. On the opposite bank, the Romans had dragged their boats down to the shore but hadn't launched them yet. Thousands of soldiers stood by their craft, waiting to embark. On our side, I couldn't guess how many Celts waited for them. The entire green space facing the Roman shore was now covered with men and women—at least triple or even quadruple the number of Romans. The Celts yelled constantly, thumped their shields, and blew on long brass horns, creating a screeching din that drowned out all other sounds.

Behind this mob of Celts stood the druids. Dressed in their gray cloaks, they raised their arms to the heavens, their lips moving in sync as they chanted. Women in black robes, who must have been priestesses, darted among the Celtic warriors. The women had their hair wildly puffed out to give them a frightening appearance, and they waved torches, inciting the Celts to battle.

My little section of the battlefield was much calmer. No druids, no shouting warriors—just a ton of women and older men and kids. It looked like a family picnic—except for the constant undercurrent of tension that permeated the air like smog. No one here had delusions of victory. Everyone knew we weren't fighting to win. We were fighting to survive.

"Okay, people," I shouted. "Let's load these things up and get some fires going. When the time comes to destroy these weapons, we'll need to do it quickly."

My helpers rushed to follow my orders, and within minutes all five trebuchets had been cranked into firing position and two bonfires raged. I moved to one of the fires, warming myself against the damp while watching the Romans wait for the water level in the strait to drop even lower.

"It's not every day someone gets to see a Roman army about to attack," someone remarked. "And if I'm lucky, I'll never see it again."

Cenacus had appeared on the other side of the fire, his gray druid cloak gone, replaced by an earth-colored one. Mud splatters covered his boots, and he panted heavily as if he had just climbed up ten flights of steps.

"When did you get here?" I asked him.

"A few minutes ago," he wheezed. He looked up at the dim sky, with water dripping from the hood of his cloak onto his face. "I would have been here sooner but my leg really bothers me when it rains."

"Shouldn't you be with the rest of the druids?"

He snorted. "Fat chance I'm going to be out there, wearing my druid grays, a juicy target for any Roman with a spear. No, I'm sticking with you." He looked around to make sure no one was listening. "The Celts may believe in all that mystical mumbo-jumbo," he whispered, "but I don't. And I know how this movie ends, so I sure as hell don't want to be around for the final credits." He scratched nervously at his beard. "The water's almost still now. The Romans will be crossing soon. Is the rod still cold?"

"Yup."

"Damn! You'll tell me as soon as we can jump out, right?"

I rolled my eyes and exhaled loudly. Cenacus's constant doubt was getting on my nerves. I knew he was worried about the Roman attack, but I was stuck in the same crappy situation as he was. "How many times do I have to say it? Yes. As soon as the rod goes warm, I'll tell you."

"Sorry! Sorry!" Cenacus raised his hands defensively. "I just—"

A cheer from the other shore made him stop. The Roman general with the gold armor had ridden his white stallion down to the beach, and his troops were cheering his arrival.

"Looks like it's showtime," Cenacus said with resignation. "That bastard Paulinus has shown up."

"You know him?"

"Damn right I do. That's Gaius Suetonius Paulinus, governor of Britain for the last two years ... and one of the biggest bastards you'll ever meet. He brings more misery to the Celts than all the other governors combined."

Although it was impossible over the wind and the distance to hear what Paulinus was saying, it was clear that he was starting the attack. He rode back and forth along the ranks, waving his sword, and everywhere he passed, Roman soldiers began dragging their boats into the water and piling into them.

As for the Batavians, half of them led their horses to the shallowest area of the strait, where the water still flowed at a furious pace. They raced their horses through the makeshift ford, kicking up a huge spray until the water began to get deeper. But even at the deepest point the water only reached to the horses' chests. The other half of the Batavian cavalry dismounted and led their horses into the deeper and smoother waters of the strait, where the Romans were now crossing with their boats. Once the animals were neck-deep, they began swimming, with their riders trailing along beside them by holding on to their saddles.

A bead of sweat trickled down my temple, and my stomach began to tie itself in knots. Hundreds of boats, rafts, and horses were now paddling slowly across the strait, struggling against the current. I began to pace back and forth, waiting for the Romans to come in range. We'd get only a few shots off—we needed to make them count.

Finally, after what seemed like forever, the Romans and the Batavians had reached the halfway point of the strait.

"Fire!" I yelled.

The five trebuchets swung as one, their massive wooden frames groaning and creaking under the strain as the counterweights plunged down. Five huge rocks hurtled through the air as I held my breath, watching their path.

Come on … Come on …

Four splashed harmlessly into the open water, but the fifth smashed through the thin wooden hull of a Roman boat. As water rushed in, the craft flooded and sank, sending twenty Romans to the bottom of the strait, dragged down by the weight of their own armor.

The Celts along the shore howled at this sight, shouting taunts and insults at the enemy. The rest of the Romans dug even more furiously with their paddles, trying to push their little boats faster across the water. With a speed born of desperation, my group reloaded the trebuchets and fired again and again, launching heavy stones in a deadly rain. With every arcing stone the soldiers in the boats looked skyward, tracking its flight.

I almost felt sorry for these guys, stuck out there in their rickety boats and watching their death descending upon them. Almost. But these were the same bloodthirsty bastards who were on their way to attack thousands of innocent men, women, and children—so with each crushing hit, I cheered along with the rest of the Celts.

Despite our barrage, the lead Roman boat made it to the beach, and the first soldier leaped out into waist-deep water. He didn't have a sword or shield, but instead carried a red banner attached to a long pole—the legion's standard. It had a large golden XX stitched on it above a picture of a boar. A second boat came to shore a bit farther down the beach, and another standard bearer leaped out, his flag depicting a horned goat beneath the number XIV. The two of them splashed farther ashore, holding their banners high, while boatload after boatload of invading troops followed.

As Romans and Batavians piled out onto the shore, I stopped my bombardment. The trebuchets were angled to fire out over the water, so I'd need to drastically change their angle to hit the beach. And, if I did, there was a good chance I'd hit the Celts also.

An overwhelming sense of frustration welled up in my chest as the Romans began to form three battle groups, each ten rows deep, with the Batavians guarding the far wings. What the hell was Prasto's problem? If I had been in charge, I would have attacked while the Romans were still stumbling ashore, knee-deep in water, exhausted and disorganized after their long paddle across the strait. But from some sense of honor or stupidity, the Celts stood there in a packed mass, far back from the beach, blowing their war horns and yelling their battle cries, trying to intimidate the Romans but doing nothing else.

Surprisingly, the intimidation seemed to be working. I could see it in the faces of the Romans in the first ranks. None of them looked confident. Men shifted and darted their heads around, searching for the first attack. The Batavians didn't look ready for battle at all as the flanks of their horses heaved from the exertion of crossing the strait.

Governor Paulinus must have sensed his men's fear. He pushed his white stallion to the front of the ranks and turned to face his men. The wind whipping off the strait and the patter of rain muted anything he was saying, so none of the words reached my ears. But the Romans heard them, and whatever he said must have been awe-inspiring, because they cheered and beat on their shields with their swords. Paulinus then retreated to the rear of their formation and raised his sword high. On this signal, Roman trumpets blared over the battlefield, cutting through the din made by the Celts.

The Romans held their shields overlapped in front of them for extra protection and began marching in unison across the beach. On either wing, the cavalry rushed ahead, spears pointed downward like lances.

Prasto, standing in the front ranks of the Celts, shook his spear above his head and bellowed at the top of his lungs. With a wild howl, the Celts launched their spears. Thousands of deadly shafts flew toward the invaders. The Romans raised their huge rectangular shields and, with a sound like pebbles banging against a wooden door, the Celtic spears clattered harmlessly to the ground. The Batavians didn't fare nearly as well, though. Spears sank indiscriminately into men and their mounts. Horses whinnied in pain and thrashed about while riders fell to the ground, but the remaining horsemen kept coming.

Prasto and his men raised their swords and charged, their battle cries drowning out all other sound. For a brief instant the Romans lowered their shields to launch their own volley of spears. Razor points ripped through flesh, and hundreds of Celts dropped to the ground.

The Romans then set their shields for the charge, hiding behind the massive rectangles.

My breath caught in my throat. The lives of thousands of innocent people depended on this one charge.

With a thunderous crash of metal and wood, the Celts hammered into the Roman line, slashing angrily at the wall of shields, jabbing with their spears, or even leaping through the air and hitting the shields with their bodies. But the Romans held their ground against the onslaught.

And then, like a huge wave smashing against a concrete breakwater, the Celtic momentum died away. The big attack that was supposed to drive the Romans back into the sea fizzled out of energy. And in the moment that the Celts were getting over the shock of their failed onslaught, the Romans counterattacked. Gaps appeared between their interlocked shields, and their short swords, designed for stabbing, thrust out, burying themselves deep into unprotected stomachs and chests. Celts crashed to the beach, their blood turning the sand dark red. The Romans then locked shields again and moved forward a step, pushing the Celts back.

I kicked at the frame of the nearest trebuchet in frustration. All those Roman boats my crew had sunk didn't matter. Celts were dying, and the battle was already turning into a rout. The Celts just couldn't break through the Roman wall of shields. They needed something heavier, like a cavalry charge or a battering ram or ...

"Turn the trebuchets around!" I yelled.

Men and women rushed to grab hold of one of the massive machines. With all the supporting beams, it was probably constructed from the trunks of ten full trees, so it weighed a ton. With everyone throwing their weight in, we managed to drag one corner of our siege weapon along the ground until it pointed to the beach.

"Load and fire!" I roared. There was a huge chance that we'd end up dropping a rock right into the middle of the Celtic army but at the rate they were dying, it was a risk I was willing to take.

The first rock sailed over the Romans, landing with a splash far into the strait.

"Heavier rock!"

The second and third rocks missed their target as well, plunking harmlessly into the shallower water.

The fourth rock was the charm. A huge boulder, about the size of a beach ball, smashed into the Roman left wing, sending soldiers flying and creating a gap in the middle of their ranks.

"Keep firing!" I yelled. We had our angle and weight. Now to see if we could turn the tide of battle more in favor of the Celts.

A tall Batavian with long braids flowing out from under the back of his helmet pointed to our position on the hill. He yelled an order, and a group of about twenty horsemen broke off from the main attack and headed along the beach, angling toward us.

Crap! Crap! Crap!

How could I have been so stupid? I'd been so focused on firing the trebuchets that I hadn't set up any defenses or assembled a screen of warriors to protect us. Except for a few knives and one or two hammers, none of us manning the siege engines had any weapons. The Batavian cavalry would scythe through us like we were blades of grass.

"Burn the trebuchets and run!" I yelled as I grabbed a torch and threw it into the pile of kindling surrounding one of them.

About half of my crew had already begun running away, but Senna and some of the remaining women grabbed torches and threw them onto the piles of twigs and kindling that lay around the other siege weapons. The flames sputtered and hissed against the tinder, dampened by the rain.

Come on ... Come on ... Light, damn it!

The women fanned the sputtering flames with just their hands,

trying to get the damp wood to catch fire. Finally, flames began crack-
ling in the tinder at the bases of two trebuchets, sending gray smoke
drifting into the sky.

The jangle of harnesses and the clomp of hooves warned me that
we were rapidly running out of time. The horsemen were halfway up
the slope already. We were going to die if we stayed there any longer.

"Run!" I yelled to Senna and the others. "Take your kids and go!
Don't look back."

"No!" Senna was adamant. "Not until *all* the fires are lit. We will
not let the Romans use these weapons against any other tribes."

Stubborn Celt. She was going to get herself killed. But she was also
right. I couldn't let these weapons fall into Roman hands and mess up
history even more. I had to do something—and fast. We had maybe
thirty seconds.

Think, Dan! Think!

"Knock this one over!" I yelled, pointing to the trebuchet we had
turned around to face the beach. It stood at the top of the hill, now
angled sideways to all the others. I grabbed a knife and slashed at the
ropes binding the beams of the trebuchet at its base. The flimsy ropes
split apart easily under the blade. The Celts who hadn't already run
away rushed over and began pushing at the heavy contraption. As they
leaned into it, I scrambled up the knobby bark of one of the main posts,
the knife clasped between my teeth. As the trebuchet began to rock
back and forth from the efforts of the Celts, I cut the ropes binding
the posts together at the top.

With a groan of wood and straining rope, the weight of the rock-
filled basket became too much, and the whole trebuchet tilted over
violently, heading for the ground. I rode the falling contraption for a
few feet before jumping on to the rain-soaked grass at the last second.
The trebuchet smashed into the hillside, its remaining ropes snapping
under the strain, and the heavy logs thudding to the ground.

Damn it! The logs remained in place.

I'd hoped for them to roll downhill into the charging horsemen, and bowl them all over. Only one thing left to do—force them. I grabbed an end of one heavy tree trunk. "Help me throw these downhill!"

My helpers instantly understood what I wanted to do, which was good, since I didn't have time to explain anything—the horsemen were almost upon us. Fear gave us strength and, with about ten people per log, we hoisted the massive trunks onto our shoulders.

"Throw!" I yelled.

Grunting with the effort, we tossed six massive logs downhill, one after the other. They sailed through the air and crashed into the enemy, knocking aside horses and men indiscriminately. Broken and bleeding men lay scattered on the hillside, screaming in pain, yet a few riders still remained on horseback, and they charged at us with fury in their eyes.

I grabbed a baseball-sized stone from the pile that had previously been in the wicker basket. The Batavians were so close now it was impossible to miss. I drilled the stone at the nearest rider, and it nailed him right in the face, knocking him out of the saddle. My second rock smashed a Batavian in the chest. He sawed at his reins for a few seconds, trying to keep his balance, before crashing sideways to the ground.

With another rock in hand, I rushed forward. The Batavian rose unsteadily to his feet, clutching his chest and gasping heavily. At the last moment he saw me coming for him and reached for his fallen spear.

Too slow.

I threw myself across the space separating us and knocked him to the ground. With both hands, I smashed my rock repeatedly against his helmeted head until he stopped moving.

Wrenching the spear from his grasp, I leaped back to my feet and searched for my next target. Of the twenty Batavians who had started the charge, only two were still mounted. They were riding hard after the women and old men, hacking with swords and laughing as they went. Three women already lay sprawled on the ground, bloody red slashes across their backs and necks.

A red haze of rage descended upon me, and I heaved my spear at one of the two riders. The blade plunged into his back and he fell to the ground with a thud. At the sound, the last rider wheeled his horse around and spotted me standing there weaponless. Snarling, he raised his spear over his head and charged straight toward me.

Time seemed to slow down as he approached. Memories of the Norman cavalry charges at the Battle of Hastings flooded my mind.

Don't run. Don't move. Just wait.

At the last possible moment, I dodged, rolling twice on the rain-slick grass as the horseman swept past me. Leaping to my feet, I scanned the area for anything that could pass as a weapon.

The Batavian wheeled his horse around and kicked into a gallop as he charged in for a second pass. I stood with my muscles tensed, ready to spring out of the way again.

Suddenly, a barrage of stones flew through the air and battered him out of the saddle. Before he had a chance to get up, Senna and the other women leaped upon him and pummeled him with stones.

Panting heavily, I surveyed the bloody scene. Twenty Batavians lay dead, and flames engulfed four of the trebuchets with the fifth strewn in bits across the hillside. Most of my group had survived this one small skirmish, but the battle wasn't over. Already another squad of horsemen, at least double the size of the first, had separated from the battle and was charging uphill toward us.

A knot formed in my throat. There was no way we could defeat these guys. I whipped my head around, desperately searching for some way out. There were a few horses left standing, but not enough to carry all of us.

"To the forest!" I yelled. The trees wouldn't really protect us, but at least they'd slow the Batavians down … and that might give me time to think of something else. Because, right now, we needed a miracle.

CHAPTER 11

I snatched up a fallen spear and raced after my little group. How was I going to save them? Hell, how was I going to save myself? I was the only one with a weapon. I couldn't take on forty Batavians by myself.

I darted a glance over my shoulder to see how much time we had, then stopped in my tracks—the miracle I so desperately needed had appeared. A large group of men had broken away from the rear of the Celtic army and was running toward us—with an all-too-familiar naked man leading them.

For the first time, an incredible sense of gratitude filled me at the sight of Atto. "Hurry!" I yelled.

The Celts sprinted across the grass, with Atto the first to reach us. He flew to Senna's side and wrapped her in his arms. "Are you all right, my love?" he asked, his breath coming out in gasps.

"For now," Senna said. "But more horsemen approach. We cannot hold out long, husband."

"That is why I am here. I have come to help." He winked at her and gestured toward the men behind him, strong warriors armed with spears and shields. Most had pants, and some even had armor. "And

I brought friends."

"Is all well?" Senna stared intently into Atto's eyes. "Why are you not in the front of battle?"

"Bah! Prasto and his followers have taken all the best spots for themselves, so we were placed in the back. I have yet to feel the clash of blades or collect a single head." He looked downhill at the rapidly approaching horsemen. "But it looks like we will get our share of glory soon." He clapped for attention. "Hear me, you heroes! Now is the time for us to charge those Batavian dogs and show them how real men fight!"

His band of warriors cheered and smashed their spears against their shields.

"Hold it!" I jumped in front of them—one stupid kid standing in the way of about fifty bloodthirsty Celts. "Have any of you ever fought this many horsemen before?" I stared down each man in turn, waiting for one of the arrogant braggarts to claim he had—I'd shoot that lie down quickly.

No one answered.

"You're all dead if you charge downhill," I warned.

"And what do you know about battle, Little Roman?" Atto scoffed.

The drumming of hooves changed to a rumble of thunder as the Batavians began their charge. We had maybe twenty seconds now before they'd be on us. "I don't have time to explain. Just stand side by side in a line and keep your spears pointing straight up."

"What fool counsel is this?" asked a shirtless Celt in blue-and-white-striped pants. "Atto, tell me you will not listen to this madman's ideas."

"Trust me," I pleaded as the earth began to tremble beneath our feet. "I've fought against cavalry before."

Atto stroked his long mustache, his eyes going from Senna and the other women to the Batavians. "All right, Little Roman," he said. "We will listen to your words." He turned to face his followers. "Spread out in a line, shoulder to shoulder, and do as the Little Roman commands!" he ordered. "And hurry!"

With a speed I didn't think possible, the Celts formed a line across the hillside, with me in the center.

"Three ..." I shouted.

"Two ..."

The jangle of harnesses and the pounding of hooves became almost deafening. The Batavians were so close I could see the bloodlust and anticipation on their faces. They expected a slaughter—and I was going to give them one.

"Spears out!" I yelled as I rammed my spear butt-first into the ground and then lowered the sharp tip so that it was at eye level with the approaching horses. In unison, the Celts mimicked my action, creating a wall of silvery points. The onrushing horses shied away from the jagged points that now confronted them, twisting and rearing to get away. The rearmost horsemen collided with those in the front, sending animals and riders crashing to the ground almost at our feet.

"Charge!" I screamed.

With a thunderous roar, Atto's band of warriors tore into the disorganized Batavians. Swords slashed, hacking limbs and cleaving skulls. Spears darted, leaving empty saddles behind. The Batavians could barely fight back—most were trying desperately to regain control of their horses. In a few short minutes the battle was over, with only a few lucky horsemen surviving our charge and reaching the safety of the beach.

"Well done, Little Roman!" Atto cheered as he repeatedly brought his sword down on a dead man's neck until he managed to sever the head from the body.

My stomach started doing backflips at this gruesome sight. "What are you doing?"

"Collecting heads, of course." He raised up two bloody trophies, holding each by the hair. "I have felled two men so far. Where are *your* heads?"

I looked around the little battlefield. Everywhere Celts stood over fallen enemies, hacking off heads. Bile rose to my throat, and I fought to keep my breakfast down. I'd seen a lot of disgusting things in battle, but this topped them all. "I don't collect heads," I replied, my tone icy.

"Then how can you prove you have killed anyone?"

I couldn't answer him. He belonged to a culture where it was normal to collect heads as trophies, while in my time the only people who collected body parts were psychopaths who were usually left to rot in a maximum-security prison. I rubbed my forehead and took a few calming breaths. A few months ago, I'd thought a boring day studying hieroglyphics in my dad's library was the worst thing imaginable. But now I'd have done anything to be back at home reading a musty book.

The clash of metal from somewhere below brought me back to my current lousy situation. We had won two small encounters, but the bigger battle still raged. I clapped my hands to draw everyone's attention. "Grab their armor and weapons," I said as I ripped the chain mail off a headless corpse, then slipped the bloody armor over my head and grabbed the man's sword. "How many of you have fought from horseback before?"

Only a few raised their hands. "Grab the horses," I ordered. "We're going to bring in some of our own cavalry." Grasping the bridle of a nearby horse, I patted the animal's neck to try and calm it a bit. After all the poor creature had been through, his coat glistened with sweat and his sides heaved in and out as he panted heavily. "Sorry, no time to rest."

Crap … How the hell do I get onto this thing?

Stirrups hadn't been invented yet, so there was no foothold to step into when trying to mount up. The saddle did, however, have these four weird curved corner posts that the Batavians used to keep themselves in place. Grasping one of the posts, I struggled to pull myself onto the animal's back. The horse danced around me, half dragging me along with him, until my grip finally broke and I fell to the ground.

"Stupid horse," I muttered, as I got back on to my feet.

Atto appeared at my side, an amused smile on his face, and I braced myself for his usual mockery. "Let me help you," he said as he cupped his hands together to create a step for my foot.

His helpfulness took me by surprise for a second, but I got over my shock, grabbed his shoulder, stepped into his hands, and got myself into the saddle easily this time. The two front saddle posts pressed down on my thighs, keeping me in place.

"Thanks, Atto."

I tugged on the reins and wheeled my horse around to see that about fifteen of Atto's band had grabbed armor and horses. The remaining warriors, including Atto, stood watching us, unsure what to do next. Seeing Atto and his men standing there filled me with a sense of dread—like watching a bunch of monkeys with lighters in a fireworks factory. I knew that if they were left on their own, they'd probably get themselves killed in some futile charge against the Romans that would prove nothing but their stupidity. "Make sure those weapons burn." I pointed to the trebuchets. "Then take the women and the children to the druid stronghold. Fight together, and you might survive."

Atto's back stiffened and he indignantly thumped his chest with a fist. "We will not run while the battle rages."

With my sword I pointed toward the carnage down on the beach. Dead and dying Celts lay everywhere. The Celts kept attacking and the Romans kept pushing them back with their shields, and then stabbing at them through the gaps. Meanwhile, at the rear of the Celtic ranks, the Batavians galloped back and forth, viciously hacking down the women, children, and old men who had stayed to watch the battle.

The Celts were in a bad place, penned in between the Romans on the beach and the Batavians behind them.

"Does that look like a battle?" I raged. "Head to the stronghold and get organized. Then you can actually turn this into a battle."

"And where do you go?" Atto asked.

"I'm going to buy us some time." I nudged my mount in the ribs and turned him toward the slaughter. "Come on!" I yelled to my group of horsemen.

Sam's words echoed in my head. *Don't be a hero.* That was the farthest thing from my mind—I just wanted to do the right thing. The Celts needed to flee this massacre and have a chance to regroup. And the only way to save them was to get the Batavians out of the way. The Celts believed that personal bravery would win any battle. It just might—as long as we had the element of surprise.

My little group circled around to the rear of the Batavian lines completely unopposed. The Batavians were too wrapped up in their slaughter to pay attention to my squad. And even if any of them did notice us, we didn't look like a threat. We wore Batavian armor, held Batavian weapons, and rode Batavian horses. Except for the sinuous blue designs snaking along the arms of Atto's men, we looked exactly like Batavians.

The jangle of my chain mail and the labored breathing of my horse were drowned out by the clang of metal and the screams of the dying. I hefted the spear over my shoulder and gripped it tightly. No backing out now. The men with me wore determined looks, their faces hard as stone. All of us knew what we needed to do.

With a bloodthirsty howl, we slammed into the rear of the Batavians. I struck a man between the shoulder blades with my spear, sending him flying out of the saddle. I kept riding at full speed, my spear darting out as fast as I could move it, stabbing countless riders in the back. Every thrust emptied another saddle. Then, with a shudder and a loud crack, my spear shaft snapped as it struck a Batavian in the shoulder blade, sending a spray of splinters into the air.

I hastily tossed the oversized toothpick aside, drew my sword, and kept riding, hacking to both sides of me. My blade threw ribbons of blood into the air with its repeated descent. Arms, legs, backs, necks—I didn't care. The sight of all those dead Celts made me burn with a hatred I'd never felt before. When the weak iron of my sword bent in half, I chucked the useless weapon into the face of the nearest rider. He ducked, and in that same moment I drew near and punched him in the jaw. His head flew backward, and as he fought to stay on his horse, I buried my dagger in his throat.

Another rider spotted me with only a dagger and came charging toward me. I drew back my arm, ready to pitch the dagger at him and hope for the best, when suddenly, he raised his hand to stop me. "Hold, Asterix!" the rider said. "It is I, Vindiorix."

A moment of clarity intruded into the haze of rage that had overtaken me. The rider's pants were red plaid, not the gray favored by Batavians. And his arms were covered in swirling blue lines. He was one of my Celts!

"What are you doing?" I asked.

He pulled his horse up beside mine. "I saw you had no weapon. Here, take mine." He passed a sword to me hilt first. "My spear still holds its strength."

"Um … thanks," I said sheepishly, embarrassed that I'd almost killed one of my own guys. I took the weapon from him and whipped my head around, searching for another target. There were none.

"They have fled." Vindiorix grinned. "Our attack took them by surprise, and they thought our numbers greater than they are."

Best news I'd heard all day. Now to get the Celts someplace safe. People were already streaming away from the battlefield, desperate to get away before the Batavians returned. But the Celts were scattered, with everyone running in different directions. I waved my sword a few times in the air over my head to attract the attention of as many people as possible, then pointed it inland. "Head to the druid compound!" I bellowed to the fleeing Celts. "There's a wall to protect you."

My words provided a bit of focus for the panicked mob, and they began running inland. As more and more of the spectators fled, some of the rearmost warriors—those who hadn't yet entered the fray—began retreating as well, with their weapons still in hand. Soon there became a clear distinction between those who were fleeing and those staying to fight the Romans.

My horsemen and I covered the rear of the fleeing Celts, providing protection in case the Batavians returned. But our protection wasn't needed—the Batavians had now joined the Romans to finish off the Celtic rearguard.

For the first time that day, a sense of optimism intruded into my otherwise gloomy thoughts. *This plan might actually work.*

The fleeing Celts, with their poor armor, were fast on their feet. They charged ahead, gradually creating a huge gap between themselves and any pursuers. They soon outdistanced even me. After a long swim and the constant running, my poor horse barely plodded along, its breath coming in gasps. Deciding that I'd be faster on foot, I leaped out of the saddle and raced us both toward the druid compound. Hundreds of Celts stood on the low earthen walls, cheering and waving their weapons. I snuck a look behind me to see only a few of my riders still on horseback; the rest had already dismounted and were running after me. But they didn't need to run; no enemies were in sight.

I leaned over with my hands on my knees, sucking in huge gulps of air as the exertion of the morning finally caught up with me. *I did it—I got through the first battle.*

Together with my exhausted riders, I entered the main gate of the compound. Celts swarmed around us, clapping us on the shoulder, offering us skins of mead or simply embracing us.

With the confident swagger of a chief, Trenus pushed his way through the crowd toward me. He must have been in the thick of the fighting at some point because his left arm was bound in a bloody sling, and a large slash split his cheek. He stopped in front of me and with a wide, flourishing gesture, unsheathed his sword and stabbed it into the ground directly at my feet. "My blade is yours, Asterix. Tell me, what would you have me do?"

Huh?

"W-w-what do you mean?" I stammered. Why was Trenus asking me what to do? He was the village leader. He should be the one giving orders, not asking for them. And especially not from me. "Where's Prasto? Isn't he in charge?"

A pained look crossed Trenus's face. "Prasto and the other chieftains lie dead." He jerked his thumb in the direction of a group arguing loudly nearby. "So now we squabble among ourselves when instead we should be fighting the Romans. We should have made you war leader from the start. If we had listened to you, we would not have been defeated at the beach." He put his good arm around my shoulders and pulled me closer to him. "Tell me," he said quietly, "is there still a chance to save my people?"

Oh geez …

What a crappy question to have to answer. Historically, the Celts got wiped out. Maybe not in this battle but, over time, their entire culture and language was erased from everywhere except a few small areas in Europe. But there was no way I could tell him that. "I don't know," I finally said. "How many warriors are prepared to follow you?"

"About half of those you see here. The rest are fools who insist we should charge again."

I sighed, raking my hands through my hair. Most of the people here in the compound were women and children, but there were still hundreds of warriors, so we had some decent manpower. But could they stop fighting like Celts and actually work together? "I need men with slings. Does anyone here use a sling?"

A warrior with a large gash across his arm overheard me and spat loudly. "Real men do not use such weapons," he shouted. "Only boys do. It is not manly to fight from a distance."

"Well, get me a bunch of boys then," I snapped. "A hundred boys with slings will kill more of the enemy than you ever will. Their horses aren't armored, and the Batavians have only small shields. Sling stones will easily break bones, or bother the horses enough that they run away."

"What of the Romans?" the warrior scoffed. "Are we to send boys with rocks after them also?"

"Use your head for something more than a target! You're faster than they are, so run away and hit them until they grow tired. Then run away again."

"You speak like a coward." His lip curled in distaste. "I will not run."

"And you speak like an idiot," I yelled back. I raised my blood-spattered hands in front of his face. "Look at me. I've charged the Batavian horsemen. I've attacked men with only rocks as weapons. And I've killed more men in the last twenty minutes than you probably have in your entire life." I glared at the moron, my hands shaking with anger. It was fools like him who were losing this battle. "Call me a coward again and I'll beat you so hard that you'll beg the Romans for help."

The man took a step back and sized me up through slitted eyes.

I dropped my fists to my side, ready to defend myself. The first rule in dealing with Celts was to never insult them, especially in front of their friends. I hadn't just broken that rule—I'd smashed it to a thousand tiny pieces. But if this guy wanted to start something, I'd gladly finish it.

He stared at me for a few seconds, neither of us moving, then a broad grin broke out across his face. "Aye, I will do as you say. Kill the horsemen and then run from the Romans." He stabbed his spear into the ground. "You have my arm!"

"And mine!" cried another warrior. More men picked up the cry, until the entire compound resounded with the clatter of spears and swords striking shields as men swore to follow me.

Seriously? Now they support me? With my fingertips, I massaged my aching temples. So much bloodshed could have been avoided if they had just listened to me from the beginning, instead of following Prasto's stupid plan. But at least they were listening now. Maybe, with a bit of luck, most of them would survive the next encounter with the Romans. And maybe—with even more luck—Sam would find that damn tablet and I wouldn't be here when that battle happened.

In the middle of the compound, a group of gray-cloaked druids tended to the wounded. I pushed my way over to them through the mass of people. "Where's Cenacus?" I asked an older druid who was busy stitching up a bloody gash in a man's leg.

"We do not know," the druid replied, without taking his eyes off his work. "We have not seen him."

Crap …

Cenacus hadn't made it back. The last time I'd seen him was at the siege hill, but in all the confusion of battle, we got separated. With his bum leg he couldn't have gone far, meaning that if the Romans hadn't gotten him yet, he was still hiding somewhere there.

Do I stay here and help the Celts, or do I go find him?

I glanced around. Most of the Celts were hastily creating slings out of whatever they could find, or scouring the ground for small rocks to use as ammunition. The rest were sharpening their weapons or repairing the few shields and pieces of armor that had survived the battle. They didn't need me here; they could figure out this next part on their own. But Cenacus? If he was hiding somewhere on the siege hill, he'd be a sitting duck when the Romans arrived. I couldn't leave him there.

"Get the men to dig a trench outside the walls and line it with sharpened stakes," I said to Trenus. "I'm going to find Cenacus."

Quickly I picked through the few horses that had made it back to the compound, choosing the one that looked the least tired. I urged it along at the fastest pace it could manage, trying not to exhaust the poor animal even further. I had to find Cenacus quickly. Below, on the beach, the Batavians and the Romans had paused to bandage their wounded or finish off any Celts still alive. This pause wouldn't last long, though, and then they'd be on the march again.

I reached my hilltop, where four trebuchets still blazed in their own funeral pyres and the fifth lay strewn on the ground in a jumble of logs and stone. The rain had finally stopped, but the sky was still dark and gray, masking everything in gloom.

I headed for the small forest near the trebuchets—which would be the best place for him to hide. "Cenacus!" I hissed into the dark trees. "Cenacus!"

"Here!" a voice answered back.

Leaving my horse tethered to a branch, I began walking through the wood. It was quieter among the trees, the roar of the ocean masked by the rustle of the wind through the pines, while the damp ground muffled my footsteps. "Where are you?"

"Over here." Cenacus lay flat on the ground at the base of a maple tree. He had covered himself in pine needles and small branches, making himself almost invisible. "I thought you'd abandoned me." He heaved himself up out of his hiding place, the forest litter falling off him as he stood.

"I told you we'd leave together. I'm here to get you."

A relieved smile appeared on his face. "You don't know how glad I am to hear that." He brushed at his cloak with one hand while pulling pine needles out of his beard with the other. "Well, pull out the rod and let's go."

"Sorry. That's not what I meant. We can't leave yet. The rod's still cold."

His face twisted as if he'd been stabbed. "What the hell's wrong with your friend?" he asked. "Why hasn't she found the tablet yet?"

"Look," I snapped. "She's doing the best she can." At least, I hoped she was. Sam had been gone a long time—too long.

From the beach, a horn sounded, followed by the rhythmic tromp of marching boots. Cenacus darted his head back and forth, a wild look in his eyes. "The Romans are coming. We need to leave. Now!"

"I know that," I said. "That's why we need to stop yakking and get moving. We're heading back to the druid compound."

Cenacus looked past me at my horse. The poor beast stood just where the trees ended, its sides heaving in and out like bellows. I knew what the druid was thinking: that tired animal didn't look like it could carry itself, never mind both of us.

"You take the horse," I said. "I'll jog along beside you."

He stood there for a few seconds, as if mulling over my offer, although I had no clue what he could be thinking about, as there were no other options available. "All right," he said finally. "But have a drink first. You look exhausted." He took a wineskin from his belt and offered it to me.

"I'm fine. Let's just go. We're wasting time."

"When was the last time you had anything to drink? Dehydration is just as dangerous as any Roman or Batavian. The last thing I want is us to run into someone and you not be able to handle things because you're too tired to fight." He pushed the wineskin toward me again. "Now take a damn drink. It's one of those awful Roman watered-down wines, but it will still replenish your lost fluids." He took a swig himself and thrust the wineskin into my hands.

Cenacus lectured just like my dad. But he did have a point: I hadn't drunk a thing in hours. "Fine," I muttered, then tilted the wineskin and took a few huge gulps. The wine was watery and tasted bad, but was somehow also refreshing. Not that I would admit that.

"There. You happy now?" I went to hand the wineskin back to Cenacus, but he had retreated a few steps beyond my reach. "Where are you going?" I took a step forward, offering him the wineskin, and then stumbled, barely stopping myself from falling. Suddenly my muscles felt like lead and my tongue grew thick in my mouth. A fog seemed to settle on my brain, and I blinked hard to stop my vision from blurring.

Cenacus put something in the wine.

"What'd you do to me?" I said, my words slurring as they came out.

Cenacus leaned to one side and spat out the wine he'd pretended to drink. Then he stood there watching me, making no effort to help as I swayed on my feet, struggling to stay upright.

Oh … damn … He wants the jump rod.

With a hiss of metal, I drew my sword from its scabbard, but my hands didn't have enough strength to hold it, and the blade tumbled from my fingers. As I helplessly watched it land in the dirt, I lost my balance and began to topple over.

I tried to raise my arms to protect myself but didn't move fast enough. I ended up in a heap on the ground, facedown—dirt on my lips. With all my strength I turned my head to glare at the treacherous bastard.

"I'm sorry," Cenacus said, his eyes pleading with me for forgiveness. "I just really want to go home. You don't know what it's like being stuck here for seventeen years."

With tentative steps he crept forward until he stood over me. My eyelids felt like they weighed a ton and my eyes kept losing focus. I didn't have much time left before whatever he put in the wine knocked me out completely. I could only see his leather boots and the bottom of his cloak, but I felt him pull the jump rod from the waist of my pants.

"No ..." I groaned.

Panic gave me strength and I tried to lunge for him. My body rose only a few inches from the ground before crashing into the dirt again. Cenacus limped quickly away from me, until he stood on the other side of the clearing.

With a swollen tongue I pushed the dirt from my mouth. "Take ... me ... wid ... you," I grunted.

He looked at me, pity on his face. "I don't know if a two-person time jump actually works."

"Please ..." I tried to drag myself across the ground, but my muscles had stopped responding, and all my fingers did was twitch.

With a hurried clicking Cenacus spun the rod's sections around to a new setting. He looked over at me, lying on the forest floor. His lips were drawn tight and his forehead creased. He stood silent for a few seconds, then began limping toward me. He had made it halfway across the clearing when a crash somewhere in the woods startled him and he jerked back. I heard voices now, but without the jump rod, I couldn't understand what they were saying.

He whipped his head around, his eyes wide with fear. "I'm sorry, I can't," he said. "The Romans are almost here."

"No!" I yelled, but the single word came out only as a moan.

Cenacus gave me a final glance of both shame and pity, then he uttered some words and vanished.

I heard footsteps approaching ... and then my world went black.

CHAPTER 12

The freshly caught trout sizzled on the campfire as soon as they hit the pan, an aroma of fish and burning wood filling the air. I inhaled deeply, letting myself relax. My muscles ached from canoeing all day, but the tents were up now, so I could just lie back, watch the stars come out, and enjoy my quiet time here in the woods.

My dad smiled at me and flipped the fish over, scraping the bottom of the frying pan with his spatula. The sound of metal on metal seemed alien in the quiet of the forest clearing. "*Surge, canis,*" he said.

Huh?

"What did you say, Dad?" My words struggled to emerge, as if my tongue was swollen.

Suddenly my ribs exploded in agony, waking me from my dream. I was lying facedown on the ground. I wasn't on a camping trip with Dad—I was in Wales, two thousand years in the past.

But why was I sprawled on the ground?

What had happened?

Damn … that bastard Cenacus had drugged me!

With a groan, I rolled onto my side. A Roman soldier stood over me, the tip of his sword aimed at my chest and his foot pulled back to deliver another kick. *"Surge, canis!"* he demanded again.

Huh? ... The words sounded so familiar. I knew I'd heard them before. But my mind was so hazy. If only I had my jump rod to help—

Wait ... Romans ... Latin ...

Like a thunderbolt, a lifetime of studying Latin in my dad's study flashed through my mind. Hundreds of long boring hours conjugating verbs, learning grammar, reading texts, and speaking Latin with my dad so he could correct my pronunciation. All so I could know what *surge, canis* meant: "Get up, dog."

Slowly I raised myself to my hands and knees, my brain still foggy from whatever Cenacus had dumped into the wine. My chest grew tight and I fought hard to breathe. I was at the mercy of the Romans. The soldier with the sword was all I could focus on—I had to get away from him.

He wore chain-mail armor, carried a heavy rectangular shield in one hand and a short sword in the other. In a fight he'd kick my ass easily. But in a race?

I swept up a handful of dirt and pine needles from the ground and pitched it at his face. Instinctively he brought his shield up to protect himself, giving me the opening I needed.

I leaped to my feet, ready to dash for freedom. Immediately, my temples throbbed, and the world started to spin around me. Before I could even manage two steps, my legs buckled and I collapsed to the ground.

"Just kill him, Gaius," another soldier suggested in Latin. "He cannot even hold his feet."

Before I could react, Gaius kicked me in the ribs again. The wind whooshed out of my lungs, and I rolled over so I lay staring through a gap in the treetops, with roots and rocks digging into my back. Gaius stood over me, his sword raised to strike.

My eyes locked onto the blade as I lay there, frozen with panic. I couldn't fight. I couldn't run. Was this how I was going to die, forgotten and alone two thousand years in the past? Weakly I raised my hands to defend myself against his blow, even though I knew they'd do little against a steel blade.

Surprisingly, my one little act of defiance made him pause, and he scanned my prone body. "He has no wounds," he said, his brow furrowing. "He probably fell over from too much drink."

"Stupid barbarians." The other soldier laughed. He said a few more things, but too quickly for me to understand in my groggy state. All I grasped was that if I couldn't walk, I wasn't leaving this clearing alive.

I almost yelled in Latin, "No, I can walk!" but stopped. I didn't want these guys to know I could understand them. I needed them talking freely so I could gather all the information I could. Instead, I struggled to my feet again, managing it slowly. The world spun a bit less when I finally stood up, but I was still a wreck. It took every ounce of energy just to stay upright.

"See, Marcus," Gaius said, "the dog can stand." He uttered another jumble of words that took me a few seconds to translate. One word stood out.

Slave.

An icy shiver raced down my spine. Slavery might be worse than simply being killed here in the forest. In the Roman world it almost always meant death. Death in the mines, death in the gladiatorial arena, or death at the hands of an uncaring owner who would work me nonstop until I died of exhaustion.

Gaius threw a rope around my neck and cinched it tight, the rough hemp cord biting into my flesh. He gave it a tug to make sure it was secure, snapping my head back.

My cheeks stung with shame. I was like a dog on a leash. If I only had a weapon and some strength, these guys wouldn't be so smug. I cast my eyes downward and searched for my sword among the fallen leaves and pine needles littering the ground. I vaguely remembered it falling from my hands just before I blacked out.

There!

It lay near Marcus's feet, half covered in faded brown pine needles. If I could just get the rope out of Gaius' hands, I might be able to grab for it. Then I'd show these guys.

Gaius kicked me in the back of the knees, yanking hard on the rope. The cord dug deep into my neck, sending me backward to the ground, choking. "Marcus! Look to your feet," he said. "Our new dog was thinking of escaping."

Marcus reached down to pick up my sword, then held it at arm's length. "Is this what you wanted, dog?" he taunted me.

I could only cough and sputter in response.

Marcus flicked at the blade with his fingernail. "Cheap barbarian weapon. Give me a good Roman *gladius* any day." He laughed and tossed the sword away into the trees, the blade crashing into the undergrowth.

Gaius tugged on my leash. "Move, dog."

I staggered to my feet before he could yank the rope again. Despite my obedience, Gaius still shoved me from behind and I stumbled forward, barely managing to stay upright.

The two continued searching the small stand of trees for anything of value, while constantly chatting about the battle, home, food, the weather. As they stomped about, the fog in my brain began to clear, and more and more of what they said made sense to me.

"There is nothing here," Gaius finally muttered. "Let us head back to camp."

As we left the cover of the forest, I saw clouds of smoke billowing from the druid compound in the distance. I stopped in my tracks, desperation gripping my heart. What had happened to all the people

I had left there: Senna, Atto, Trenus, and all the families? Were they dead? Were they slaves? Or had they somehow fled and were now safely hiding?

"Keep moving." Gaius cuffed me on the back of the head. "Nothing but death for you over there. You have a nice life of slavery ahead of you."

"Stop talking to the dog," Marcus said. "He is an ignorant savage; you will have more luck talking to a tree."

"What harm is there in talking to this savage? It amuses me."

"Bah! Next thing you will want to keep him." Marcus rapped his shield with his spear. "You know the rules. We all split whatever coin this slave will bring. I will not lose out on some extra coin just because you want someone to polish your armor."

"Do not worry, my friend. I do not want this slave. But one day I will have a nice villa, a good wife, strong sons, and fifty slaves to work my land."

"I share your dream. But we need to fight more barbarians if we want all that. This raid was poorly rewarded."

Gaius sighed loudly. "Aye, all we have to show for our plunder is this one captive. And he has no gold arm rings or neck rings. Hopefully the rest of the legion has fared better."

Marcus gestured toward me. "How much do you think this one is worth?"

Gaius stopped and squeezed my cheeks, forcing my jaws open so he could peer into my mouth. "He has good teeth, and his body seems strong. He should be worth at least a hundred denarii."

"A hundred denarii?" Marcus scoffed. "Has your brain gone soft? Do you remember the village we took last year? The merchants paid only ten denarii per slave there."

"Which left a poor profit when all the coins were finally counted." Gaius tugged on the leash and continued walking again, while I was stuck following behind him like an obedient poodle. "If we really want to make ourselves rich, Marcus, we need to find a chief. They wear so much gold that no one would notice if a bit went missing. Then we could quit being soldiers."

Marcus snorted, slinging the spear over his shoulder. "You really think you will find a chieftain? Those damn Batavians took most of them already. With their horses they find all the good ones before we have a chance to get there."

Gaius turned his head up thoughtfully. "We may not get a chief, but hopefully we will have our pick of those barbarian women. My bed has not been warmed for many nights."

"We might have to wait our turn for the prettiest ones." Marcus snickered. "They will be bedded many times today."

I felt like puking. This was the Roman Empire that the history books ignored, an empire built on cruelty, plunder, and slavery. The same Roman Empire where an unknown slave like me would be quickly forgotten.

My captors dragged me toward the freshly built Roman camp that lay on the plain between the druid compound and the beach. A low turf wall enclosed a large square containing thousands of tents. Two main paths crossed each other to split the encampment into four quarters. I was led toward a fenced-in pen outside one of the gates. About a thousand Celts already sat huddled together inside the pen, all of them teenagers and younger adults—basically those who could work hard for many years to come. Roman soldiers stood stationed around the pen to make sure no one escaped.

Some of the captive men glared in defiance, but most had their eyes lowered, the fight beaten out of them. The few women in the pen either wore torn garments or were naked, their clothing long ago ripped off by soldiers. A few sobbed while others stared with a fierce hatred at any passing Roman. But most just sat there unmoving, an empty look in their eyes.

Gaius removed the rope from around my neck and shoved me inside the pen. All eyes turned toward me, but shame forced me to stare at the ground to avoid meeting anyone's eyes. I had tried to save these people but failed them—and myself. Now we were stuck here like cattle waiting to be sold off into slavery.

A hand clapped down on my shoulder, startling me. I spun around to see Vindiorix, the Celt who had given me his sword in the battle against the Batavians. His red plaid pants were torn, and his bare chest and arms were covered in scrapes, but otherwise he looked okay.

"Asterix," he began, his eyes wide with surprise. He then uttered a long sentence of Celtic, all of it unintelligible to me because I no longer had the jump rod translating.

I hadn't imagined it possible, but in that instant the reality of slavery became so much worse. I pointed to my throat and shook my head, hoping he'd figure out what I meant.

"Asterix?" he pressed, his voice now sounding bewildered. He uttered another slew of words that again meant nothing to me. I had never learned even the basics of ancient Celtic—there was no language for my dad to teach me. The Romans had so completely erased the Celts from history that only a few words and inscriptions of their various ancient dialects had survived to modern days.

Silently I shrugged, then walked away. Without language I felt so alone, so totally apart from all these people who yesterday had been my friends.

Vindiorix and the other Celts watched me, looks of confusion on their faces. They had no clue what was going on, and I had no way of telling them. I sat on the ground with my back resting against a fence post, far away from the others, and stared at my hands. There was nothing else I could do. There were too many Romans to fight, and I was too weak to run. I was powerless and alone.

Where are you, Sam?

A long sigh, full of despair, escaped my lips. Our plan had been so simple: I'd stay back here with Cenacus while Sam dug up the hidden tablet. Then we'd all jump out together. Seemed easy but, unfortunately, it hadn't been easy enough. Now I faced a lifetime of slavery.

My fist slammed into the soft earth. Why had I drunk that stupid wine? Sam hadn't trusted Cenacus from the start; I should have followed her lead and been more cautious. But no, my trusting nature had done me in. I was such an idiot.

Hopefully Sam had avoided all the crap going on here and made it safely back home. Would I ever see her again? It had taken years for Cenacus to create a phony time glitch, and he'd done it as a free man. I'd have to somehow escape slavery first, which could take even more years. If by some miracle I made it back home and found Sam again, would she even recognize me? Because of the difference in the way time flowed between the past and the present, Sam would still be young and beautiful, and I'd be some decrepit old guy like Cenacus.

I shut my eyes, trying to envision how my dad would get out of this situation. He had always pushed me to think outside the norm. "There are always answers," he'd say over and over again, whenever questions stumped me.

A knot formed in my throat. Dad wouldn't have an answer for this one; he was stuck in a coma in modern time. He couldn't even breathe without a ventilator. Along with Sam, there was an excellent chance I'd never see him again either.

An overwhelming wave of despair washed over me, and tears began to stream down my cheeks. I was utterly screwed.

CHAPTER 13

Throughout the rest of the day I sat silently as the soldiers assigned to guard us gathered around and hurled rocks or clods of dirt into our slave pen, laughing whenever they struck someone. When the occasional rock hit me, my eyes would water from the pain while my body trembled with rage and humiliation. As much as I wanted to grab the same rock and pitch it back so hard that it caved a Roman's skull in, I always held back and uttered only a small cry. That seemed to be the best response. Anyone who tried to hide the fact that they were hurt had more rocks thrown at them until they finally cried out. I could only imagine what would happen if I dared throw a rock back.

No matter how badly the other men and I had it, the women had it worse. A steady stream of soldiers came barging into the pen and grabbed any female available. The unlucky woman would scream and fight as she was hauled off to a nearby tent or a clump of trees, only to return later, bruised and crying, with her eyes cast down in shame. We all knew what was going on, but none of us could do anything to stop it. One brave Celt did leap up and try to protect his wife from being taken, but the Romans beat him with their spear shafts until he crumpled to the ground, bleeding and unconscious. So the rest of us sat there like cowards, hanging our heads.

When night descended, the Romans finally left us alone, as the air grew cooler with the wind gusting in from the coast. Our guards gathered around large fires to keep warm, while the Celts were left huddling together for warmth in the center of the pen. I still sat by myself, my woolen cloak pulled up tightly around me to ward off the cold. My stomach ached from hunger and my lips were cracked from thirst.

The Celtic men had gone into battle shirtless or dressed only in the lightest of garments, while very few of the women had any clothes left. Yet while they shivered from the cold, I was warm in my tunic, pants, boots, and a full cloak. The more I thought about this, the more embarrassed I became.

At almost glacial speed, an idea began to form. It wasn't much of an idea but, after a day spent sitting alone in the slave pen, it seemed my one little chance to salvage something from a disastrous day. I hadn't been able to save the Celts from the Romans. I hadn't been able to protect any of my fellow slaves from abuse. But I could still do one small thing to help—and the Romans couldn't stop me.

I stood up and headed toward the huddle of Celts, who watched me warily in the flickering torchlight. I stopped a healthy distance away from them and took off my woolen cloak. The air felt cold through my thin tunic, but I could live with it. In the midst of a group of women sat a blond girl who looked just a bit older than Sam. Whatever dress she had once worn was long gone, and now she had only her hands to cover her nudity. Throughout the day she had been continually dragged away by the soldiers, more than any other woman here. Despite the bruises on her arms and legs, and the dirt covering her, she didn't cry or hang her head in shame. She sat with her back straight, her eyes burning with hatred. I crumpled my cloak into a ball and tossed it at her feet.

Without taking her eyes off me, she snatched up the cloak and pulled it around herself. She didn't thank me or even nod. She just kept staring, her piercing blue eyes boring holes through me.

My one little act of defiance against the Romans done, I turned and headed back to my fence post.

"Asterix," someone called out.

I stopped and turned to look. Vindiorix waved at me, then uttered a slew of words that held no meaning for me.

I shrugged and continued walking away.

"Asterix!" he called again.

Geez … I was never going to get rid of this guy.

I turned around, hands on my hips, trying hard to figure out how to explain that I had magically lost my ability to understand or speak Celtic.

He smiled and patted the ground next to him.

Maybe I couldn't understand a word he said, but his message was clear—I was one of them. His act of kindness was like a beacon of hope burning through the darkness of my misery. At least I wasn't alone. I settled down beside a hairy man with a bloody cloth wrapped around his hand. The smell of sweat and fear was thick in the air, but I didn't care. Exhaustion and starvation took their toll, and I fell asleep immediately.

I woke to drops of water falling on my face and trickling across my lips.

Rain!

Gray clouds filled the sky, obscuring the morning sun. The rain drizzled down, soaking us as we huddled together. I held my mouth open, trying to catch a few drops and slake my raging thirst.

Vindiorix nudged me and pointed to my tunic. As usual, I had no clue what he meant. He sensed my lack of comprehension and grabbed a corner of my tunic and twisted it. A few drops of water oozed out.

Of course!

I took my tunic off and began wringing it out over my mouth, squeezing every last drop of rainwater I could from it. The water tasted like sweat and dirt but, after almost a day without drinking, I didn't care—it beat drinking out of puddles like some of the Celts had been reduced to doing.

A trumpet blared from the camp the Romans had built on the large island, and all of us in the slave pen jerked upright. With a tromp of boots, a column of legionaries marched out of the camp, headed straight for our pen. In front of them, on his white horse, rode Governor Paulinus. Beside him, on a brown mare, rode a Roman with short dark hair, wearing a green cloak trimmed with fur. He was dressed way too fancy to be a soldier, so he had to be a nobleman or a merchant.

This can't be good.

The two horsemen stopped outside the pen. Even though Governor Paulinus was just surveying us lowly slaves, he still wore his golden breastplate with a red cloak hanging soggily from his shoulders. Cenacus had called him one of the biggest bastards he'd ever met, and Paulinus looked the part. He was probably around fifty, with thinning gray hair, permanent worry lines etched into his forehead, and his lips curled in a sneer. Despite his age, he held himself upright in the saddle as he gazed imperiously over us.

The soldiers spread out around Paulinus and his guest, guarding them in case any of us got the stupid idea to attack. Not that we had much strength left. I hadn't eaten in a day; I barely had enough strength to stand.

"These are the ones we have captured so far, noble Varus," Paulinus said in Latin, waving his hand toward us.

The man in the green cloak scowled. "I traveled all the way from Londininum for this? I expected to see thousands of strong men and women, not a handful of half-dead captives."

Paulinus's eyes narrowed, and he gave an irritated flip of his reins. "If you do not want these, I will find another slave merchant willing to take them."

Varus raised his hands apologetically. "I beg your forgiveness, honorable Governor. I meant no harm. I will take these. How many are there?"

"Twelve hundred. Almost all men." Paulinus answered. "They have strong backs and simple minds; they will make good workers."

Varus dismounted and walked among us, four guards plodding just behind him and a dark-skinned man with the downcast eyes of a slave holding an umbrella over his head. "Stand up, dogs!" Varus yelled.

Roman soldiers began kicking and dragging Celts to their feet. Not everyone could get up, though—a bunch of them hadn't survived the night, dying from their wounds or the cold. Varus personally inspected each of us as if he was buying fruit at the market. I shuddered as his appraising eyes passed over me, but thankfully he didn't poke me, he merely nodded and moved on to the next person. After a few minutes he headed back to Paulinus.

"I will give you two hundred aureii for the lot," he declared.

"Two hundred!" Paulinus scoffed. "That is only four denarii per slave. A strong worker will get you five hundred denarii in the markets. And there are some women here who should fetch at least a thousand." Paulinus crossed his arms over his chest. "Two hundred is impossible. My own men will hang me if I let these slaves go that cheaply."

Varus bowed deeply. "The wise governor clearly knows the prices of slaves. However, this lot will only fetch such lofty sums if they ever reach Londinium. Most of them will die from the cold in these blasted mountains or on the long journey south. And I have to guard and feed them as well." Varus tapped his chin with his finger. "But since I am a fair and honest man, I can give you two hundred and fifty ... or else you can always find another dealer ready to take this many slaves from you."

Paulinus's face twisted as if he had just bit into a lemon. He raised his fist as if he was about to haggle some more, but then thought better of it. "I accept your offer," he grumbled.

Varus bowed again to Paulinus and then turned to us. "Do any of you ignorant savages speak a civilized tongue?" he asked us in Latin.

No way I was stepping forward. The only way to survive this was to keep my head down and not draw attention to myself. To my right, a man slightly older than me stepped forward. He was shorter than most Celts, but still had the wild hair and bushy mustache common among their men. "I speak your language," he said in Latin.

Varus snapped his fingers and two guards dragged the Celt forward. They held him by both arms and shoved him to the ground so that he was kneeling in front of Varus. "Where did you learn to speak our tongue?" Varus asked.

The trembling Celt kept his eyes fixed on the ground. "My—my mother was a servant in the house of a Roman lord," he stammered. "I lived there until the lord died and his villa fell to ruin."

The slaver nodded and motioned for his guards to haul the Celt up. "Translate for me," Varus ordered him, then threw his arms wide to gather everyone's attention. "I am Quintus Varus, and you are all now my property. Whatever past life you have led, you can forget. If you listen, and are obedient, you can expect to lead a long and happy life as a servant of the Empire."

As the man translated these words, an angry mutter rose from the prisoners.

"If you attempt to escape," Varus continued, shouting over their rumbling, "then you will be tortured upon your recapture. If you kill a member of my household, then you and ten others will be killed. I expect to be obeyed at all times. Failure to obey me will result in instant punishment. You can cry to your friends, your ancestors, or your gods, but none of them can help you. From now on there is only me."

So that was it. I was no longer a slave of the Roman army, I was now property of Varus and headed for the slave markets, where someone else would buy me. Since the moment I'd been captured, I'd known this would be my fate, but hearing it put into words crushed any lingering hope that might still have lurked within my head. I was a slave. I would probably never see my home—or Sam—again. I'd end up in the mines, in the gladiator arena, or if I was lucky, in some rich man's villa as a servant. My life as I knew it was over.

Varus clapped his hands and a small man in a gray tunic bowed in front of him. "See that these slaves get water and food," Varus ordered. "I want them ready to sail by the time the channel calms."

The servant started barking orders, and soon we had buckets of water and gruel. The water was brackish, with things floating in it, and the gruel was probably the stuff the Batavian horses had refused to eat, but I was ready to eat anything.

There were no bowls or utensils. Everyone just had to reach into the slop buckets and grab handfuls of mush. I barely had a chance to wolf down a few sloppy fistfuls before the guards began walking among us and tying us together with a rope fastened around our necks. There were twenty of us per rope, with a guard firmly holding the end. My hands trembled with rage and shame as the coarse noose was cinched tight around my neck, tying me up like a dog again. All I wanted to do was rip the hateful thing off me, but I knew better. The moment the rope left my neck, it would be considered an escape attempt, and I'd be tortured.

The only bright spot—if there was such a thing as a bright spot in slavery—was that Vindiorix was tied up directly in front of me. With him around, at least I wouldn't feel so alone.

Once all of us slaves were secured together, the guards started herding us toward the beach along a path littered with heaps of Celtic dead.

"Stupid barbarians," one of our guards chuckled. "Too dumb to know when they are conquered."

I kept my eyes focused on Vindiorix's back, trying to forget the slaughter. But the closer we got to the shore, the more corpses we passed. As we skirted the site of the main battle, the dead lay in piles, and the stench of blood hung thick in the air. The endless cawing of crows and ravens drowned out all other sound as the birds picked over the dead. Their raucous calls seemed like a final mocking laugh at the futility of the Celtic resistance.

I was almost glad when we reached the shore and the noise of the wind and the waves drowned out the birds. A variety of boats waited for us: a large ship with twenty oarsmen that could only have been intended for Varus, smaller rowboats for the guards, and the flat-bot-tomed boats that the Roman army had crossed on, great for slaves.

"Pack them in!" Varus ordered.

The guards pushed and bullied us, cramming us into the boats until each craft rode precariously low in the water. I didn't know much about boats, but even I recognized that the danger now wasn't the Romans but the surrounding water—one large wave could swamp an entire vessel. And since we were all tied by the neck, and most people in ancient times couldn't swim, if this boat started sinking, I'd be dragged straight down with the rest of the helpless slaves attached to my rope.

Luckily our hands were left free so we could paddle. And if this boat did start sinking, I'd have at least a chance to untie myself before I drowned.

Just as my boat was pushed off from the shore, and we began row-
ing out into the channel, a voice somewhere inland cried out. "Hold!"

Varus, who was standing on the shore supervising the whole load-
ing process, wheeled around. "What is the meaning of this?"

"Orders from Governor Paulinus," a breathless soldier explained.
"The Third Century of the Second Cohort of the Twentieth Legion is
to accompany you. We have a special shipment intended for Rome."

A group of a hundred or so legionaries came marching down the
hillside where my trebuchets had stood. Between them they carried
the logs, ropes, and wicker basket of the shattered trebuchet.

Crap …

The sight of my creation coming down the hill was like a final kick
to the face. I was trapped two thousand years in the past, stuck as a
slave, and had no way of going home but, impossibly, my situation had
just gotten worse. The Romans had my trebuchet—which meant I'd
also massively screwed up history.

CHAPTER 14

About a hundred paces ahead of me, the wagon rumbled along the plank road, carrying my trebuchet deeper into Roman-held territory. I'd been following that wagon and its protective cohort of armed Roman infantry for six days. Six days of dreary plodding through the Welsh mountains, where the rain never ended and the nights froze your skin. Six soul-crushing days of watching people fall by the roadside, never to get up again. Six soggy, sunless days of beatings if we moved too slow, beatings if we made eye contact with any of the guards, and beatings if the guards just needed someone to beat.

Another hacking cough tore through my chest, leaving me breathless and weak. I was so freakin' tired, and every part of me ached. But I trudged onward, forcing one foot in front of the other over the rain-slicked path. The rope around my neck tugged me along, not giving me a chance to stop. Either I kept pace with the nineteen other slaves in my chain or I died, plain and simple. The caravan guards had zeroed in on me at the first cough, watching me from the comfort of their saddles, expecting me to fall. I'd seen what happened to those who couldn't keep up. One quick spear thrust—one less slave in the ranks slowing down everyone else.

Over two hundred had died so far on this terrible march, and if I didn't lose this cough, I would join them. I didn't need a doctor to tell me that I was in bad shape. I could feel it with every wheezing breath I took, in the chest pain that grew worse every day, the hacking cough that never let up, and the constant fever that sapped my strength and made even the simplest of thoughts difficult.

So tired. So cold.

For the hundredth time, my thoughts turned to somehow escaping this nightmare. Over the past week I had envisioned countless half-formed plans and barely sensible ideas, all ending in the same conclusion: there was no escape. Even if I did free myself from this leash around my neck, I wouldn't get far. I could barely manage walking—running was impossible. My eyelids felt too heavy to keep open, so I shut them and continued trudging along, one foot after the other.

My attempt at sleepwalking lasted only a few steps. One moment I was moving upright, the next I lay on the ground with the rope around my neck nearly strangling me.

I rolled onto my side, trying to push myself to my feet. The clop of hooves grew louder as the guards neared. My hands slid over the muddy road, and I fell again.

A pair of hands reached down and pulled me to my feet. "Keep walking. No rest," Vindiorix urged.

I nodded in thanks and continued stumbling forward again. How many times had he dragged me out of the mud so far? Five? Ten? I'd be dead if it wasn't for him.

I owed Vindiorix so much, yet he'd annoyed the hell out of me at first. When the boats had crossed the strait and we'd begun our death march through the Welsh countryside, the guy had just kept talking and talking. Morning, afternoon, evening—even when we stopped for the night and were all huddling together for warmth. He just didn't shut up. When he continued talking that first night, even as I was falling asleep, I finally snapped. "Don't you get it?" I yelled at him in English. "I can't speak Celtic!"

His mouth had gaped at my response, and I figured I had finally stopped his annoying chatter. But then he snapped his mouth shut and tapped his forehead with his finger, like a man with a genius idea. He scanned our group of huddled slaves, watchful guards, and the Roman soldiers in their own separate camp until finally his eyes lit on Varus's horse, tethered outside the slave merchant's tent. "*Epos*," he said, pointing at the horse.

"*Epos*," I repeated, just to humor him.

A huge smile spread across his face, and he started pointing with his hands at more things in our camp. *Carros*—wagon. *Scutum*—shield. *Sagum*—cloak. *Bracea*—pants. *Gaesum*—spear. The words kept piling up. And, like a parrot in need of a cracker, I repeated them all back to him. With each word, I realized how much I had missed talking to someone else.

The next day, as our endless marching resumed, we continued our lessons. He never asked why I'd lost the ability to speak Celtic; he just seemed happy that I was learning to speak again.

As the days wore on and we trekked deeper into the Welsh mountains, my language skills improved and, through a combination of words and a ton of hand motions, I learned how Vindiorix had ended up stuck as a slave, like me. Before the Romans came, he had been a farmer, with a wife and three kids. Then, from what I could understand, a neighboring tribe had called in the Romans to settle an argument. This was typical of the Romans. They had built their huge empire by regularly offering to "help" one group of people against another. Once both were weak through constant fighting, the Romans would swoop in and conquer both. For Vindiorix, the end result was that Roman soldiers burned his village. He'd been away when the Romans came, so he returned to a house in ruins and his family all dead. Ever since then, this simple farmer had turned to war—fighting Romans when he could, but running from them even more.

After six days, I still couldn't understand the majority of what he said, but I at least understood the important bits—and I knew he wanted me to keep moving. With my teeth chattering, I stumbled back into line and continued shuffling onward. How much longer could I last?

For the hundredth time I looked with envy at the other wagon in our caravan. This one held an iron cage in which fifteen female slaves huddled under blankets. Varus, the slave merchant, clearly knew which slaves he had to pamper. Only the prettiest women rode in this caged wagon, because they could be sold for the highest amounts in the slave markets. Varus didn't want to risk losing them to cold or hunger, so they had warm blankets and even extra food. While I choked down a few handfuls of slimy boiled grains every day, they got bread.

I remembered bread: the smell of it, the warm softness. My stomach growled just thinking about it.

Comux, the only Celt who knew how to speak Latin, was the one I despised the most. He had turned traitor faster than you could say *sellout*. He followed Varus around like a lapdog, translating for him and serving him. For his faithfulness he had been rewarded with a warm, fur-lined cloak and the scraps from Varus's table. He got to eat meat!

I shook my head. Was this really what my life had become, envying someone because he got table scraps and I didn't? I imagined this was exactly how Victor Stahl would model the world if he and the rest of his band of time jumpers succeeded in their plan. Victor at the top—the emperor—with all the lackeys around him well rewarded. Then there'd be the rest of us, fighting each other for the scraps.

Vindiorix nudged me, breaking my train of thought. He was pointing to a trio of crows perched on a branch overlooking the road. The large black birds leaned from their branches and cawed noisily as we passed underneath. "The gods send word," he said in a hushed voice. "Battle comes soon."

The Celts might have believed in such omens and superstition, but I didn't. The gods definitely weren't going to swoop down and save me. But despite my lack of faith, the other slaves seemed to hold the same view as Vindiorix. They all were pointing to the crows and speaking in whispers to each other, glancing expectantly into the forest. Whatever the Celts thought was lurking out there, I couldn't see it. Nothing moved in the trees except for the leaves, as rain drizzled down. The only sounds were the constant drip of water and the drumming of feet on the slick road.

Ahead of us, the trail slithered down the mountains and entered a long narrow valley lying between two hills covered in thick trees and underbrush. Some part of my sickness-riddled brain was still alert enough to recognize that this spot would be the perfect place for an ambush. My breath hitched in my throat. Was Vindiorix right? Was something about to happen? I peered into the thick forest cover, trying to spot any sign of movement, but saw nothing.

Ahead of me, Vindiorix stumbled and fell.

"Get up," yelled a guard in Latin as he rode his horse near and raised his spear above his head.

Vindiorix pulled himself to his feet and continued walking, his eyes now focused on his feet. Every few seconds he'd peek up to see if the guard was watching, then he'd look down at the ground again. When the Roman finally turned away, Vindiorix glanced over his shoulder to catch my attention. He winked and opened his clasped hands. Nestling in his palms he held an apple-sized rock. He motioned with his chin at the guard. His message was clear.

I stifled a cough before it knocked me to the ground again. Vindiorix was nuts if he thought he could attack one of the guards.

They were mounted; he was on foot. They had spears and shields; he had a rock. Bad idea all around. When he failed, the rest of us would suffer. Everyone in our chain of slaves would be beaten for not stopping him. Varus might even kill some of us off as a lesson to the others.

But I knew Vindiorix wasn't crazy. So why did he think he could get away with it? I looked again toward the forest. Were those eyes peering out from the bushes over on the right? I stared at the spot, but all I could see now were moisture-beaded leaves. Was my fever making me see things?

As the cohort of Roman infantry escorting the pieces of my trebuchet made it to the bottom of the valley, I held my breath, clinging to the hope of an attack. I waited and waited, but nothing happened. My shoulders slumped. No matter how much I didn't believe in omens, I had hoped that Vindiorix was right: that some huge army would burst out from the trees and save us all. I sighed, my breath coming out in a ragged gasp. *Just keep walking.*

Ahead and to the right, a bird chittered in the woods, an alien sound in the rain-soaked forest. Almost instantly, its chirp was answered on the left.

Huh? Birds don't call to each other in heavy rain.

Then the quiet hills erupted as sling stones flew out from the forest on both sides and pelted the legionaries. Men screamed in pain as rocks whistled through the air and shattered bones.

My body tensed and my heart beat quicker. *Ambush!*

"Guard the slaves!" Varus yelled.

The guards wheeled their horses around, pointing their spears toward us, watching for anyone trying to flee. There were about sixty guards, so we heavily outnumbered them, but as long as we remained tied together by the necks, escape would be almost impossible.

"Form the turtle!" a centurion yelled.

With a rustle of chain mail and a stomping of feet, the Roman soldiers quickly formed into a tight square, the men standing shoulder to shoulder. Those on the outermost edges overlapped their rectangular shields to form a wall, while those within raised their shields protectively above their heads. Once all the shields were locked into place, the legionaries crouched so that not even their feet were visible—just a solid square of red-painted shields.

I closed my eyes and hung my head as my feeble hope of being rescued evaporated. Whoever had planned this battle had no clue what they were doing. Only a few Romans had fallen in the initial attack, and now they were all massed together into a tight block that could defend itself against any assault. The Celts in the forest kept firing away with their slings, but the stones now clanged off the wall of Roman shields and fell harmlessly to the ground.

Wait a second …

Something didn't seem right about this. But what? It was so hard for me to think—exhaustion and sickness made even the simplest thoughts an effort. Then it hit me. Celts would never attack Romans with slings; they thought such weapons unmanly. And where were the shouts and the blare of trumpets? Celts would never be this quiet.

Suddenly the distinctive creak of straining ropes came from the woods, followed a second later by the rustle of bushes and saplings as if they were being slapped aside by something massive hurtling through the brush. My eyes shot open in time to see two huge logs secured with ropes swing out from the trees on either side of the road and go smashing into the Roman formation. Soldiers flew into the air like bowling pins, their swords and shields tossed aside.

For a second I stood slack-jawed, staring at the destruction. I'd never been more wrong in my life. Whoever had planned this ambush was a total genius! They had attacked the Romans first with slings, knowing they'd form a turtle, and then smashed them.

Another volley of sling stones flew out from the trees, felling even more soldiers, and then the forest erupted as Celts rushed from the trees, spears and shields in their hands.

No, not just Celts—Celtic *women*. There were hundreds of them, all in dark gray and green cloaks and with their arms and faces smeared with mud to add to their camouflage. Uttering savage war cries, they attacked with a ferocity few men could match. The first Romans fell quickly before their attack, too surprised to raise their shields in time.

"Form up! Form up!" the centurion yelled.

The remaining soldiers struggled to obey his command, hurriedly shifting position and trying to link shields, but the warrior women wouldn't let the troops close ranks. They jabbed at every opening with their spears, sending even more Romans to their deaths.

"Now!" Vindiorix yelled, yanking at the rope that joined us. He rushed forward, almost dragging the rest of us behind him. He smashed his concealed rock into the front leg of the guard's horse, and the animal reared in pain, dumping the Roman to the ground. A second later the valley rang with a sickening crack as the rock came down hard on the fallen guard's face. As the man slumped lifeless to the ground, Vindiorix grabbed the Roman's sword from its sheath and severed the ropes linking our two necks in one blow. A few more slashes and he had completely freed our line. Slaves ran at the other guards, dragging them from their horses.

I grabbed the frayed end of the rope and just stared at it. The feeling of not being tied up to the man in front of me suddenly felt odd, like I was doing something wrong and would be punished.

"Move, Asterix!" Vindiorix yelled as he headed for the next group of roped slaves.

His words snapped me out of my stunned confusion. I plunged into the underbrush at one side of the road, holding my hands up in front of my face to ward off the branches. I managed to get a few steps in before my foot slipped on the muddy hillside and I collapsed in the muck. My lungs ached for air—I couldn't run farther. Closing my eyes, I lay there exhausted, too tired to even roll over. At any moment I expected to feel a Roman spear plunging into my back.

A few seconds passed before I realized that no guards had followed me. I dragged myself back along the muddy ground to peer out through the bushes. The slave caravan was in chaos. Vindiorix and the other freed slaves ran around, either attacking guards or setting more Celts free. Like me, some slaves didn't know what to do: they remained in place, eyes cast downward and a kind of lost expression on their faces. A few ran off into the forest while others grabbed rocks and sticks and attacked the guards.

"Kill all who try to escape!" Varus yelled, wheeling his horse in a tight circle.

This was the order the guards had been waiting for. They rode among the Celts, hacking and stabbing at any slave who was not still tied to another. The freed slaves fought back with whatever was at hand, hurling rocks, swinging branches as clubs, or using weapons they had managed to take from fallen guards.

My fingers drummed restlessly on the wet soil. No matter how crappy I felt, I should be out there helping. I shook my head to clear the thick fog that had settled over my brain. It didn't matter that I could barely stand; if the Celts lost this fight, the Romans would find me and I'd either be stuck as a slave again or executed. I needed to get out there and fight.

My muscles groaned as I grabbed a muddy rock and dragged myself to my feet. Maybe I didn't have strength, but I still had stealth. A few paces ahead of me a guard was hacking away at a group of slaves who had been freed. His back was toward me—an easy target.

Slowly I crept out of the bushes, any noise from my movement masked by the drumming of rain and the clash of battle. Suddenly, an all-too-familiar tickle started in my lungs.

No! Not now!

Clenching my throat muscles, I tried to control my breath, but my chest still exploded in a huge coughing fit. The guard wheeled around, his eyes widening as he saw me and the rock in my hand.

I stood frozen in place. I knew I had to run, but I could barely move as the coughs racked my body. With my heart pounding, I looked around for a better weapon. Nothing. Not even a bigger rock.

The guard raised his spear, ready to plunge it into me.

So this is it. This is how I die.

I didn't feel fear. I didn't feel sadness. I just felt … tired.

CHAPTER 15

Time seemed to slow. Everything grew quiet, and all I could see was the snarl on the guard's face as he thrust his spear toward my chest. Then suddenly there was a gray-fletched arrow buried halfway in his side, and his mouth was gaping with surprise and pain. The spear dropped from his fingers and he fell face-first into the mud at my feet.

For a second I just stood there, too stunned to do anything. Then something seemed to switch on in my head, and I experienced a brief moment of clarity. Only one person in this time period used a bow.

I whipped my head around, desperately searching for her. *Come on, Sam. Where are you?*

But she was nowhere to be seen in the chaos of the battlefield. Muddy slaves were attacking caravan guards. The Celtic women were still battling the Roman soldiers. Everyone was running around, shouting and trying to be heard over the clash of weapons and the screams of the dying.

Sam wouldn't be in a fight.

I wiped the sweat and rain from my eyes and scanned the hillsides. Midway between the legionaries and the slave caravan, I spotted her.

She stood partly obscured by the trees, only her bow and the folds of her drab-green cloak visible. With cold accuracy she leveled her bow at another two guards, and with a pair of rapid shots dropped them both.

My legs felt as heavy as tree trunks, but seeing Sam gave me the strength to run. "Sam!" I gasped. "Sam!"

She didn't hear me over the din of fighting. Her bow just kept sweeping over the two battles, finding a target in any Roman who had his back turned to her.

My lungs gulped for air, setting me coughing again, but I kept pushing myself onward. I had to get to her. "Sam!" I croaked as I lurched onward.

She swung her bow toward me, ready to fire. For a second we locked eyes as I stared down the shaft of her arrow. My heart pounded in my chest. Would she recognize the weak mud-stained slave in front of her?

Her green eyes widened, and she lowered the bow. "Dan?" she asked incredulously.

I nodded.

"Dan!" She rushed over and threw her arms around me. "You're alive!" she said, her voice cracking as she clung to me.

"Barely," I said as I collapsed into her arms, with my head resting on her shoulder.

Sam's here. I'm safe.

Sam half led, half dragged me into the bushes at one side of the road. "Rest here," she said as she eased me to the ground. She pulled a knife from her sheath and placed it in my hands. "Stay low. I have work to do." Without another glance at me she raised her bow and sighted along it, before releasing an arrow at a nearby Roman soldier. The arrow hissed through the air and buried itself into his back, sending him to the ground.

This was all wrong. I shouldn't be hiding here in the bushes while the Celts and Sam did the fighting. Yeah, maybe I was feverish and weak as a newborn kitten. But we were fighting for our lives here. There had to be something I could do.

Using a tree for support, I dragged myself up to a standing position to survey the scene. In the main battle the Roman soldiers still fought with discipline and bravery against the Celtic women, but their numbers were decreasing. This is where Sam focused most of her arrows. Any time an opening appeared behind a shield, a gray-feathered shaft would strike. As for the battle between the slaves and the guards, it was almost over. The last remaining guards fled on horseback down the forest road, their cloaks flapping soggily behind them. The rest of them lay dead, overrun by the mass of freed slaves. Varus the slave master, caught in the space between the two battles, was the only slaver left alive.

"You cannot do this!" he howled as he wheeled his horse in circles, trying to find a way to escape the angry mob that surrounded him. He lashed around him with a short staff, batting away the spears and sticks poking at him.

In my former life I might have felt pity for him. I might even have jumped to my feet and told the Celts to leave him alone. But after six days of being his slave I knew what he was and how little the Celts meant to him. He deserved whatever punishment they doled out. I even caught myself smiling as a hand reached up, caught the hem of his dark green cloak, and dragged him out of his saddle into the mob of slaves below. His howls of fear and pain ended quickly. Too quickly. He should have suffered longer.

Varus's screams had barely stopped before the former slaves streamed past me and Sam to join the fight against the Roman soldiers. I studied each angry and determined face, trying to find Vindiorix among them.

Where is he?

Beside me, Sam shifted from side to side, trying to angle a shot through the flood of freed slaves that now blocked her view of the battle. "Crap," she muttered to herself as she lowered her bow.

"Come with me," I said, heading as fast as my aching legs could carry me away from the battle.

"But the fighting's that way." Sam jerked a thumb over her shoulder.

"The Celts don't need our help—they're going to win. This is more important."

Sam followed me to where the battle against the slavers had happened. Dead or dying Celts lay everywhere, each of their moans and cries of pain like a dagger in my heart. So many people who needed help, but I couldn't help them—not until I found Vindiorix. I headed to the middle of the battlefield, where the fighting had been the thickest.

Please, don't be here.

"What are we doing?" Sam asked.

No ...

A man wearing familiar red-plaid pants lay facedown on the ground. I knelt and rolled Vindiorix over; which set me violently coughing from the effort. Cuts and stabs covered him, but his chest faintly rose and fell. He was still alive—but wouldn't be for long.

A weak smile appeared on Vindiorix's face when he saw me. "Asterix ... you still live," he said, his voice weak.

"You'll live too," I said. I tried to sound encouraging, but his wounds looked so bad. "Just hold on."

To my surprise, my words came out in Celtic. And not the awful, bumbling Celtic I'd picked up in the last six days—but proper Celtic, as if I'd been speaking it since birth.

The smile on his face grew larger. "You speak our tongue again ... Good ..." He coughed and his eyes focused past me on Sam. "And you found your woman ... Live well together ..." His breathing slowed.

"Come on, Vindiorix. Stay with me!" I pleaded.

Sam's comforting hand gripped tighter on my shoulder. In that instant I understood why my Celtic had been restored. Somehow, by touching me, Sam had transferred her jump rod's translation ability to me. Not that it mattered right now—I needed to save my friend.

I tore a strip off the bottom of my tunic and pressed it against the largest gash across his chest. Bright red blood gushed out of the wound, dripping to the muddy ground beneath him. My ragged cloth did little to stop the flow, so I tore off another strip of my tunic and added it to the first one.

Sam shook her head grimly. I knew what she was thinking—that Vindiorix was beyond help—but I couldn't just let him go. I pressed both cloths down on to his wounds, trying to stem the flow of blood. So many wounds. So much blood.

Vindiorix raised his hand weakly and rested it on my arm. "Stop, Asterix … I head to the otherworld …" His head rolled to the side, and he stared down the road to where it disappeared into the forest. A huge smile appeared on his face. "My wife and children beckon me …"

"I can't let you go. You saved my life."

"Nay … You owe me no debt." A coughing fit racked his body and blood dribbled from his mouth. "Good bye, Asterix."

He took two more ragged breaths, then the spark of life faded from his eyes.

Tears blurred my vision and I felt like a part of me had been ripped away. Vindiorix, my friend, was gone.

Sam knelt beside me and wrapped her arms around me. "I'm so sorry."

I buried my face in her shoulder and cried, each sob cut short by another hacking cough rattling my lungs. Sam said nothing, just held me close.

We probably sat like this for a minute or two until a loud chorus of shouts and cheers emanated from down the road.

"Looks like we've won," Sam said.

With the palm of my hand, I wiped the tears from my eyes and looked up. The last of the Roman troops lay dead, but they hadn't gone down easily. Dead Celts lay strewn everywhere along the road. Victory had come at an awful price.

Slowly, painfully, I dragged myself to my feet. The forest seemed to be spinning around me and I reached out to prevent myself from falling. Sam grabbed me and held me upright.

"Are you going to be okay?"

Another bone-shaking cough rattled through me, and dark spots swam before my eyes. "I'll be fine," I wheezed.

"Are you sure?"

"Positive."

Then the world went black.

CHAPTER 16

Something woke me. A bird? Voices?
Where am I?

A crushing weight of blankets or furs covered me, leaving only my face exposed to the chilly air. My skin was clammy from the sheen of sweat covering it, but I still felt like I was lying on a bed of ice.

So thirsty. So cold.

My eyes flickered open, and I stared at the leafy canopy of trees above me. It moved slowly across the sky, accompanied by the creak of wagon wheels and the thump of feet.

"He wakes. Give him some more of the mixture," a man said.

Was he speaking Celtic or English? I couldn't tell.

Other people lay next to me, but opening my eyes had taken most of my strength, so I couldn't turn to see them—though I could feel them. Their bodies blazed with heat like furnaces, spreading their warmth over to me. I cracked open my parched lips, and a thick liquid trickled into my mouth. It tasted like a mixture of lawn clippings and cough syrup, but it soon spread its warmth through me, sending me back to sleep.

My chest erupted with a hacking cough, waking me again. My eyes remained glued shut, and I moaned softly. Everything hurt.

A hand stroked my forehead with a damp cloth. "Go back to sleep, Dan," came Sam's soothing voice.

Where is she?

Beside me, one of the other bodies was now cold and stiff.

"Put her on the other wagon. She has gone to the otherworld," said a man with a deep, stern voice.

The weight of blankets was lifted, exposing me to a blast of frozen air and filling my nostrils with the stench of sweat. I shivered from the cold and my teeth chattered. *What are they doing to me?* With a rustle of hay, the body beside me slid away.

Someone else crawled into the wagon and curled up against me, their bare skin next to mine, sharing their body heat. The blankets and furs returned, wrapping us in a warm cocoon. The man shouted something and the ground under me jerked forward and then started swaying, lulling me back to sleep.

My thoughts drifted between sleep and consciousness. *So tired. But I don't want to sleep anymore.* The gentle rocking had stopped; I wasn't on a wagon anymore. The people next to me were also gone. With one hand I reached out and felt a bed frame.

"The sickness has passed; he will live," a man declared. "He will be weak for some time, though." A patter of footsteps and the banging of a door followed his words.

Where am I?

Every part of me felt tired. If someone told me I'd been hit by a truck, I'd believe it. The pain in my chest was gone, though, so my breath came out easier. My eyes cracked open, and I stared up into the wooden rafters of a cone-shaped roof. Smoke clung to the thatching, obscuring the dark recesses at its peak.

"Welcome back," Sam said softly.

The sound of her voice instantly made me feel better, and I turned my head to find her. I was lying on a short bed, just a few inches off the ground. She was sitting next to me, on a pile of furs strewn across the floor. Her hair looked wild and knotted, as if it hadn't been brushed in years, and her eyes, usually sparkling with life, had dark circles underneath them. She probably hadn't slept in days, but she was still the most beautiful sight I'd ever seen.

"Glad to be back," I croaked, my voice straining through a parched throat. We were in a large circular room that had four doors positioned evenly apart. Sun shone through the woven branches forming the doors, letting in a weak light. The walls of the room were painted a chalky white that reminded me of the stuff Atto put in his hair. A series of low beds like mine, just inches off the ground, butted the walls, and in the center of the room burned a large fire.

"Where are we?" I asked.

"We're in a village about two days' travel away from the ambush site. You're in the healing hut." Sam put a hand behind my head and raised it so I could drink from her water skin.

No foul lawn juice this time, just cool water. I gulped at it greedily, sloshing it everywhere.

"Easy," Sam said. "Don't make yourself sick."

I drank more slowly, relishing the coolness until I was finally sated. "Are we safe?" I asked her, my stomach knotting.

Sam replaced the stopper on the water skin, then pushed the sweat-soaked hair away from my eyes. "Safe enough. Some of the slave guards managed to get away, so the Romans will soon know about the ambush. But this village is hidden pretty deep in the Welsh highlands, so if they come looking for revenge, they're going to have a hard time finding us."

I exhaled slowly. "I can't wait to get out of here."

Sam winced.

"What's wrong?" I asked.

She stroked my forehead with her fingertips. "Nothing that can't be fixed once you get better. You were pretty sick back there."

"I've never felt so bad." I glanced at the other beds around the room, which were all empty. "What about the people who were with me on the wagon?"

"The girl died. The other guy is better; he left yesterday."

I concentrated hard, trying to figure out what was memory and what had been only fever dreams. "I remember the girl dying and them taking her away. Then someone else took her place beside me. Who was it?"

"Catia," Sam replied. "She stayed beside you constantly. Said she owed it to you." Sam tilted her head and looked at me with curiosity. "She wouldn't say why she owed you, just insisted on lying beside you to keep you warm."

"Catia …" I tried to remember anyone with that name. Nothing. "What does she look like?"

"Young. Blond. Pretty."

I remembered Senna by the pond, topless, asking me for help. Then I thought of all the other Celtic women I'd seen during the days leading to the battle. "Doesn't help. A lot of women here fit that description."

I panned hazy memories, remembering times where I woke up for a few seconds and felt the warmth of bodies on either side of me, blasting me with their heat. I became suddenly aware that I could feel every fiber of the coarse blanket against my skin. "I'm not wearing any clothes, am I?"

"Nope." Sam shook her head. "You soaked them through with sweat on the first day. Catia and I took them off so you wouldn't cool down and get even sicker."

She said it so matter-of-factly, as if two women stripping me naked while I was unconscious was the most important advancement in medicine since penicillin. My cheeks burned with embarrassment and I pulled the blankets over my head.

Sam yanked the blankets away from my face. "Don't be embarrassed. Neither of us looked"—she grinned slyly—"much."

"And whose genius idea was it to strip down the sick guy?"

"I was just following doctor's orders." Sam raised her hands defensively. "One of the slaves we freed earlier was a healer. He told us how to treat your fever. He also mixed a potion from some plants that he found in the forest. It kept you sleepy, but it worked to clear up your chest."

Despite all the water I had drunk, the taste of that foul potion still lingered on my tongue. No wonder I'd slept so much. "Great," I responded sarcastically. "Some backwoods witch doctor told you to strip me naked and force liquid lawn clippings down my throat. Sounds like I'm lucky to be alive," I grumbled.

"Stop being such a baby." Sam's eyes sparkled with amusement. "The Celts were supposed to be the best doctors in the ancient world—and he did as much as he could with the resources at hand." She wagged a finger at me. "Without antibiotics, we had to keep you as hot as possible and let your fever fight off your sickness. That meant stripping you naked and sharing body heat. It's not like we could have had a nice fire blazing away in the middle of the cart." She shrugged. "And hey, it worked."

I had to admit that I was genuinely feeling better. Good enough to leave the bed? With all my strength I pulled myself into a sitting position, the effort forcing a raspy cough from my chest. My ribs felt a twinge of pain, but my cough seemed much less forceful than before. *So far so good.*

Sam pointed to a small metal cauldron suspended by a hook over the fire. "You hungry? You haven't eaten in days."

My stomach growled in response. "Starving."

She grabbed a bowl from next to the fireplace and spooned some gruel into it. With slow, tentative steps I got up from my pallet and shuffled over to the fire, the blanket wrapped tightly around me both for warmth and for modesty. Sam took a seat beside me and handed me the clay bowl. The aroma of oatmeal mixed with honey and berries wafted from it. I gulped down a spoonful and felt its warmth spread through me, giving me strength. A low moan escaped my lips. I'd never been more appreciative of oatmeal.

"How did you know where to find me?" I asked as I scooped up another spoonful.

"I didn't." Sam tapped the archery bracer on her left forearm, where she kept her jump rod hidden. "The women were following the slave caravan to see if they could rescue their husbands, and I went chasing after a new time glitch that had suddenly appeared. We just happened to have the same target. We followed it for days and ended up finding you."

I thought back to the ambush in the forest: the dark clothing and muddied skin of the women. The logs swinging through the trees and crushing the Roman turtle. Everything had been so well planned. "The ambush was your idea, wasn't it?"

"Yup. Worked pretty well."

I nodded appreciatively. "It was a beautiful thing to watch. So well done, especially since the Celts are almost impossible to lead."

Sam chuckled. "That's because you tried organizing the men. They only want to show off their bravery. But the women just wanted to rescue their people and avenge the attack on the island."

"I wish I'd had more women fighting for me on the island. We might have saved more Celts." I looked up from my food. "How did you even get off the island? Isn't it crawling with Romans?"

"They're everywhere," she said, in a voice filled with disgust. "Like cockroaches. But they don't go out at night—at least not in small groups. The Celts who survived taught them how deadly that can be. So we hid during the day and crossed the strait in the moonlight on some boats we stole. It was rough going in places, but we made it." She stretched her legs out across the floor, the toes of her brown leather boots resting on the rocks of the fire circle. "That's my story. So what happened to you?"

Between spoonfuls, I told her everything that had happened to me after she had left. I told her about the trebuchets, fighting the Batavians, moving the Celts back to the compound, and ended with Cenacus drugging me, stealing my jump rod, and leaving me for the Romans.

"That bastard," she said. "I knew we couldn't trust him."

I tapped the wooden spoon nervously against the rim of my bowl. "How am I going to get home?"

Sam rested her hand on mine. "Cenacus said he wanted to do a dual jump with you. Maybe it actually works?"

"Have you ever heard of a dual jump?"

She shook her head. "No, but I'm willing to try it. Cenacus might have been a deceitful bastard, but he wouldn't have a reason to lie about that. Of course, if I'm the one initiating the jump, it would probably mean that we'd both end up back at my house. But I guess you could figure out a way home from there."

Home.

It would be so awesome to see my little apartment again and to visit my dad in the hospital. Hopefully his condition had improved since I jumped out. I really missed him. Life just hadn't been the same for me since Victor came into my life and messed everything up.

Victor ...

A cold chill ran down my back. "Damn it!" I yelled.

Sam eyed me quizzically. "What's wrong?"

"Cenacus knows who I am!"

"So? He only knows your first name. He doesn't know your last name or where you live. What do you think he's going to do?"

"What if he tells Victor he saw me?"

Sam held her hands out as if pleading for more information. "You really have to be more specific here. What are you so worried about?"

"When Victor broke into my place, I flat-out lied to him and said I didn't have any other jump rods. If Cenacus tells him about me, Victor will know I lied. And he warned me that there'd be consequences for lying. What if he's waiting for me when I get home?"

Sam's face went pale. "He knows who I am too."

"No he doesn't. You were at least smart enough never to give him your real name."

"You don't get it," Sam said emphatically. "My dad and brother were both red-haired like me. There can't be that many redheaded time jumpers out there. If Cenacus rats you out to Victor, he's going to rat me out too. And I can guarantee it won't take long for Victor and his pals to figure out who I am and how to find me. What if they try to take us both out?"

I squeezed the bridge of my nose to fight the pain rapidly forming in my head. "Look. We have no clue what Cenacus will say or do once he gets back home. He said he only wanted to watch football. We might be just making ourselves worry for nothing. He might already be sitting at home in front of the TV."

Sam's eyebrow rose. "Are you willing to risk our lives on that?"

"No," I said glumly. "But if we get back now, we might still be able to cut him off before he does anything serious. Don't forget that events move slower in real time than they do while we're on a jump.

So probably only a day has passed in our time back home. Cenacus won't have had much time to do anything yet. So let's get our things and get the hell out of here."

Sam wandered over to one of the four doorways and stood in the center of it, looking out. "We can't jump out," she said quietly.

"What! Why not? You burned my trebuchet, didn't you?"

"I did … but I never destroyed the tablet."

"What? Was it not there?"

"No, it was there. It even had a marker stone showing exactly where it was buried. But I dug for hours and got nowhere. The stupid thing was buried in deep clay—the ground was hard as a rock." Her voice dropped to just a whisper and she continued staring out the doorway, as if making sure to avoid looking at me. "Then the shovel broke."

"How does a shovel break?"

She wheeled around, grabbed the pot from over the fireplace and smashed it against the hard packed-earth floor of the hut. The side of the pot caved in under the impact. "That's how," she said, frustration in her voice. "You don't know how hard I tried to dig with that crappy shovel. I realized you were waiting for me, so I just kept digging, and the stupid shovel kept bending. I tried digging with my hands, or a stick, or anything, but I just couldn't do it!" She held up both her hands, revealing half-healed blisters all along the pads of her fingers.

I felt like howling at the top of my lungs. I had spent a week in slavery all because of a too-well-buried tablet and a poorly made shovel. I wanted so badly to get out of this miserable time period. To see my dad again. To sleep in my bed and not freeze at night. To eat a pizza. To not live the daily fear of the Romans finding me. Now all these things would have to wait.

"I'm sorry about your hands," I said.

"They hurt like hell for a while, but they're better now."

"If it makes you feel any better, the same thing happened to me.

My sword bent all out of shape while I was fighting. I guess we'll just have to head back there with more shovels." I drew in a deep breath, inhaling the scents of wood smoke and musty earth. Breathing was easier now, but the sickness still lingered in me. "Give me a few days to regain my strength, then we'll go back to the island and dig up that stupid tablet."

Sam stared into the fire. "I guess that's the best I could hope for."

I thought back to the Roman invasion and the huge fleet of boats that carried them across the strait. "Any idea how we're going to make it back to the island?"

"Same way I left—by boat. The Celts hid the boats we stole in the reeds along the shore. We just need to find one, row it across in the dark, sneak ashore, and avoid all the Roman patrols."

She made it sound so simple. But then, stealth was her strong point. I was more of a bull-in-a-china-shop type of guy. Hopefully she was right, though, and sneaking back onto the island was going to be easy, because the one thing keeping us from escaping this time period was practically sitting in the middle of a Roman army.

CHAPTER 17

The distant thump of drums—like the faint beating of many hearts—drifted in through the doorway. "What's going on out there?" I asked.

"The village is having a party," Sam explained.

"A party? After all they've suffered?"

"That's exactly why they're having the party. They know that tomorrow can bring even more suffering and death, so today they celebrate life." She raised an eyebrow toward me expectantly. "Do you think you're strong enough to go join them?"

With one hand I clenched my blanket so it wouldn't fall, and with my other I grasped Sam's shoulder and pulled myself to a standing position. My vision blurred as a wave of dizziness washed over me, and I clung to her to stop myself from falling. Slowly the world returned to normal, and I let go of her shoulder to test my balance. Like a newborn giraffe, I took a few hesitant steps, wobbling less and less with each one. "I think I'm good. I need some clothes, though."

Sam reached for a pair of brown pants and a tunic lying neatly folded on the floor by the foot of my bed. "We got rid of your old clothes; they were pretty ragged," she explained as she handed them to me.

To Sam's amusement, I grabbed the pants and pulled them on underneath my blanket, making sure not to let it drop.

"Aww … you're no fun," Sam teased.

"Didn't you see enough already?" A guy deserved some privacy.

The wool pants were scratchy, but they were better than running around pantsless. I cinched them at the waist with a broad leather belt, and then shrugged off my blanket. The sudden bite of cold air shocked me, but after days sitting in a sweaty cocoon, it also made me feel more alive. I finished dressing by pulling on the shirt, a loose-fitting burgundy thing.

Sam tilted her head and looked me up and down. "If your hair was a bit longer, you'd look just like a Celt. You ready?"

"I think so." I grabbed for her hand. "Just remember that I can only speak and understand Celtic as long as I'm touching you."

"I remember," Sam said. "And *you* remember: no matter how much we hold hands, we're not dating."

"Yeah, yeah, I know," I said.

"And you're on your own for bathroom breaks," Sam added with an amused grin.

I chuckled and pointed to the door. "I'll survive any short breaks either of us might need to take. Now let's get out of here."

With Sam leading the way, I walked barefoot out of the hut.

The sun was blazing, a first for me in Wales. After all the rain of the last few days, the sun seemed almost like an intruder. It shone down on thirty or so roundhouses with whitewashed walls and thatched roofs. A small stream ran through the middle of this cluster of buildings, and right past the healing hut. I expected the village to be crammed with Celts, but only a few chickens and goats wandered around, scrounging for food. From behind a small rise the sound of drums came stronger, now mixed with singing and flutes.

We crested the hill and saw a huge field filled with hundreds of people all dressed in vibrant blues and yellows and reds. Gold neck rings and bracelets sparkled in the sunlight as the villagers danced and mingled around an open pit. My spirits lifted at seeing everyone having fun. After days of misery, this party was exactly what I needed. What better way to banish the nightmares of the island and of slavery than to be with Celts having fun? I craned my neck to peer past all the people, trying to see what was in the pit.

I wished I hadn't.

About fifty men and women lay there side by side, pale in death, with their daily goods—like pottery and beadwork—lying next to them.

"A funeral?" I asked Sam, my good mood rapidly vanishing.

"For all those who died during the slave raid."

The corpses lay as if sleeping, their bodies washed and clothed and their hair brushed straight or braided. I recognized most of them; they had been slaves like me on the march. I couldn't recall their names, but I remembered their faces. The villagers danced on past the huge grave to the screech of the pipers and the furious beating of the drums. Occasionally someone paused to pour in some mead or toss in some flowers. Not a single person seemed sad; everyone had smiles on their faces, as if the death of all these people was the best thing to ever happen.

A horrified shudder ran through me and the little bit of oatmeal in my stomach felt like it was going to come up. "This is all wrong," I said, waving my arm at the pipers and the dancers. "Why is everyone so happy? All these people are dead. They're never coming back."

Sam pulled me by the sleeve so she could whisper in my ear. "The Celts don't view death like we do. They see it as a time to rejoice. They believe a person's soul goes off to the otherworld to join the gods and be reborn."

The Celts might have felt that death was a happy occasion, but I couldn't forget that all these people would no longer dance or sing or drink mead, or feel the sun on their faces. So many lives senselessly snuffed out, all because of the Romans. I looked at each body in the grave, searching for one corpse in particular. "Where's Vindiorix?" I asked, panic rising in my voice. "What happened to him?"

Sam pointed to four holes near the mass grave. Each one was about the diameter of an extra-large pizza and had a wooden frame standing above it. All four frames were decorated with severed Roman heads. Despite the bruising on their lifeless features, I still recognized almost all of those faces staring blankly back at me as guards of the slave caravan. "They put Vindiorix in a hole all alone? And why are there heads set up over them?" I asked. "He didn't deserve this!"

Sam rested a hand on my arm. "Easy, Dan. They buried him as a warrior—with honor."

Frantically I dashed from hole to hole, searching for Vindiorix. In each one was a corpse standing upright, spear in hand, shield at his side. Vindiorix's body stood in the hole that had the most Roman heads displayed above it. The sight of him standing there in death, like some weird wax figure, filled me with anger and I sank to my knees next to the pit. "The Celts honor him by burying him standing up?" I snapped. "Why does he get stuck like this while everyone else is buried lying down?"

Sam sat beside me and clutched my knee. "They've given him the greatest honor of all. Only their bravest warriors get standing burials. The Celts believe the spirit of a warrior will live on after death, guarding the living. That's why he's facing south—he's on eternal guard against the Romans."

I thought of my conversations with Vindiorix, about his farm, his family. "He wasn't a warrior," I said gloomily. "He was a farmer. He just wanted peace."

Sam patted my leg. "He might have been a farmer at one point in his life, but not anymore. War changes everyone."

I shook my head. I was like Vindiorix: just a guy caught up in events, doing more than he ever imagined. Wiping a tear from my eye, I turned to Sam. "Can we go now? I don't want to be—"

"Have my eyes seen into the lands of the undying?" a familiar voice said. "That looks like the Little Roman."

Atto? Alive? An odd feeling of happiness—something I'd never associated with Atto—filled me. I darted my head around, searching for him, and finally spotted him by the tree line. He wore pants, thankfully, and even a yellow-and-green shirt this time. Most noticeable about him, though, was his right arm; it was gone. A bloody cloth covered the remaining stump just above his elbow.

"Atto!" I yelled, as if he was my long-lost best friend. I grabbed Sam's hand and pushed my way through the crowd to get to him. I hugged him tightly and he returned the hug as best he could with his surviving arm. "What happened to you?" I asked.

"You mean this?" He waved the bloody stump. "A small disagreement between me and a Batavian. He wanted my head, but I was only willing to give him my arm." He chuckled. "No matter. I still have one arm to drink with. Although it does make it hard to hold my woman and drink at the same time." He turned his head toward the funeralgoers. "Senna! Senna!" he called. "Come see who has finally joined our celebration!"

Senna emerged from the circle of revelers, with Vata and Cario following close behind. She wore a long green dress, and her blond braid hung straight down her back. A glimmer of surprise flashed in her eyes when she saw me. "You are well now, Asterix. My heart feels joy." She threw her arms around me and kissed me on the lips. Not as deeply as when she had kissed me by the pond, but she still lingered over it, as if she didn't care that Atto was standing right there or that Sam was holding my hand and squeezing harder with every second Senna kept her lips on mine.

Awkward.

With a jerk I pulled away from her. "It's great to see you again," I said quickly, a warm flush of embarrassment stinging my cheeks.

Senna grabbed my hand and placed it over her heart. "I thank you for all that you have done. But Atto has returned, so what was pledged before between us shall not come to pass." She let my hand drop.

I tensed as I waited for Atto to smack me or at least yell at me for making moves on Senna. Instead, my jaw dropped as he threw his one good arm around my shoulder and gave me a playful shake.

"Too bad, Little Roman," he chuckled. "You almost had for yourself the queen of all women."

Sam glanced from me to Senna to Atto, and back again to me. "Can someone tell me what's going on here?"

"I'll tell you later, I promise," I said quickly. "So, Atto, what are you and Senna going to do now?" I asked, trying to move the conversation away from this painfully embarrassing territory.

His shoulders slumped and he kicked absent-mindedly at the dirt. "I promised Senna we would find a village that will take us," he said with no enthusiasm. "We will create a new home, and I will farm the land. If all goes well, I will grow fat and old and die in bed like a farmer—not on the battlefield like a warrior."

"But at least we will be together, my love." Senna gave him a huge, warm smile.

"Aye," Atto replied glumly. "And together we will build a new life in a new village, only to run again from the Romans while they take whatever they want of ours."

Senna's smile vanished and she jabbed a finger into his chest. "Do not think of changing your mind, Atto, son of Dunorix! We have an agreement."

"We do. We do." Atto chuckled softly and put his arm around her waist. "And I will hold to it." He twirled Senna around once. "But now the drink flows and the music plays. Come, let us dance!" He dragged her, with Vata and Cario, toward the ring of dancers. "Genovefa! Little Roman! Join us!" he shouted over the lively music.

I had to hand it to him: no matter what crappy hand life dealt him, he knew how to make the most of it.

Sam nudged me in the side and gestured toward a woman flitting in and out among the dancers. She was probably about twenty years old, with long blond hair that had wildflowers woven into it, and she wore a flowing red dress. The most remarkable thing about this woman was her smile—she exuded peace and happiness. She chatted with everyone she passed, touching them on the shoulder or arm, and making them smile in turn. Oddly, a dirty and torn gray cloak was draped around her shoulders, looking out of place with the colorful dress and the flowers.

"That's Catia," Sam explained. "The woman who insisted on lying next to you in the cart to keep you warm."

"It is?" I peered closer at her, trying to trigger some sort of recognition. "Nope, I have no clue who she is."

No sooner had I spoken than Catia turned and caught me watching her. For the briefest moment the smile faded from her face and her eyes held a hunted look, filled with anger and shame.

That look …

I'd never forget it. I'd seen it on the face of the cold and naked slave back in the slave pen.

Just as quickly the smile returned to Catia's face, and she angled herself over to where Sam and I stood. "Genovefa. It is good to see you again," she said warmly. "And Asterix, I am glad to see you well."

"Th-th-thank you," I stuttered, still trying to get over my shock that this was the woman from the slave pen. "I heard you helped me recover from my sickness."

"Yes, I did." With careful movements Catia removed the cloak from around her neck, rolled it into a ball, and then held it straight out in front of her. Turning her hands over, she dumped the bundle at my feet. "And now my debt to you is paid."

I smiled as I bent down to pick it up. *Okay, I guess I deserved that.*

As I stood up again, Catia threw her arms around me and kissed me with even more intensity than Senna had. When she finally broke off the kiss, I could only stand there panting heavily.

"Be well, Asterix." She reached over to caress my cheek just once, and then began lithely walking back to join the other dancers.

"What the hell is going on here?" Sam asked in bewilderment.

"What?"

"First Senna, now Catia. Why is every woman we meet trying to stick her tongue down your throat?"

Oh, geez … where do I even start?

"Do you remember that day Senna and I went to get water?" I began hesitantly. When she nodded, I then launched into the whole story about how Senna had tricked me into agreeing to marry her if Atto died. I didn't spare any of the details, even the ones that made me look just plain stupid. And there were a lot of those—Senna had completely played me.

"And that's it," I said, at the end.

Sam rolled her eyes and shook her head in disgust. "Typical male. Show them some skin and their brain shuts off completely." She crossed her arms over her chest. "And what about Catia? You said you didn't know her. Are you trying to hide an even more pathetic story?"

"No, I really didn't know her—at least not her name. I met her the day I was captured. She was just a naked and cold slave who had been abused repeatedly by the bastard Romans. I couldn't stand seeing her exposed like that, so I gave her my cloak."

Sam's stance softened and she uncrossed her arms. "Oh. Well, that was very nice of you." She sounded almost thankful.

I just shrugged. It seemed like such a paltry gesture next to all Catia had endured.

"So did you get involved with any more two-thousand-year-old women while I was gone?"

"None!" I raised my hands. "I swear!"

She smiled and grabbed me by the wrist. "Come on, let's go back to the celebration."

Atto saw us approaching and waved us over to where he and his family were sitting by a roaring fire. "Little Roman!" he bellowed over the pipers and the drums. "You look like a man who needs a drink."

"And some food," Senna suggested. "Come feast with us. What better way to celebrate the journey of all these people to the otherworld?"

The smell of roasted goat wafted through the air, making my stomach growl. The half bowl of oatmeal I'd eaten for breakfast couldn't compare with this. "We'd love to," I said.

Sam and I found space by the fire and sat down, with Sam resting her hand on my arm. Even though I knew she was only doing it so I could stay in the conversation, her touch still raised goose bumps.

As soon as we were settled, Senna passed us wooden platters with goat, wild onions, and barley, then Atto came over and thrust a clay jug of mead into my hands. "Drink!" he said. "A sober man brings no joy."

Food was one thing, but it just didn't feel right to be drinking at a funeral. "I'll pass."

"Nonsense! We insult the dead if we do not raise a drink in their honor." He lifted his jug high. "To Tasulus, my brother in battle, slayer of countless Romans. May the otherworld welcome you." He took a long swallow and raised his jug high once more as if offering a drink also to the spirit of his friend. "Now you." Atto motioned to me with the jug.

No getting out of this one, so I stood and raised my pitcher, my other hand resting on Sam's shoulder. "To Vindiorix, husband of Senovara. Farmer. Friend. Hero. Thank you for keeping me alive. May you find warmth in the arms of your loved ones." I drank deeply, the sweet Celtic mead spreading its warmth through me, numbing my aches. Surprisingly, it felt right toasting Vindiorix this way. I could almost imagine him smiling in the otherworld as we shared a drink at last.

Between mouthfuls of food, Atto and I drank to many others. The men of his war band who didn't survive. The women who died on the siege hill. The slaves who died on the march or in battle. Both our jugs were almost empty by the time we were done toasting them all.

As I sat there next to the fire, a warm, sleepy feeling spread through me, and my limbs felt heavy. Either because of my illness, or lack of food—or both—the mead was affecting me hard. I was probably drunk, but I didn't care—I'd earned it.

"So, Little Roman, where will your travels take you now?" Atto asked as he drained the last drop from his pitcher and tossed it aside.

"Back to the island." I raised my jug to him.

Atto clapped me hard on the back, knocking me forward and nearly spilling my remaining mead. "I was wrong about you, Little Roman. You are a warrior after all. What do you plan to do there? Kill Romans? Burn their camp?"

Sam elbowed me in the ribs before I could drunkenly blurt out anything else. But the damage was already done. Atto staggered to his feet and raised his remaining arm. "I will go with you!" he shouted.

"No!" Senna yelled. She leaped to her feet and beat her fists against his chest. "You promised me!" she cried. "You said we would leave this village and find a new home, somewhere safe for Vata and Cario. Some place where we can farm and be out of the grasp of the Romans."

Atto stroked Senna's cheek. "We will still do that, heart of mine. But first I will help the Little Roman exact his vengeance on the invaders."

"We're not fighting anyone," Sam said. "We just kind of … forgot something there, so we have to go back and get it."

"Ah! You move by stealth." Atto thumped his chest. "Well, no man knows how to move more silently in a forest than me."

Sam nudged me again and motioned with her hand to Atto. "Say something!" she hissed. "He's your friend."

Friend?

I'd never thought of Atto as that. Loudmouth, drunk, braggart, annoying pain: those were the words I'd use to describe him. But friend or not, Sam was right—Atto couldn't come with us. "Look, Atto," I said. "It would be better if you stayed here. I know you can move silently, but we still might run into trouble. And I can't fight and watch out for you at the same time."

Atto's body crumpled as if I had punched him in the gut. The fire went out of his eyes, and he looked gloomily at the bloody rag that covered the stump of his right arm. "Is that what you think of me? That, because I am missing an arm, I am a babe who needs minding?"

"No! No!" Using Sam's shoulder for support, I pulled myself unsteadily to my feet. *What the hell did I just say? I challenged a Celt's ability to fight.*

"Of course you aren't helpless … but you're missing an arm. Even you'd have to agree that you probably aren't as good as before. So it—"

Sam punched me in the calf to shut me up.

But it was too late. Atto inhaled sharply and his back stiffened. He raised his fist in front of his face and clenched it until the knuckles cracked. "Tomorrow, Little Roman, after the sun has risen, you and I shall fight. Then, I will show you that I am no babe who needs to hide behind his mother's skirt, and you will agree to take me with you." He grabbed another jug of mead, drank a huge gulp, and thrust it into my hands. "No more talk. Now is the time to drink!"

I clutched the ceramic pitcher and stared through the opening at the dark liquid within. *In vino veritas*, the Romans said—in wine there is truth. They forgot to mention mead was just as dangerous. Unfortunately, the damage was done—I'd made an ass of myself and challenged Atto's honor. I pretended to take another swig and passed the jug back to him.

Senna grabbed my arm. "Asterix," she said, through gritted teeth. "I would have words with you—alone."

"Hell no!" Sam said firmly, not giving me a chance to answer. "He's not going anywhere alone with you, especially when he's drunk. Who knows what other mess he'll get himself into?"

Senna looked from Sam to me, and then back to Sam. Neither of us said anything. Sam wasn't going to budge. And I needed Sam for translation.

"Fine," Senna snapped. "Then I will speak with *both* of you." She whirled on her heel and headed toward the village. Sam and I followed until she halted behind one of the roundhouses.

"What do you want to talk about?" I asked Senna.

Her hand whipped out and slapped me across the face. "How dare you ask Atto to fight again!" Her voice cracked with anger and frustration.

My cheek stung and I blinked back tears. "I didn't. He volunteered."

She raised her hand to slap me again, but Sam caught her arm. "That's enough!" Sam snapped.

Senna tried to yank her arm away from her grasp, but Sam wouldn't let go.

"Yeah, Asterix is drunk and said some things he shouldn't have," Sam continued. "But Atto is the one who wants to go. Now back off!"

Senna and Sam glared at each other like two proud tigresses. For a few seconds neither moved nor spoke, then Senna bowed her head. "Apologies. You have it right. My husband lives for the fight. He will never be content as a farmer." She snatched her arm free from Sam's grasp. "But I still cannot be happy about his choices."

"Look," I said to Senna, "we don't want him with us either. We want him to stay with you and the kids. Tomorrow, when we fight, I'll just make sure to beat him, and then I can force him to stay."

"Thank you, Asterix. I am sorry for striking you. It is my husband who should have felt my anger—not you." Senna gently caressed my cheek. "May the gods bring you a swift victory so my husband will give up his fool's quest." Without another word she headed back to the celebration, leaving Sam and me watching her retreating figure.

"Do you think you're strong enough to beat Atto?" Sam asked.

I flexed my fingers and curled them into a fist. I felt stronger than I had in a long time, but also really, really sleepy from all the mead I had drunk. "I don't know," I confessed.

Sam pointed to the healing hut. "You better get some rest, then, because this is a fight you can't lose."

Even though it was only late afternoon, I had to agree with her: I needed rest. So much depended on my fight with Atto. He didn't know the meaning of subtle—there was no way Sam and I would be able to sneak back onto the island if he was with us. And even worse was the potential blow to my pride. Atto was already enough of a loudmouth and a braggart. I couldn't let him beat me—I'd never hear the end of it. This was one fight I really had to win.

CHAPTER 18

The first rays of dawn snuck through the woven branches of the door, shining right in my face. Groggily I raised a hand to shield my eyes from the light. A dull ache pressed against my skull, and my mouth felt like I'd swallowed cotton.

"Well, look who finally decided to wake up," Sam said cheerily. She knelt beside the fire ring, blowing on the previous night's embers, trying to coax them back to life. After a few long, steady breaths, the dry leaves and twigs crackled and caught fire, a cloud of gray smoke rising to the thatched reaches of the roof.

Sam stood up and wiped her hands together to dust them off. "How are you feeling?"

"Awful," I groaned. "My head is killing me, and I feel like I'm going to puke."

"Maybe you shouldn't try to outdrink a Celt." She gave me a knowing smirk before nudging my feet aside and sitting down cross-legged at the end of my bed. Her usually fiery red hair lay flat and wet against her head, looking almost brown. Dark water marks spread over the shoulders and back of her loose-fitting tunic where her hair had touched it.

She placed her backpack on her lap, rummaged around in it for a few seconds, then passed me two tablets of different colors. "Take these," she said as she handed me her water skin. "It's ibuprofen and a multivitamin. We need you feeling your best when you face Atto."

Atto.

The sharp pain in my head got worse. I was in no shape to face him—even lying down hurt. I couldn't imagine picking up a weapon and fighting.

Sam must have sensed my reluctance to move. "Come on, up!" she ordered.

There was no chance of me winning this argument. Groaning, I pulled myself to a sitting position and winced. My head felt like it was going to explode. With a shaking hand I tossed the pills into my mouth and swallowed them. "Have you seen him yet?"

"No. The village is just waking up, but I'm sure he'll be around soon."

I motioned to her still dripping hair. "Where have you been?"

"I took a bath in the creek. If you go downstream a bit there's a bend that's hidden from view." She pulled a bar of soap from a pocket in her backpack. "It'll take me a few minutes to get breakfast ready, so why don't you go for a swim? It'll make you feel better."

I eyed the soap. "Don't you mean 'Dan, you haven't bathed in a week, so please use some soap before I pass out from the stench?'"

Sam put her hands up. "Your words, not mine."

Grumbling, I grabbed the soap and headed outside. My steps were shaky at first, each footstep sending a jolt through my body that reso-nated in my skull. After a few minutes the ibuprofen must have kicked in because my headache lessened, and I found I actually enjoyed being outside. The Welsh mountain air felt crisp and clean, bringing with it the earthy scent of the forest. I took my time walking down the narrow path that ran alongside the creek, just appreciating the tranquility.

The forest reminded me of camping back home with my dad, and my thoughts drifted to him. How was he? Had he woken up yet? Was he wondering where I went? I was so lost in thought I almost missed Sam's secluded area. No one else was there, and the forest was quiet except for the ripple of water as it flowed over rocks.

I stripped off my clothes and tossed them on the bank, then dipped a toe into the stream. The water had no warmth to it, only a freezing bite that sent a chill down my back.

How badly do I need a bath? I sniffed my armpit and nearly gagged. *Really badly.*

Clutching the soap in one hand, I clenched my fists by my side and took a deep breath. *One ... two ... three!*

With an icy splash, I jumped into the stream and dunked myself in the deepest spot. My skin felt like it was burning from the cold, but at the same time my heart pounded with exhilaration. I quickly scrubbed myself all over with the soap, washing away a week of sweat, dirt, and grime. When I stepped back out of the water, I felt not only clean but stronger, like the mountain runoff had washed away my sickness.

With teeth chattering, I dressed and hurried back to the hut, where Sam had prepared a breakfast of boiled grains and berries.

"Eat." She passed me a steaming clay bowl. "It'll make you feel better."

I really doubted that. My headache was fading, but I still felt nauseated. Just the thought of food made me feel queasy. To make her happy, though, I swallowed a warm mouthful of breakfast—and grimaced as it turned my insides upside down.

"Oh, yeah," I groaned. "I feel better already."

Sam grinned smugly. "And that's why I never drink."

I choked down another small spoonful of mush—and then rode the wave of nausea that followed. Not drinking? That was starting to sound like a really good idea.

Despite the continuing protests of my stomach, I finished the rest of the mush. Sam rinsed our bowls outside in the stream, and together we headed into the village looking for Atto. People were up already, gathering their meager belongings or trudging off down the road that led away from the village.

"Genovefa! Little Roman!" Atto shouted. "My day is better for seeing you." He stood, shirtless as usual, beside the hut of the village blacksmith, a pair of dull practice swords tucked under his stump.

How can the guy be so damn cheerful? I felt like a shambling zombie, but he sounded like last night's drinking binge had only increased his annoying happiness.

He strode toward us and offered me the hilts of both swords. "Choose your weapon. Although it shall matter not, both blades are sound. I just do not wish you to fault your sword when I trounce you." He winked at Sam. "Do not worry, my beautiful Genovefa. I will not hurt him too much."

I snatched one of the swords and tested the blade with my thumb: dull and heavy, like a practice sword should be. "Where are we doing this?"

"Follow me. I have just the spot."

He led us back to the clearing where the previous night's celebration had taken place. It was empty of people now, and the graves had been filled in. Only flattened grass and freshly-turned earth remained. "Is everyone gone already?" I asked.

"Of course. This village does not have the supplies to support so many. The people here were most excellent hosts, providing us with food and drink, but now we must be excellent guests and go find other homesteads before we eat and drink all their stock." He pointed to the masses of men, women and children shuffling away from the village. "Many do not have homes to go to, but they will seek out other villages to house them."

He stopped on a level green space and raised his sword. "Shall we begin?"

I let go of Sam's hand and held my sword in front of me, its wrapped-leather grip snug in my palm. Sam leaned in close and pulled the jump rod from her sleeve. "Here, you might need this," she said. I tucked the jump rod into the back waist of my pants and turned to face Atto.

This was it. I let all distractions flow from my mind. The only things that existed now were me, Atto, and our swords. My hands trembled in anticipation. *Time to kick ass.*

Atto let out a yell and lunged at me.

Rookie mistake.

You don't yell before you attack, it tells the defender that you're coming. My blade knocked his aside easily and I countered, aiming a slash at his right side. His sword swung up to parry my blow, but without enough speed or strength. With a clang of metal my blade forced through his weak block, drawing a scrape across his ribs.

Yes!

"Ha, ha! The gods are kind to you, Asterix. They granted you the first strike, but the rest shall be mine!"

He yelled again and slashed at my head. A quick sidestep and the sword hissed past me, leaving Atto wide open for a lunge. My dull point took him in the chest, managing to draw a small trickle of blood.

He grimaced at that, and the look of confidence faded from his eyes. "You are better than I thought." He waved his sword at me. "But now you shall face *all* my skill."

He attacked again—three strikes at my head, chest, and legs. If he had been attacking with his right arm, I might have had to worry, but with his left the blows were slow and inaccurate—like someone who had written all his life with one hand suddenly trying to write with the other. I'd spent years training with my dad in our basement, learning the finer points of sword fighting. One-handed, two-handed, fighting from my knees, fighting with my off hand, I'd done it all. My blade weaved around Atto's, smacking him on the thigh, drawing a grunt from him.

"Stand still," Atto panted. "We do not dance. We fight."

A sinking feeling grew in my gut; this wasn't fun anymore. Here was a man trying his best to deal with the loss of his arm, and I just kept smacking him around like some bully picking on a helpless kid. I needed to end this—for both our sakes.

As Atto attacked again with a wild overhand swing, I deflected the blade and kicked him on the side of the knee. His leg crumpled beneath him, sending him tumbling into the dirt.

I pulled up my blade and stopped next to Sam so I could grab her arm. I wanted her to understand what was going on. "We're done, Atto." I bent over and placed the other hand on my knee, trying to recover my breath. Sweat dripped from my brow. *Too much. Too soon.*

Panting like an aging lion, Atto pushed himself to his feet, every movement drawing out a groan of pain. Bruises covered him, and he bled from a number of small cuts. "No! We are not done," he shouted as he held his sword out in front of him. "I will still fight you."

"Give up, Atto," I said. "You should be finding a new home for your family, not following us back to the island. There's nothing for you there."

Atto bowed his head and lowered his sword. "Aye, there is nothing there. But there is nothing for me here either."

"What do you mean?" I asked as I stood up straight. "You have a beautiful family who love you and need you. You should be spending every moment with them."

Atto looked at the sword in his hands and then looked at me. The laughter was gone from his face, and his brow creased with concern. "I know you are a smart man, Little Roman. You can see what I also see. Our people will not be free much longer. The Romans treat us as mere beasts. They herd us away from the best farmland, the best grazing ground, the richest mines." His lips drew thin and he shook his head slowly. "I may not be the smartest of men, but I can tell you that running and hiding with my family will not bring me a longer or happier life. We already tried that, and my village and farm still lie in ashes. If we run now, the Romans will find us, wherever we are, and they will take whatever we have and force us to move again." He tilted his head and eyed me. "Is that the type of life I should give to Vata and Cario? A life of Roman slavery or constant running?"

He jabbed his sword toward the south, in the direction of Rome. "The day I stop fighting the Romans is the day that I have given up and let my children become slaves," he spat. "I know my family needs me, to farm the land and build them a shelter. But the Romans have already stolen my crops, destroyed my village, and now taken my arm." He raised his bandaged stump defiantly. "What type of man would I be if I suffered all these slights and then turned and fled? What example would I provide to my children? No, it is better to fight the invader, no matter how bad my chances, than to accept defeat." He raised his sword again and shakily pointed it at me. "And that, Little Roman, is why I will not give up."

I looked at Atto as he stood there, pleading with his eyes. He just wanted to make a difference, to know he could protect his family in whatever way necessary against the overwhelming forces of Rome. He was homeless, armless, and just trying to prove he wasn't useless. I tossed my sword to the ground. "You win, Atto. You're coming with us."

He didn't smile or joke or do any of his usual antics; he merely nodded. "You will not regret having me with you, Asterix." He turned to head back to the village. "When will we leave?"

I thought of how much walking we'd have to do to get back to the coast. If a little sparring tired me out this much, I obviously wasn't ready to travel yet. But we'd need to leave soon; time was running out in the real world. "Four days," I answered. "Maybe five." I needed to get better quickly.

"Excellent!" Atto said, his enthusiasm returning. "I will tell the others."

"Others!" Sam exclaimed. "What others? We're just bringing you."

"Of course there are others, my sweet fiery maiden. Does either of you know how to cross that strait so your boat does not get crushed by the rocks or swept to sea?"

Sam and I both shook our heads. "All right," she said, "so we need one guy to navigate."

Atto chortled. "What about the boats? Do you plan for just four of us to row one of them across?" He waved his stump. "I will not be much help, and we will need at least ten men to row us across."

"Is that true?" I glanced at Sam. "Are all the boats that big?"

Sam shook her head in resignation. "Unfortunately, he's right. We're going to need lots of rowers."

Our group of two had just ballooned to ten. "All right, Atto, get whoever you have to. But no more! Remember, this is all about stealth."

"Have no fear. I will not disappoint you. Let your worries fly away like birds, because Atto is now in charge!" He thumped his chest with his fist and began sprinting back to the village.

His reassurances left me with the cold, clammy feeling of disaster. "We're doomed," I said to Sam.

CHAPTER 19

S am and I watched Atto climb the crest of the hill rising between the field and the village. "Who knows?" she said as I shook my head. "Maybe he'll surprise us."

I snorted. "If he doesn't yell out at the top of his lungs 'We're coming to get you, Romans,' *that* will surprise me."

"Look, he just has to get us there. After that it'll be up to us."

"I guess so," I replied half-heartedly. With Atto, anything could go wrong at any time.

"How are you feeling? You looked pretty tired there."

"Stronger, but not full strength."

"If you're up to it, could you, um ... do me a favor?"

"If it's about Atto, I'll do my best to keep him alive."

"No. It's not about him." She twirled a strand of her hair in her fingers and stared at it intently, almost as if she was too embarrassed to look directly at me. "Can you teach me how to fight?"

"What? You don't need me to teach you anything. I've seen you in tons of fights."

"Yeah, but I only ever used the bow. I know nothing about

hand-to-hand fighting. Like I told you in England—my dad never wanted me to time-jump. He spent all his time in the backyard with my brother, teaching him to fight." Her lip began to quiver, but she clenched her fist and drew her mouth tight. "It wasn't fair that my brother got to have Dad all to himself. I needed a father too!" Her eyes grew misty. "It was only because I kept barging in on their training sessions that he finally tossed me a bow. He figured that would keep me out of trouble."

I put my arms around Sam. "Boy, was he wrong."

For a few seconds Sam let me hold her, but then she twisted out of my embrace and wiped her eyes with the heel of her hand. "Anyway, I need a crash course in fighting because we'll be back home soon, and if Cenacus is as big a dirtbag as we think he is, Victor's men might be waiting for us."

I closed my eyes, trying to envision what sort of ambush we'd be heading into. "Where did you jump out from?"

"From the forest behind my mom's house ... I always jump from there. My mom doesn't know I'm a time jumper, so I just tell her I'm going camping. That way, if I'm gone for a few days, she doesn't start wondering where I went." She snorted. "Not that she cares. She's just happy I'm out of the house and not trying to 'seduce' her stupid husband." She retched dramatically. "So I wander into the woods, change my clothes, and jump out."

Even though I'd been to Sam's only once, I could picture it perfectly, right down to her disgusting stepdad, who was one step above cockroach on the evolutionary scale.

"Okay, if Victor is planning anything, it definitely won't happen there. I can't imagine him standing around in the middle of a forest getting his fancy shoes all dirty."

"Great." Sam nodded gloomily. "He'll be inside my house—where my bow will be useless. That's why I need to learn how to fight for real."

"If Victor's in your house, swords are going to be useless too. He'll bring guns."

"What am I supposed to do, then?" Frustration and anger made her voice crack. "Just let him kill me?"

"All right. I'll teach you." I broke off two branches from a nearby tree and stripped away all the twigs and leaves. "First things first. This is your sword." I handed her a branch as my thoughts drifted back to my lessons with Dad. How every day he made me go through my sword forms, sparring against him.

This one's for you, Dad. I hope I can be even half the teacher you were.

I waved my branch. "First rule of sword fighting: stick the pointy end into the other person, while keeping their pointy end out of yourself."

"Dan! I'm serious. I want to learn how to *fight*."

"And I'm serious too. That's the first rule my dad ever taught me. And if you master this one simple rule, you'll master sword fighting." I held my branch in front of me. "Now hold your sword up."

She held her own branch in front of her. Awkwardly. Too much to one side and too close to her body. Worst of all, her drab-green cloak hung loosely around her, impeding the motion of her arms.

"You need to lose the cloak," I said. "It might help you hide in the woods, but that thing will only get in the way of sword fighting."

She dropped the mock sword at her feet, took off her cloak and tossed it to the ground.

"Better?" She held out the branch again, but for some reason the angle of it just didn't seem right. It could have been the way she tilted her wrist or the bend of her elbow, but because her tunic was so bulky, I wasn't sure.

"Your tunic will probably have to go too," I said.

Sam's eyes narrowed suspiciously. "How is me getting undressed going to help my sword fighting?"

"Sword fighting is all about positioning your arms, legs, and body correctly. Your tunic is so thick and baggy that I can't tell if your arms are bent at the wrong angle, or your shoulders are too high, or if your stance is just wrong."

Sam lowered her branch and chewed her lip uncertainly.

"Look, I'm not trying anything. But I can't help you if you don't work with me."

"Fine," she said miserably. Reaching down with both hands, she pulled the tunic up over her head, revealing a simple white sports bra. "How's this?" she asked as she retrieved her tree branch.

Whoa ... "Much better," I said, my voice cracking. My eyes traced along her smooth neck. Her pale, freckled arms, slim yet muscular from using the bow. The way her top clung tightly to—

Without warning, her tree branch darted out and smacked me on the side of the head. "If you're done staring at my chest, can we start the lesson?"

"Uh ... uh ... right," I stammered. "Um ... point the tip of your weapon at my face or chest. You always want to make sure that you are one quick thrust away from ending my life."

She held her sword in front of her, and I corrected its height and angle.

"We'll have Celtic weapons," I explained. "They're mostly suited for slashing. So I want you to take a swing at me."

She swung at my head. A hard, baseball-type swing that completely turned her body around. I ducked under it and smacked her on the butt with my branch.

"Hey!" Sam yelled. "What was that for?"

"You forgot the first rule already," I chuckled. "You're overswinging, which leaves you open to attack." I mimicked her swing and spun around. "Don't think baseball. You're not trying to hit a home run. Think of a quick strike from the arms and wrists—like swatting a fly."

I went through a few swings to show her what I meant.

"Like this?" she asked, as she struck quickly at my shoulder. I knocked the branch aside and swung at her. She instinctively sprang back out of the reach of my mock sword. Not surprisingly, she moved with a cat-like grace.

"Good reflexes."

"Thanks. My dad tried to get me into all the girly things when I was a kid: ballet, gymnastics, horseback riding." She spun around on one foot, her soft leather boot making almost no noise.

"Sword fighting and dancing have a lot of similarities. You constantly need to keep yourself balanced, and you always need to shift your weight as you move." I raised my stick. "Now I'm going to attack you slowly, and I want you to move to block all my swings."

I began swinging at her. Her feet slid across the grass with a fluidity most men could only dream of. I couldn't take my eyes off her: the way her feet danced into position, the smooth movement of her arms as they slid from form to form, the shimmering copper highlights of her hair, the rise and fall of her chest as she began to breathe harder from exertion.

I stabbed low, and her block was too slow. My branch hit her just above the belly button. She grimaced and lowered her branch. "Do you really think I can learn all this in four days?" she asked.

"I can't turn you into a master in that short a time, but you'll learn enough to keep yourself alive. Just remember to always bring your weapon back to the center, and you'll be fine." I moved around behind her and grasped her wrist, angling it slightly, my other hand on her hip. I pulled her wrist gently back. "This is where you need to keep your sword. And now move a half step back with your left foot. That way, you present a smaller profile."

She shifted her foot and moved back into me. Our bodies were so close, I could feel my breath ricocheting off her neck while her hair tickled my cheek. My heart thundered in my chest, and all I could think of was the smooth curve of her hip underneath my fingers.

Back off, Dan!

Sam had already told me a thousand times she wasn't interested. Just because I felt this way about her didn't mean she'd melt at my touch and fall into my arms if I tried to kiss her. Nope. I'd probably get an elbow to the gut and maybe a knee to the groin as well. Not to mention that the awesome trust we'd built would be shattered.

"Asterix!" Senna's shrill voice yelled out, thankfully throwing a bucket of cold water on my thoughts.

"What's up, Senna?" I asked. She was running down the hill, her skirt hiked up in one hand and her blond hair streaming behind her. I'd seen her looking mad before, but never like this. Her jaw was clenched, and her cheeks burned with rage.

Senna stomped closer until she stood right in front of us. With hands on her hips, she glared at me. "Have your wits left you, Asterix? Do you not remember I have seen you in battle? You faced the charge of mounted warriors. You killed horsemen with only a rock in your hand. Even Atto does not have the skill to have bested you." She wagged her finger in my face. "So tell me why is he now preparing to go with you back to the island?"

I placed a hand strategically over my groin and prepared to be kicked, punched, beaten, slapped—or all of the above. Sam shifted to position herself slightly in front of me, but grabbed my hand so she could understand what was going on. I sensed she was getting ready to protect me if Senna started smacking me again, but I hoped she wouldn't have to fight my battles for me.

"He didn't beat me," I replied. "I told Atto he could come."

If Senna looked mad before, she was livid now. She drew in a sharp breath, balling her hands into fists. "Do you plan for my children to be left fatherless? Is that what you wish?"

"What sort of man is Atto?" I asked her. "Is he the sort of man who will be happy farming? Will he go off to some village, build a hut, and then talk about growing grain and vegetables for the rest of his life?"

"No," Senna snapped, as she glared at both me and Sam. "He is a stubborn goat of a man who will constantly pine for his lost glory."

"Exactly," I said, trying to keep my tone level and calm. "We're giving him one last chance to do something heroic before he begins a farming life. A small group of us, under cover of darkness, are sneaking back behind the Roman lines. He will have his last chance to fight the Romans so that he can tell tales to his grandchildren about how he bested them. And his last memories will not be about losing his arm during a Roman attack, but instead will be about beating them." I reached a hand out to her. "Isn't that how you would want it for him?"

Senna's face settled into a stony mask. She glanced from me to Sam and back again before finally releasing a long-drawn-out breath. She unclenched her fists as her shoulders sagged. "You have it right, Asterix ... But this still does not mean that I approve or accept it." She jabbed a finger toward the ground beside her feet. "I want my husband by my side, not lying dead on a battlefield. The glorious dead do not feed starving families. They only feed the worms in the dirt."

I grabbed both her hands and held them in mine. "I will do my best to bring him back."

Senna wrenched her hands away. "I grow weary of your promises."

"I mean it," I said. "I'll watch over him."

She shook her head slowly. "If you had truly meant that, you would have won the fight against him."

She had me there. I could have beaten Atto. But when I really got down to it, Atto was a decent guy; he didn't deserve to fade into the sunset. And in some cruel twist of fate, I needed him now—he knew how to get us to the island. "I'll do my best."

Senna's lip curled in a sneer. "I hope your best will leave me with a husband." Before I could respond she turned and began heading back to the village.

Sam crossed her arms and watched her walk away. "So I guess that marriage between you and Senna is off?" She smirked. "That's too bad. I was going to get you two a really nice clay pot as a wedding gift."

I picked up my tree branch and took a swing at Sam. She was too quick, though. She leaped backward and grabbed her own branch.

She stuck out her tongue. "Missed me."

I gripped my branch and tried to ignore her graceful, catlike movements and the way her breasts rose and fell with each breath.

Come on, Dan. Focus.

I had told Atto we'd leave in four or five days. That wasn't much time to take a complete newb and teach her sword work. But if Sam was right, and Victor and his men were waiting for us, then our lives depended on her becoming at least a decent sword fighter in less than a week.

I flicked out with my flimsy tree branch and caught Sam on the side of the leg.

We had a long way to go.

CHAPTER 20

S am held her metal practice sword in a low guard position, her
torso turned sideways to give me less of a target. Beads of sweat
glistened on her brow.

I slowly circled her, waiting for an opening to attack. My sword
felt comfortable in my hand, like a part of me. I had missed the weight
of real steel. Branches were all right to teach the basics, but there was
nothing like a real metal sword to teach proper fighting.

Sam's feet slid smoothly along the ground, keeping me a safe distance away, her sword constantly aimed at my chest, tracking me. Its
tip wavered slightly as her muscles strained to keep the heavy weapon
on target.

Sweat dripped down my forehead and I wiped it away from my
eyes. The noonday sun was brutal, but we didn't have time for a break.
Despite four solid days of practice, Sam needed more.

The days had passed in a blur, just the same routine over and over.
Get up, train, go to sleep, repeat. Teaching turned out to be a lot harder
than I expected; my dad had made it seem so easy. I wondered what
he would have done in my situation. Would he have been able to teach

Sam more than I'd managed?

I'd told Atto I'd be done recovering and ready to head out by tomorrow. I felt great physically, but every time I thought of Sam facing Victor's men, a hollow ache formed in the pit of my stomach. She was nowhere near ready. She kept making the same mistakes.

Sam inhaled and held her breath, her eyes focused on my wrist. *How many times is she going to do that?*

"Stop staring at my wrist," I snapped as I stepped backward to move out of range. "I've told you a hundred times, look at my eyes. That way you won't give away your intended target."

Sam lowered her sword and pushed her hair back from her eyes. "And I've told you a hundred and *one* times," she said, her voice thick with irritation, "I'm an archer. Archers look at their target."

"You're going to be a dead archer if you keep that up," I grunted. "You can't let people know where you'll strike."

"Whatever," she mumbled, her lips curling in annoyance.

"No. I'm trying to keep you alive. Stop looking at your target and stop holding your breath just before you attack. This is sword fighting, not archery."

"I'm trying," she said sharply.

"Well, try harder. If Victor's men are waiting for us, they're going to kill you."

Sam gritted her teeth and pointed her sword at me. She shifted slowly from side to side, looking for an opening. She struck quickly but, after days of recovery, my strength was back, so my block was even quicker.

Sam slammed her sword to the ground. "It's no use! I can't fight like you. My shoulders and arms are killing me from all this stupid practice. And I'm getting worse, not better."

I picked her sword up and held it out to her hilt-first. "Come on," I insisted. "Our time here is running out."

She glanced at the sword as if I was offering her a piece of moldy cheese. "Time's already run out. Cenacus left here two weeks ago. And it'll take us half a week to get back to the island, and then who knows how long to get past the Romans and destroy the tablet. Even with the different time flows between here and home, he and Victor will have had more than enough time to find out where I live."

"That's exactly why we need to keep practicing."

Sam crossed her arms over her chest. "Do you *really* think one more day is going to turn me into a sword fighter?" She shook her head. "I can't push myself anymore. I'm exhausted."

"So that's it?" My back stiffened with indignation. "You're just packing up and quitting? How is that going to help?"

She stabbed the air with her index finger, her cheeks suddenly red with anger. "I'm *not* quitting! I'm just sticking with what I'm good at." She snatched her tunic off the ground and pulled it on.

"Where do you think you're going?" I snapped.

"Into the forest. I need to make some new arrows." She pulled out the jump rod and threw it at my feet, next to her sword. "Here. You'll need this so you can tell Atto we'll be ready to leave tomorrow." She stomped toward the trees without another word.

How could she just quit like that? This had been her idea in the first place. With a grunt, I hurled my practice sword across the clearing. It flew, end over end, in a glittering arc and landed point-first in the ground.

Damn.

I picked up Sam's sword and her jump device. No matter how much my better judgment screamed against it, now was the time to find Atto and tell him we were ready to go. I hadn't seen him at all the last few days. Now that I thought about it, that was a little strange.

Crossing the practice field, I climbed the low hill separating the field from the village. Atto didn't seem like the type to be off helping the villagers in the fields, weeding the crops. And with only one arm, he definitely wasn't in the forest chopping wood. If there was a town bar, that's where I'd expect to find him, but this village didn't have anything like that.

As I crested the rise, the distinctive peal of clashing swords, followed by loud drunken cheers, rose from the village. Inwardly I cringed at the racket—that had to be Atto and his friends.

I quickened my pace and followed the noise until I spied Atto and a group of men in the village center practicing their sword work. None of them had spotted me yet, so I crept into the shadows of a nearby roundhouse to watch them sparring. They fought with swords and shields, usually just two men at a time, while the rest stood in a circle watching. They held their weapons with the ease of men who had fought often. There were eleven men in total, all shirtless and with long hair. Some already had blue designs painted on their chests and arms in anticipation of our journey over to the island. That wasn't a good sign—they were preparing themselves for battle, not stealth.

At least they're wearing pants.

I stayed in the shadows watching, hoping I was wrong about this group. But with each mock fight, a sinking feeling grew in my stomach—they were just so noisy. Every successful strike was met with shouts of encouragement and long swigs from the many clay jugs that littered the ground. If these were the men bringing Sam and me to the island, the Romans would hear us coming even before we crossed the strait.

I massaged my temples and winced. This mission had *doomed to fail* written all over it. All signs pointed for me to just run away from Atto and his noisy friends. But I had no choice: either I went with them, or Sam and I remained stuck here forever. I took a deep breath, stepped out from behind the hut, and headed toward their group.

Atto stopped at the sight of me. A smile lit up his face and he waved me over. "My heart soars with the birds that you are here, Little Roman!" he shouted. "Today is the fourth day, so tell me, when do we leave?" The clearing became quiet as the other men with him stopped their practicing and turned to watch me, their faces bright with anticipation.

"Um ..."

Last chance to tell these guys they're noisier than a herd of elephants and the plan is canceled.

"Yes?" Atto asked.

"We leave tomorrow ... if you're ready."

I'm doomed.

Thunderous cheering filled the air as the men rattled their swords against their shields and clapped each other on the back. Atto threw an arm around my shoulder. "Excellent! We will be ready to leave at dawn!"

"I need to find at least four strong shovels before we go," I said. "Ones that won't bend the first time they hit a rock."

"I will find them for you," Atto assured me.

"And what about food?" I asked. "Did you get that?"

Atto winked at me. "Did I not tell you to leave everything to me? I have spent much time in preparation for our journey. We will have food."

"And mead!" another man roared. "Killing Romans is thirsty work."

"You know this is a stealth mission, right?" I reminded them. "You're just supposed to sneak us back to the island and drop me and Genovefa off."

An older Celt with a large scar across his cheek nodded. "Aye, Atto told us that we will sail to the island with only the moon and stars to guide us. Do not fear, young one, we will remain quiet when we set you upon the island." He pointed to a cart filled with clay jars. "But what we do after is entirely our concern."

"Death to the Romans!" one man shouted. The cry was picked up by the others, and they all gulped more mead.

I looked over at the cart, which carried about twenty clay jars, each with a thick wax stopper. Normally I'd assume Atto was just bringing plenty of mead, but these jars were shorter and had a much wider mouth. "What's in those jars, Atto?"

Atto wagged a finger and winked. "We have a surprise for the Romans," he chuckled. "They will finally learn what it feels like to have their own homes burned down around them." He picked up a nearby jug of mead and thrust it into my hands. "We can talk later, for now we must celebrate! And no man should ever be quiet while celebrating!"

The sweet smell of mead wafted out of the jar, and my stomach recoiled from the memories of my last drinking binge and the resulting hangover. But with Atto and his friends watching me intently, I took a sip and then I passed the jug back. "Okay, I'll see you guys tomorrow," I said with little enthusiasm as I turned to walk away.

A hand clamped down on my shoulder. "You leave us? What manner of deed draws you from our midst?" asked the man with the scar.

I didn't really know. Sam was off in the woods somewhere, most likely pissed at me, and the only other people I actually knew were Atto and Senna. My options were pretty limited. "I'll probably grab some lunch and go for a walk or something."

The man's mouth gaped. He held this look for a second, then he roared with laughter. "Ah! You jest!" He slung an arm around my shoulder. "Atto, you did not tell me that the Little Roman had such a sharp wit." He picked up another jug and placed it in my hands. "Come, sit with us as we celebrate our last day of comfort together. We shall drink like brothers!"

Great ...

Just what I needed—a sweaty half-naked man who reeked of stale booze draping his arm around me. For half a second, I flirted with the notion of emptying the jug over his head. But I really didn't feel like getting my ass kicked for insulting a bunch of drunks, and I *did* need them to get me to the island. So instead I tilted the pitcher back and pretended to drink deeply. The Celts cheered again as I passed on the jug and wiped my mouth with my sleeve. Like it or not, I was stuck with these guys.

What followed ended up being one of the most miserable afternoons of my life. The more the mead flowed, the louder these guys became, with their nonstop barrage of drunken boasts, good-natured insults, and unbelievable tales of heroism in battle. Any time I got up to try to sneak away, someone would shove a jug in my hand and demand I stay. I couldn't even take a bathroom break—these guys just stood up and pissed on the fire.

Hanging out with Atto and his pals did give me a lot of time to think about my argument with Sam. I'd been an idiot to actually think I could teach her to be a good sword fighter in just a few days. It had taken me years to learn, so I never should have pushed her so hard. And I shouldn't have accused her of quitting. She was the strongest person I knew.

Sometime after sunset, Atto and his friends had gotten drunk enough that I hoped they wouldn't notice me slipping away. Darkness cloaked the village, with only the stars and the fire giving any light. I began inching away and, after what seemed like an eternity, I made it safely out of the circle of firelight without anyone calling my name and demanding I return.

I pumped my fist into the air. *Free!*

With careful steps, I meandered through the darkness, back to the healing hut. A warm orange glow emanated from it, seeping through the cracks in the door. Sam was back! Now what was I going to say to her?

I nudged open the door and peeked into the room. She was sitting on the pile of furs by the fire, her knees pulled up under her chin and a blanket wrapped around her. She had her arms tight around her knees and her bare feet stretched toward the flames.

At the squeak of the door, she looked up. Even in the dim light I could see that her eyes were red. My chest tightened at the sight of Sam looking so sad. Of all the dumb things I'd done in my life, how could I have hurt her this way?

"I'm sorry, Sam," I said as I moved closer to her. "I never should have said those things."

She wiped her eyes on the blanket. "It's okay," she said softly. "We've both been under a lot of stress."

"How are you doing now?" I asked.

With a distracted wave she motioned toward the bow lying next to her bed. A quiver of freshly made arrows lay beside it. "As ready as I'll ever be, I guess," she sighed.

"You know that's not what I meant." I sat down next to her. "The thought of facing Victor again scares the hell out of me, but I shouldn't be an ass because of it. And I shouldn't have expected you to become something you aren't."

She tilted her head to face me and rested her chin on her knees. "I'm scared too. I've always stayed on the outer edges of fights. As soon as things look bad, I bolt. But if we get home and Victor and his men are waiting for us, there will be no place for me to run."

"That's why you've been learning how to protect yourself," I said optimistically.

She raised her head and her green eyes bored into mine. "Tell me the truth, Dan. Do you really think I'm good enough to fight off a bunch of people at the same time?"

She'd be lucky to last a minute.

"I'll protect you," I said, trying to radiate confidence.

Sam groaned and rolled her eyes. "I don't *want* your protection, Dan. I need to be able to take care of myself. We don't even know if you'll make it. We have no proof that double jumps work. You could end up stuck here forever."

I shuddered. Romans, Batavians, even Victor—all of them could be fought. Good solid steel would bring them down. But how could I fight the jump rod? Whether I made it back home or got trapped here forever was entirely up to the whims of one stupid hunk of metal—I was at its mercy. "What do you want me to say, then?" I grunted. "That you're right? That I'm going to die a lonely death here, while Victor and his morons slaughter you back home?"

Sam grabbed my hand. "No, sorry, you don't need to say anything. I spent a lot of time thinking in the forest about what could happen—I've made my peace. If Victor's men are waiting, I'll just have to face it. I've had a good life and done and seen things that most people never will." She waved her hand toward the walls of the roundhouse. "Look at this! We're in a Celtic village! How awesome is that? I've traveled through history, met kings and queens, saved history, and seen battles that everyone else has only read about."

I let out a long breath, releasing my anger. "Don't talk like that. Everything will be fine. Hell, Cenacus probably didn't even go to Victor. He's probably just sitting back home, watching TV."

"Yeah, but you don't know that for sure. We have to face the fact that we might not survive." She put her hand on my knee and gave me a small smile. "Either way, thanks for being with me these past months. I started out time-jumping alone, to get revenge. I never thought I'd meet my best friend."

I never would have imagined that Sam calling me *friend* would feel so good. We were best friends: we told each other everything, shared everything from food to sleeping quarters, and saved each other's lives. I put my arm around her shoulder and leaned my head in against hers. We sat there in the quiet room, staring at the orange flames and listening to the crackle of the burning wood.

"You're my best friend too, Sam," I said softly. "And whatever happens in the next few days, I wouldn't want to face it with anyone else."

CHAPTER 21

S am and I crouched in the reeds by the shore, eyeing in the distance the dark outline of the Island of the Druids. The moon snuck through the clouds, its light reflecting off the choppy waters of the strait like shards of a broken mirror. The wind whipped across the waves, bringing the taste of salt and the smell of algae. Across the narrow waterway in the Roman encampment, fires burned in braziers high atop watchtowers, shedding light into the darkness. The flames sputtered in all directions as the wind gusted. After four days of creeping like ghosts through the hills and forests of Wales, we were back where we started—and closer to leaving Celtic times.

"Ready to get your feet wet?" Atto said, his voice loud over the wind.

I startled at Atto's voice. "Shhh," I said. "The Romans will hear us."

Atto shook his head and snickered. "The Romans could not hear an entire field of bulls bellowing." He cupped his hands around his mouth and turned to face the Roman camp. "Helloooo ... Romans ...," he shouted across the water. "Can you hear me?"

"Are you crazy?" My shoulders tensed as I expected a call to arms to sound from the fort.

Sam and I had been holding hands nonstop for the entire trek to the coast. Nothing romantic, of course—only so that both of us could understand Atto and his friends. They mocked our closeness constantly, with more than a few suggestions that we should be doing more than just holding hands. Now she gave mine a reassuring squeeze. "It's all right," she whispered in my ear. "They're too far away and the wind's too strong."

Okay, maybe I was being a bit antsy, but we had made it this far without running into any Romans, and it seemed stupid to risk everything now.

Atto pushed on through the long reeds lining the shore. He had only the moonlight to guide him, but he walked with confidence as if he was moving in broad daylight. A second later, a dull thud echoed through the air, and a stream of curses flew from Atto's mouth.

"Looks like Atto has found the boat," a man said with a laugh.

"And yet you stand there like sheep and let the one-armed man try to pull it into the water," Atto jibed. "No fear, Gavo, I do not need your help. Even with only one arm I am still stronger than you."

Gavo chuckled again and went over to help Atto with the boat. Together they hauled the craft out from its hiding place alongside the shore and pushed it into the water. It rocked gently as the waves slapped against its side.

"How much longer, Ollocus?" Atto asked.

Another Celt sniffed the air and then knelt to feel the water with his hand. "Soon enough. By the time we get our goods on board, the water will be calm."

"Well let us get moving then!" Atto motioned to our two-wheeled cart piled with shields, a sack of grain, mead jugs, the twenty clay pots, and two long slings. Leaving the grain and mead in the cart, the men carefully loaded the melon-sized pots into the boat, making sure to keep them separate so they didn't bang together.

"Can you tell me what's in those pots now?" I asked.

Even in the moonlight I could see him smile as he tapped one side of his nose. "Just a while longer, Little Roman, then you will see the surprise I have brought." He placed the last pot in position and hopped into the boat. He looked at us all still standing on the shore. "Do you wait for a sign from the gods?" he asked. "Get on board, you slow-moving sons of she-goats! There are Romans to kill!"

The other men shouted in response and then clambered aboard the low skiff. Sam and I grabbed our shovels off the cart and found ourselves spots near the stern. Just like on our first boat ride to Anglesey, I found myself at the side again, so I gripped one of the wooden paddles and prepared to push off. Sam squeezed in just beside me with her hand resting on my shoulder, two fingers just touching the skin on the back of my neck.

The dark shape of the island loomed ahead. The flaming beacons on the towers glowed like eyes, watching in the darkness. I swallowed hard and tried to stop thinking of everything that could go wrong. Only the thought of Sam by my side and the two swords strapped across my back gave me courage.

"Dig hard, you miserable dogs!" Ollocus yelled. "The water is ready now."

With a chorus of grunts, we pushed off from the shore and dug deep with our paddles. The boat edged forward, picking up speed as all of us got into a rhythm of paddling. Atto held the tiller and kept us heading for a point just to the left of the Roman beacons.

The men fell silent as we rowed, the only sounds the never-ending wind and the quiet splashing of our paddles. The boat seemed to nearly fly across the water, but it was still too slow for me. The waves in the strait glowed white with moonlight, and I felt like our little boat was a huge black mark in the middle. As we neared the island my palms grew sweaty and my breath emerged in ragged gasps. All it would take now was one guard to look out and see us, then Romans would be swarming over the approaching shore. We'd never be able to turn the boat around in time—we'd be captured or killed for sure.

With a crunch of gravel, the boat came to an abrupt halt on the shore. Silently the men hopped out of the boat and into the shallow water, their swords and shields at the ready. Sam drew her bow and stepped over the side, while I unsheathed one of my swords. Carefully I lowered myself into the knee-deep water next to her and grabbed her hand. I scanned the dark beach, looking for anything out of the ordinary. But, in the eerie half light, all I could see were the black shapes of trees and rocks. Anything could be hiding there in the shadows.

Atto splashed through the surf toward us. "Well, Little Roman and beautiful Genovefa," he whispered, "we have brought you to the island. Where do you go now?"

Sam motioned toward the interior with her bow. "We have to go inland and find something we lost. After that, we're going home."

"How long will you be?"

"We don't know," Sam said. "Probably a few days."

"Shall the men and I await your return?"

"No. We can find our way back home. You just get yourself back safely to Senna."

Atto grinned and pointed to the new fort on the hilltop. "Aye, I will, but not until I go play with the Romans first."

He removed one of the clay pots from the boat and carefully unsealed it, then held the open clay jar in front of me. A smell like lighter fluid filled my nostrils. "Pitch and birch oil," he said, a wicked grin on his face. "It took us days to collect enough from the nearby villages, but it was a worthy task. The Romans are going to find out they are not the only ones who can bring fire and ruin."

A strange feeling of admiration filled me. I'd always thought of Atto as some loud buffoon whose boasting was ten times bigger than his actual skill. But what he'd done was pure genius—he had basically scoured northern Wales and found twenty jars full of gasoline.

"Just don't do anything stupid," I said. "Senna and your children need you."

"Do not fear." He tapped the skiff with his toe. "I will be on this boat as soon as the water is ready again. But until that time"—he hefted the pot—"I plan to have some fun."

After all I had been through with this loud-mouthed, half-crazy, braggart of a Celt, I realized I was actually going to miss him.

"It was great knowing you, Atto," I said. "You've been a good friend."

Atto put his clay pot on the ground and hugged me with his one remaining arm. "You have been a most excellent friend, too, Asterix." He patted me on the back. "If we meet again in this life, I will tell you of my fight here and how I left this island victorious, with a host of dead Romans behind me."

I doubt that. But, then again, Atto did have an uncanny knack for survival. Maybe he really would make it out of this one alive? Too bad I'd never know.

A sudden thought hit me. "Could you do me a favor?"

"Name your boon."

"Do you remember the hill where we fired those weapons at the Romans? If you ever get the chance, can you set up some sort of marker up there to tell me you made it safely back to your family? It doesn't have to be right away—you can do it five years from now. Ten. Just you know … if you ever find yourself back on this island and without Romans trying to kill you, could you put up a pile of stones or something that will tell me you made it out all right?" The idea seemed stupid even as the words tumbled out of my mouth. Atto's chances of survival were poor. And even if he did survive, nothing he could build there would last two thousand years.

"You still worry that I will not win the day? It will take more than a fort full of Romans to kill me. They sent two full legions and only got one arm. Tonight I will show them what I am capable of." He chuckled and gave me a playful punch on the shoulder. "But, yes, I will do as you ask. When the smoke has cleared and the heads are counted, I will set up a grand monument of my triumph here, so you will have no doubt who won."

He turned away from me and put his remaining arm around Sam. "And you, Genovefa of the fiery hair. Knowing you has brought joy to my soul; but now my sorrow grows that we must part." He kissed her on the lips. "May the gods grant you speed on your journey." He pointed to the fort up on the hill. "We go now to make sure the Romans have other plans than chasing after you." He picked up his pot and turned to his companions. "Let us go bring them fire and death!"

"Fire and death!" the others whispered as they slung their shields over their backs and grabbed their own pots, while one of them carried the two long slings. One by one they started up the hill, crouching low and slinking furtively from tree to rock to bush, with Atto bringing up the rear. He turned back one last time and saw us watching him. "What are you waiting for?" he whispered. "Go!" He then faded off into the darkness, a dark splotch against the gray trees.

Good luck, Atto, my friend.

"Come on, Dan," Sam urged as she wiped her eyes with the heel of her palm. "Try to keep up."

Her leather boots barely nudged aside a single pebble as she moved across the beach. I wasn't nearly as quiet. No matter how carefully I stepped, my foot always managed to dislodge stones or find the one stick lying on the beach. Even in the dim light I could see Sam shaking her head at me, as my feet finally hit the part where the rocks gave way and the grass began. "I think you might have missed a stick or two on your way here," she muttered. "Do you want to go back and stomp on them, too?"

"Excuse me for having a little *urgency* to get the hell out of this time period."

She grinned and headed for a nearby stand of trees while I trailed along, trying to be quiet. Now that we were off the stones, it was a lot easier. The swords across my back were wrapped in fur so as not to bang against each other, and Sam and I both wore dark cloaks so we could blend into the background. For once in my life, I actually felt somewhat stealthy.

Sam stopped at the far side of the trees and motioned me close. "Are you ready for one hell of a run?"

Before us stretched nothing but wide-open fields of grain dotted with the occasional clump of trees. Sam had told me that the tablet was buried in a mound on the far side of the island, almost at the coast. If we cut across the middle of the island, we could make it there by tomorrow night. Unfortunately, we'd have little cover, so we'd be traveling at night and sleeping during the day, to avoid Roman patrols.

I checked my swords one more time to make sure they wouldn't bang together as I ran. "All right. Let's—"

To the north, the night suddenly lit up: the watchtowers of the Roman fort were ablaze, huge tongues of flames climbing up their wooden structures. Even at this distance I could hear the Romans in the towers screaming as the flames burned them out. Within seconds the fires spread to the walls of the fort, and another explosion of flame lit up the gate. A trumpet sounded, calling the men from their beds. Two more explosions lit the night, and more screams were carried on the wind.

"Come on," Sam said. "Every Roman on the island is going to be busy putting out that fire. Which means they won't be looking for us."

I took one last look at the destruction, a feeling of cold satisfaction flowing through me as I imagined Atto and his friends using their slings to hurl pots of liquid fire at the Romans, getting revenge for some of the suffering the Romans had brought.

Sam and I raced into the night. The endless fields flew past under our feet, and the crash of the waves and the smell of the sea soon faded away, replaced by the rustle of the long grass and the scent of earth and greenery. We had probably been running for about twenty minutes when Sam dived to the ground. "Down!"

I hit the dirt faster than a drunken groundhog. The long grass blocked my view, but from somewhere to the south came the stomp of marching feet and the clink of metal. Slowly Sam and I popped our heads above the grass to look. In the distance a column of Roman soldiers quick-marched in the direction of the burning fort.

"There must be another fort over there." Sam gestured into the darkness from where they had come.

"There are probably a few of them," I replied. "The history books say that after the Romans attacked the island, they left behind a garrison to make sure the survivors didn't cause any trouble."

Sam watched the Roman column pass. Once they were safely out of sight, she sprang to her feet. "That was close," she said. "*Too* close. We might not be so lucky next time."

I nodded silently and pulled myself up. We were traveling under terrible conditions—the moon was almost bright enough to read by, and it cast ghostly shadows everywhere in the grass. A nice storm would have been great right now—something to reduce visibility and our chances of being spotted. But, no, the universe had a cruel sense of humor. After giving me nothing but rain the last time I was on this island, now I had beautiful clear skies.

Sam and I began walking again, passing through fields and circling low hills. We kept our eyes and ears alert, but it seemed we were alone. After a few hours of walking, Sam finally called a stop. "We need to make camp. I'm totally beat."

"I'm good with that," I said, trying to sound cool, though in reality

I could barely contain my relief. My legs felt as heavy as tree trunks, and it was taking all my willpower to keep my eyes open.

We headed for the only group of trees in the middle of a vast plain. Nothing too big, maybe thirty clumped together—an island in a sea of grass. We found a flat spot among the trunks, with few rocks and little underbrush—enough space for two people to lie down. Sam sat on the leaf-strewn ground and looked out past the dark branches. "Do you want first watch?" she asked.

Hell no. "Yeah, I'll take it. You get some sleep."

She curled up into a ball, and I leaned against her to share our body heat. As soon as I sat down, I knew it was going to be a long night. My eyelids kept drooping, enticing me into sleep. I tried keeping one eye open and then the other, but I only got sleepier. The thick canopy of branches hid the night sky, so all I could see was blackness above me. Just a warm black blanket ... covering everything ...

I caught myself napping and jerked awake. I listened for threats, but heard only the hum of insects and the rustle of leaves.

Nothing out there. My lids grew heavy again.

CHAPTER 22

My eyes flew open to the pounding of hooves.

Oh crap! Oh crap! Oh crap! The first light of dawn was peeking through the trees.

I hastily shook Sam by the shoulder. "Wake up!" I whispered.

Her eyes cracked open. "Is it my turn to keep watch?" she asked groggily.

I put a finger to my lips, but she heard the hooves and froze. Four horsemen with long hair and mustaches appeared just beyond the fringe of our stand of trees—Batavians.

I didn't dare move; even the slightest stirring might draw their attention. They rode at a slow pace, chatting with each other. I couldn't hear their conversation, but they had their swords sheathed and their spears held loosely in their hands, as if they were out on a casual ride. I exhaled slowly. They weren't even looking our way.

With glacial movements I stretched myself flat on the ground next to Sam. We lay facedown in the dirt, only the top of our heads visible as the Batavians came closer.

"Wait here," one of the men said as he reined in his horse. The other three pulled up their mounts while the first Batavian jumped from the saddle and headed toward our grove. He didn't carry his spear, but left it rammed point-first in the ground next to his horse.

Sam slid her bow along the ground so it lay in front of her. Ever so slowly she drew an arrow from her quiver and nocked it to the bowstring. "If he spots us, kill him. I'll take the guys on horseback."

I licked my lips and carefully drew one of my swords from its scabbard on my back, making sure the metal didn't rasp as it left the sheath. The Batavian walked as far as the edge of our mini forest, grabbed a handful of leaves off a nearby tree, then dropped his pants and squatted in the bushes.

Seriously? He chose our grove as a bathroom?

The Batavian was only about ten paces away, but he had his back to us. He whistled to himself, oblivious to our presence, while the other three remained seated on their horses and chatted. We just had to wait them out, and then they'd be on their way.

Behind me, a squirrel chittered in a tree. The Batavian grabbed a stone, glanced over his shoulder, and chucked the stone at the creature. A loud thunk rang out as the stone hit the tree and then bounced into the underbrush. The squirrel chattered in annoyance and then its clawed feet scratched against the tree trunk as it fled. The Batavian chuckled and picked up another stone. He turned and searched for the squirrel. Then his eyes locked with mine and his mouth dropped open.

Crap …

I leaped from my hiding position. At the same time Sam sprang to her feet and drew her bowstring to her cheek.

The Batavian shouted a warning to his friends as he fumbled for his sword.

I wasn't the type of person who normally would attack a man with his pants around his ankles, but this was different. I covered the ground between us in seconds and swung my blade upward, tearing though his unprotected midsection, killing him instantly.

I whipped my head around to see how Sam was doing. One Batavian was already on the ground, an arrow in his chest, while the other two were galloping away. One rider jerked backward as an arrow appeared in his back. He pulled desperately at the reins, trying to hang on as his horse galloped a few more steps, but his grip weakened and he fell out of the saddle.

The last Batavian crouched low over the neck of his horse, giving the smallest target possible for Sam to hit.

"Get him!" I yelled.

Sam drew an arrow to her cheek and sighted along the shaft. "I got him," she said as she released the bowstring. Her arrow zipped through the air, striking the fleeing horse just beside its tail. The animal reared in pain, dumping the Batavian out of the saddle.

The rider sprang to his feet and began to run. He pulled a horn up to his lips and blew out two long notes that rang out over the fields. As he started a third note, Sam's next arrow hit him in the back. He slumped to the ground, the horn tumbling from his lifeless fingers.

I scanned the horizon, looking for any more Batavians, my heart pounding in my chest. "Do you think anyone heard … ?" My question died on my lips as another horn answered from the east.

"New plan," I said, glancing over my shoulder. "Grab their horses and ride like hell." I grabbed our shovels and, using a tree for support, awkwardly pulled myself up on to the nearest horse.

Sam rushed over to the fallen Batavians and yanked her arrows out of the three corpses. She slammed the bloody arrows back into her quiver, slung the bow over her shoulder, and grabbed the saddle post of a horse. With her foot she reached for the stirrup but found only air. "How do you get on this stupid animal?" she asked frantically.

I rode over and leaned down to help raise her into the saddle. "No stirrups," I barked. "Hold on with your thighs."

Sam adjusted herself so she wouldn't fall off, then held her left arm out in front of her and turned it in a slow circle, feeling with the jump rod for the location of the time glitch. "That way!" she cried, pointing to a spot in the distance. She slapped her reins against the horse's neck and galloped away.

I raced after her. "Don't go too fast," I said. "If we burn out the horses, we'll end up walking."

She leaned low over the neck of her horse and urged even more speed from it. "And if any other Batavians see us, we're dead," she yelled over her shoulder. "So either save yourself or your horse."

No arguing with that logic. I leaned low and slapped the reins, urging my mount to gallop as fast as it could. Without stirrups, I couldn't raise myself in the saddle, so every step the horse took sent a jarring pain through my thighs and butt. And Sam didn't seem to be doing much better. She bounced in her saddle, her bow and quiver smacking her repeatedly in the back.

After the gloomy mountains and forests of the Welsh mainland, riding across this sunlit plain was like being the only performer on stage. In broad daylight, anyone could see us, and there wasn't a single place to hide. I patted my horse's neck and willed it to be strong. Every few seconds I looked over my shoulder, expecting to see a horde of Batavians charging after us.

When the little clump of trees was long out of sight behind us, our horses were lathered and panting heavily. "We have to slow down," I yelled. "The horses can't take any more."

Sam slowed her horse to a walk. "These saddles suck," she moaned.

I shifted in mine, trying to find a comfortable position. But no matter how I sat, everything hurt. "Do we have to go much farther?"

"We're about halfway across the island," she said. "If we ride at a decent pace, we'll be there in about two hours."

"Two hours ..." I repeated. I could do that.

For about another hour we rode, skirting all the hills, keeping low, and staying out of sight. We kept the horses moving at a slower pace, and they gradually began to recover from their hard gallop. As we rounded another small hill, Sam pulled up on her reins. "Listen!"

I pulled my mount to a stop next to her. From far behind us came a sound I'd heard only in movies before: dogs baying as they chased their prey.

With a growing sense of dread, I looked over my shoulder. On the horizon, a long line of horsemen was barely visible, just a group of black dots against a sea of green fields and gray sky.

"Go!" I yelled.

We pushed our horses again, their period of rest over now. I kept low in the saddle, letting the wind whip over me as the hooves of our horses churned the ground. It felt like we were flying across the fields and hills, but every time I peeked over my shoulder, the Batavians were closer. I urged my horse along, trying to coax even more speed out of it while not falling out of the saddle. The poor animal plunged ahead, clods of dirt flying from its hooves as it ran. I bounced in the saddle, clinging with all my strength, one hand on the reins, one hand on a saddle post, and my legs spasming.

Still, minute by minute, the Batavians gained on us. There were about twenty of them, a pair of dogs running ahead, leading them in the chase.

Sam pointed to a low hill no higher than a man and about ten steps across, with a freshly dug hole on one side. "Over there," she panted.

I reined in my horse just short of the hole, tossed the shovels to the ground, and hopped off, then started digging frantically. The blade seemed to barely chip the hard ground, the handle vibrating in my hands from each impact. "It's like concrete," I muttered.

"That's why I never finished," Sam said as she pulled the quiver off her back and began stabbing her arrows into the dirt around us.

"Aren't you digging?"

"Not enough room. You dig. I'll fight."

The baying of dogs came louder now, the sound sending a surge of primal fear through my system, giving me strength to dig faster. "How long before they're on us?" I asked, not wasting time to look for myself.

"The dogs are almost here," Sam said, an uncharacteristic shake to her voice.

The dogs bayed again, sending their howls out for the Batavians to follow. The bowstring twanged once and a howl ended in a yelp. A second later and the other dog was silent.

"Dig faster!" Sam urged.

I glanced up for the briefest of moments and immediately wished I hadn't. The Batavians had their spears raised and were charging toward us. We had maybe two minutes. "How many arrows do you have?"

"Less than thirty."

I slammed the shovel back into the earth and swore as it hit a rock and the blade curled up from the impact. Without hesitating I tossed the shovel aside and grabbed the next one.

"You fight them off until you run out of arrows," I panted. "Then we switch, okay?"

She didn't answer.

"Okay?" I grunted, as I heaved another shovelful of dirt out of the hole.

Sam reached down and lifted my chin so that our eyes met. "If we don't make it through this, I just want you to know that I always thought you were a great guy," she said breathlessly. "And if we'd met in a normal way, in a normal life, I probably would have gone out with you."

I stopped my shovel in mid-swing and gawked up at her, astounded by this admission after all these months of her pushing me away.

She leaned down and kissed me quickly on the cheek. "Uh, I didn't say stop digging!"

"Right!" I threw myself back into my work. Dirt flew and the hole grew deeper, but still no tablet. The air now rang with the jangle of harnesses and the thunder of hooves, sending a shiver down the back of my neck. Ever since the Battle of Hastings, I'd hated that sound—it meant death was on its way. Over it all came the almost constant twang of Sam's bow. Every time she fired, a man screamed or a horse whinnied in agony.

"Hurry, Dan!" Sam yelled.

"I'm digging as fast as I can!" I panted. A huge pile of earth lay next to the hole, but nothing to show for it. "How much longer until they're on us?"

The Batavians let out a huge cry as if in response.

"Duck!" Sam yelled. Suddenly her body crashed into me, knocking me face-first into the ground so that my mouth filled with dirt. Spears hissed overhead, their points thudding into the earth around the hole.

Instantly, Sam leaped up again and fired, and a man howled.

I grabbed my shovel and attacked the hard ground with renewed fury. Sam had probably just saved my life, but this muddy pit could still become our grave if I didn't step up. Sam's bow twanged a few more times, and then the sound of her bowstring stopped.

"What's happened?" I asked.

"Out of arrows!"

I tossed the shovel aside, grabbed my sword, and leaped out of the hole to stand beside her. Sam's arrows had reaped a bloody harvest. Half the Batavians lay dead or wounded across the field. The remaining ten riders circled their horses and regrouped.

"What are you doing?" Sam yelled. "Keep digging!"

"But you suck at fighting. You'll get killed."

"I suck even more at digging." She grabbed one of the Batavian spears that had embedded itself into the hillside. "At least I have spears now."

I stood there for half a second, long enough to realize she was right. With a quick glance at the remaining Batavians, I jumped back into the hole and attacked the earth again with my shovel. My jaw clenched in frustration; every bite into the ground hit a rock. With another shuddering impact, my shovel hit a large stone and the edge curled up.

I tossed the useless tool aside and started clearing away dirt with my sword. The narrow blade dug deeper into the clay, and I dug faster than I had with a shovel. I slammed my sword again into the ground, and the distinctive thunk of metal hitting wood rang from the hole. "I think I got it! How much longer?"

The Batavians shouted again as they began another charge.

"Twenty seconds max!"

As dirt flew out of the hole, I could make out the outline of a small wooden chest.

"Ten!"

I didn't need her telling me now. The horses were so close I could hear their labored breathing.

I yanked the chest out of the hole and tore open the lid. A small golden tablet lay inside the box. Whoever had created this must have been a master smith. The workmanship was incredibly detailed. It would be the main attraction in any major museum.

My sword smashed into it, denting it.

"Five seconds!"

I hacked again and again, completely destroying the markings etched into the tablet.

Sam jumped into the hole, knocking me to the ground.

"*Azkabaleth virros ku, Haztri valent bhidri du!*" she yelled, as she threw her arms around me.

Please don't let me be stuck here.

I shut my eyes as the rod hidden beneath Sam's bracer began to glow like a thousand suns, bathing the clearing in light.

CHAPTER 23

For a few seconds the familiar glare of the time stream pressed against my eyelids, then suddenly it stopped. It was as if someone had been shining a million-watt spotlight into my face and then decided to switch it off. I cracked my eyes open—a universe of blackness surrounded me.

What the … ?

Where was the light? To see nothing but emptiness seemed … wrong.

Oddly, and against all the laws of physics, Sam and my own body were still visible to me. It was as if we were the only two specks of light and color passing through an ocean of dark.

For a few seconds more, I floated along in this blackness, and then, from out of nowhere, a howling wind began tearing at me with the force of a hurricane. It whipped my hair into my face and wrenched violently at my cloak. My head and neck arched backward under the strain, and I wrapped my arms tightly around Sam to keep from tumbling off into the void.

"Help me!" I yelled, but Sam seemed oblivious to the evil wind attacking me. Her eyes remained shut and her hair hung loosely and unruffled over her shoulders.

Fear snaked through my gut. The phantom wind was targeting only me—as if I was an intruder who needed to be destroyed.

Slowly, one finger at a time, my grip on Sam began to slip as the wind continued yanking at my cloak. Spots began to form in my vision and I twisted my head sideways, struggling to breathe.

With a strength fueled by panic, I clenched my hands tighter until all my knuckles cracked under the strain. This only seemed to anger the wind, and it pummeled me even harder. One by one, my boots were yanked off my feet, sailing off into the blackness. A second later one of my swords flew out of its sheath and tumbled end-over-end after my boots.

I was barely holding on when the pin holding my cloak snapped, releasing the pressure on my neck and giving me a chance to breathe again and retighten my grip. The gray cloth whipped away into the darkness, hurtling toward a white dot in the distance. The dot rapidly grew in size, increasing from baseball-sized to basketball, to beach ball.

No freakin' way ...

I was either going crazy or my eyes were playing tricks on me, because I could have sworn that the little white dot had grown into an ancient Greek city, complete with white columns and tiled roofs.

The bigger the city grew, the more the wind tore at me, trying to rip me away from Sam. Terror gripped me as my fingers again began to slip from Sam's tunic. I scrambled to hold on, but my hands were so slick with sweat and the wind so powerful that her tunic sleeves slid from my grasp.

Frantically I grabbed at her cloak but felt it skim past my fingers. With a last desperate lunge, I caught hold of Sam's belt, clenching the leather so hard that my fingernails dug into my palms and drew blood.

A bright light exploded in front of me, throwing purple spots before my eyes. The howling wind vanished, replaced by a cold breeze. Through my near blindness, trees and blue sky appeared, and underneath my bare feet I felt the frozen ground.

We made it. I let out a huge sigh of relief.

But my elation at surviving the latest time jump lasted only a split second—Victor and his men could be out there. As a wave of dizziness sent my senses reeling, I pushed Sam to the ground and whipped out my remaining sword, straining to hear any sound.

Nothing. No snapping of twigs. No rasping of metal. No shouts.

Gradually the dizziness passed, and the spots faded from my eyes, revealing orange and yellow fall colors. We were in a small clearing surrounded by trees. A one-person tent stood in the middle, with a cold fire pit next to it.

Sam sprang to her feet and pulled out her bow. She reached over her shoulder for an arrow, but her hand stopped above the empty quiver. Shaking her head, she pulled out her knife and crouched behind a large maple tree. "Do you see anybody?" she whispered.

"No. Where are we?"

"In the forest behind my house." She pointed to the tent about ten paces away. "That's where I go to change."

"Anything look wrong?"

Slowly she scanned the forest. "No," she said finally. "Everything looks exactly like it did when I left."

I peered past the gray trunks, my breath frosty in the near-freezing temperature. A few gold and red leaves fell lazily from their branches, but otherwise nothing stirred. "I don't see anything either."

Sam bit her lip and stared off into the woods. "If there's trouble, it'll be in my house. I'll have to check things out there."

"*We'll* have to," I corrected.

She gave a half-hearted smile and crept over to her tent. From inside it she removed a pair of sweatpants, a sweater, and a hooded sweatshirt. She tossed me the sweatshirt. "Here, put this on before you freeze."

I pulled on the sweatshirt while Sam changed into her normal clothes. When she'd finished, she grabbed a pair of running shoes from inside the tent and jammed her feet into them, then stashed her bow and time-jumping gear in the tent. But she tucked a knife with a wicked six-inch blade into the back of her pants, right next to her jump rod.

"Ready?" she asked.

"Ready," I answered. Despite the sweatshirt, my teeth chattered from the cold seeping into my bare feet.

She turned and began creeping through the trees, each footfall silent and her head always in motion, searching for anything out of the ordinary. Every now and then she would stop and crouch to examine the ground, then get up again. I followed along just a step behind her with my sword drawn.

Soon we could spot the back of her house through the trees. Same run-down bungalow with a roof badly in need of some new shingles. The back screen door hung partly open, banging weakly in its frame as the breeze rocked it.

"So how are we going to do this?" I whispered as we crouched low just inside the tree line.

"I'm going inside to check out the house." Sam motioned for me to stay behind her. "You cover me—but stay back. If you see me running out, get the hell out of here as fast as you can. And if you hear me screaming, just run. It'll probably be too late to save me."

"That's a terrible plan. There's no way I'm letting you go in there alone."

"Yes, you are." Sam gripped my arm, her eyes blazing with intensity. "Because one of us has to survive. And this is *my* house, meaning *I* have to go in, not you." She got up from her crouch. "Now quit arguing and cover me."

There was no winning this one. "Fine," I muttered.

I snuck up behind the half-fallen shed in the backyard, breathing in the smell of rotten wood and mold. I leaned against the moss-covered siding and watched as Sam crept from tree to tree toward her house. Midway across the backyard she stopped and reached for her knife. My muscles tensed as I prepared to leap out and attack whatever Sam had seen.

With her knife clutched in front of her, Sam turned the corner of the house. A few seconds later she reappeared on the other side of the building. She caught my eye and shook her head. Nothing wrong yet.

Gingerly, she climbed the concrete steps at the back of the house and with a creak of hinges opened the screen door. She tried the doorknob, but it was locked, so she banged on the door a few times.

After a few seconds it swung open, revealing an older woman with long black hair, wearing a pair of ripped jeans and a low-cut, flowery shirt. "Jesus, Samantha, three days?" the woman snapped, flicking ashes from her cigarette. "Where the hell have you been?"

"Camping, Mom. I left you a note."

Sam's mom crossed her arms over her chest. "You and that damn camping. I don't know how you and your father ever found fun in that." She stood blocking the doorway and glanced back over her shoulder toward the interior of the house. "School called today. Said you wasn't there."

"It's Monday?"

Sam's mom looked hard at her. "Are you on drugs? Is that what you do when you're out 'camping,' you get high?"

"No, Mom. I don't. I swear," Sam pleaded. "Look, did anyone come by the house this weekend?"

Sam's mother took a long pull on her cigarette before exhaling a cloud of smoke. "Billy had his buddies over last night ... and Bobbie-Jo come by after bingo on Saturday."

"Anyone looking for me, I meant."

Her mother snorted. "Who'd be looking for *you*?" She grabbed a handful of Sam's hair, raised it and let it drop a few strands at a time. "Do you even brush your hair, girl? You ain't gonna get no boyfriend looking like this."

Sam—who had confidently held her ground against a charge of twenty Batavians and who I had never seen back down from anything—bowed her head, and her shoulders slumped. "Can I just come in, Mom, please?"

"I guess," her mom sniffed, without moving aside. "Now, Billy's treating me to Chicken Shack tonight. You can have some, but you'll have to pay for your share."

Sam pushed the hair back from her eyes. "Mom ... can a friend of mine come in for a bit?"

"She don't want no chicken now, does she?"

"I'll pay for whatever we eat," Sam sighed.

"Fine. When's she coming over?"

Sam turned around. "Dan, it's okay. You can come out now."

I tossed my sword out of sight behind the shed and, with tentative steps, came out into the open. I was acutely aware that I was giving the worst possible first impression. I should have arrived at the front door, politely knocking and dressed in some decent clothes, or at least wearing shoes, not coming out from behind the shed like some barefoot hillbilly stalker.

Sam's mom looked me up and down, her face twisted into the type of grimace that most people reserved for things stuck to the bottom of their shoes. "Samantha Evelyn Cahill! Have you lost your damn mind?" She gestured toward me. "That boy's a bum. He don't even have shoes. He ain't setting one foot inside my house."

"Mom! This is Dan, the guy who took me to the homecoming dance.

He's just a bit dirty from camping and … uh … he lost his shoes in the creek. Please let him stay for a bit."

"You went camping with *him*?" Sam's mom asked incredulously. "You never told me you got yourself a boyfriend."

"He's not my boyfriend. He's just a friend."

Sam's mom opened her mouth to speak but Sam jumped in. "No, he doesn't do drugs either. And no, we're not having sex." Sam flung both her hands up in the air. "We're cold, we're tired, and we just need a place to wash up. Can we *please* come in?"

Sam's mom glanced down at my dirt-encrusted fingers, my mud-stained pants, and my bare feet. I didn't need to be a rocket scientist to figure out her answer.

"I'll give you this week's paycheck," Sam blurted.

Her mom took a slow drag on the cigarette. "And you're still buying your own dinner?"

"Yes, Mom," Sam said in a sad monotone.

"Fine. But y'all steer clear of Billy. I don't want you getting him upset like you do." She stepped aside, allowing Sam and me to enter the house. The warm linoleum of the kitchen was like heaven for my freezing feet. I just stood there for a moment, relishing the warmth seeping up through me.

"Come on," Sam said.

Sam's room was a small one at the back of the house. It had a single bed pushed against the wall, a bookshelf, a dresser, and a night table with a uniform from a local pizza joint folded neatly on top of it. What took me by surprise, though, were all the unicorns littering the room. Unicorn posters and pictures adorned the walls, and figurines covered both her dresser and bedside table. Meanwhile, the largest assortment of unicorn plush toys I'd ever seen covered her bed. Small ones, big ones, medium ones, in all colors.

"Unicorns?" I chuckled.

"Yeah. And?" she snapped.

"Nothing." I raised my hands defensively but couldn't stop snickering. "Nothing at all. I just didn't have you pegged as the type."

Sam sat on the edge of the bed and hugged a large plush unicorn to her chest. "My dad brought me my first unicorn when I was about five," she said, looking sadly at the stuffed animal while she stroked its fuzzy mane. "And it just kind of snowballed. Birthdays. Christmas. On random days when he just wanted to bring me a smile. They're all I have left of him. They remind me that at one point in time I had a parent who loved me."

"Sorry," I said, as I sat down next to her. "I wasn't making fun of you."

Sam kicked off her shoes and flopped back onto the bed so she was staring up at the ceiling. A shudder ripped through her body, and she clutched the unicorn even tighter.

"Are you okay?" I asked.

"No ... yes ... I don't know." She didn't say anything for a few seconds as she continued staring up at the yellowed stucco. "Now that we're finally safe, I keep thinking back to that last fight." She exhaled slowly and her eyes grew haunted. "They kept on coming and I just kept firing," she said, her voice distant. "I killed so many. Men ... horses ..." She swallowed hard. "I even killed two dogs."

I placed a reassuring hand on her shoulder. "You had to, Sam. If you hadn't, it would be us lying dead in that field."

"I know. I told myself the same thing after the battle against the Romans. But it doesn't make me feel better." She held her hands in front of her face as if expecting to see blood on them. "So many people died because of me this time."

I thought back to my own battles. The Romans who died from the trebuchets. The Batavians who fell under my blade. In the heat of battle, I'd cheered their deaths. But now my stomach churned at the memories. "Yeah … this one was bad," I said quietly. "We're both gonna have nightmares for a long time." I shrugged. "But at the end of the day, we're alive, we managed to save history, and there's no sign of Victor or his guys anywhere. Isn't that good enough for now?"

"I guess," Sam said without conviction.

"And what about that trip through the time stream?" I said, trying to change the subject. "Wasn't that the wildest thing ever? That wind was vicious. If it wasn't for your belt, I'd be a goner."

Sam sat up and peered at me, her eyebrows raised. "Huh?"

"You know … the wind in the time stream. It took my boots, one of my swords and my cloak. Didn't you see any of that? What about the city?"

Sam stared at me as if I was crazy. "What are you talking about? All I saw was the usual blinding light, so I shut my eyes. I didn't feel any wind, and I definitely didn't see any city. But I did feel you fidgeting like mad and then grabbing hold of my belt."

There was no way the wind had been a figment of my imagination; my bare feet were proof of that. But whatever I'd experienced in the time stream had been clearly limited to me. Sam wouldn't be any help figuring things out. And me trying to press the subject would only convince her I was crazy. My stomach rumbled, reminding me I hadn't eaten since yesterday. "As much as I would love eating dinner with your mom, who clearly hates me, and your human cockroach of a stepdad," I said, "how about we do *anything* else for dinner?"

"What do you have in mind?"

"I don't know," I shrugged. "Burgers? Pizza? Maybe even go catch a movie? Is there a theater around here? And it won't even be a date," I added quickly, before she could say no. "Just two heroic time jumpers celebrating the fact they aren't dead."

Sam smacked me playfully with her unicorn. "You make it hard to say no."

"So don't."

She tugged on a strand of her hair as she mulled over my offer. "All right," she decided. "Let's celebrate. But we should probably get cleaned up first."

"Umm ... one slight problem," I said sheepishly. "I have no clothes, money, or shoes. Think you might be able to help me out?"

"Some *non*-date this is turning out to be," Sam chuckled as she hopped off the bed. "Don't worry, I have some cash. As for the clothes ..." She rummaged around in her dresser and tossed aside a few items before pulling out a pair of gray sweatpants. "These should fit." She tossed them to me.

I held up the pants, which were huge, even for me. "You really like baggy clothes, huh?"

The humor faded from her face, and she slammed the drawer shut. "My stepdad would like it if I didn't."

"Oh, geez, Sam ... I'm sorry."

"He's such a dirtbag. He's always barging into my room, trying to catch me changing."

"Why don't you put a lock on your door?"

"I did. Bastard took it off while I was at work. He convinced my mom that it wasn't 'safe' to have a lock on my door. You know, in case of fire." She snorted. "This place is so leaky it would take a blowtorch to set it on fire." She shook her head sadly. "But let's not waste time talking about that loser."

She turned away from me and rummaged again in her dresser until she found a pair of socks. "Here. Shoes might be an issue, though. I'll probably have to steal a pair of butthead's. He never gets off the couch, so he won't miss them." She grabbed an armful of her own clothes. "I'm gonna shower now. Feel free to admire my unicorn collection while I'm gone."

"Uh ... thanks. Can I use your phone? I want to find out how my dad is doing."

She plugged her phone into the wall to charge it, waited a few seconds for it to come back to life, then punched in her password. "Go ahead."

As Sam headed toward the bathroom, I sat on a corner of her bed and dialed the hospital. A picture on Sam's dresser showed a roughly ten-year-old Sam in front of a Christmas tree with two red-haired men who could only be her brother and her dad. All three of them were smiling, as if they had just shared a joke.

The phone clicked as someone picked up. "Intensive Care Unit. How can I help you?"

I recognized the voice. Nurse Flores was one of the main nurses on the floor, and I'd seen her often whenever I went to visit my dad. "Hi, Nurse Flores, this is Dan Renfrew. How's my dad doing? Any change?"

The phone went silent for a moment. "Daniel, let me get the doctor for you." Her voice sounded shaky, hesitant.

My throat tightened. The doctor only spoke with me when things were bad. "What's wrong?" I asked.

"I'm sorry, Daniel. The doctor needs to speak to you in person," she insisted. "Can you come in?"

I fought the panic rising in me. "No, I can't. I'm in Virginia right now. I won't be home for days. Just tell me what's wrong."

Another silence. "I'm sorry, Daniel, but I can't give out that information. Just let me get Dr. Onakanyan. I have to put you on hold for just a minute. Don't hang up, okay?"

"Okay." I sat there numbly on the end of the bed, slowly rocking back and forth, while listening to the terrible hold music. Something had obviously happened to Dad. Did he have another heart attack? Did they have to do surgery again? I stood up and began pacing, my mind jumping from one horrible thought to the next with each footstep.

The phone finally clicked. "Daniel?"

"It's me, Dr. O. What's wrong with my dad?"

"Daniel, I would prefer not to discuss this over the phone. Can you come in?"

"Please, just tell me. I'm nowhere near home. I'm in Virginia."

Dr. Onakanyan sighed—the type of sigh you hear in movies and TV shows. It was the sigh of someone about to deliver bad news. "Son, I regret to inform you that your father passed away early this morning."

"No ... No ... You're wrong ..." My chest felt like my heart had just been ripped out of it. Dad couldn't be dead. The doctor had to be mistaken.

"I'm sorry, Daniel."

"But a few days ago you said he was stable!"

"He was," Dr. Onakanyan said calmly. "But sometime during the night his respirator stopped functioning, leading to cardiac arrest. We did our best to resuscitate him, but he didn't respond to our efforts."

"How does a respirator just stop functioning?" I snapped, trying to make some sense of everything. "There's always tons of people at the nurse's station—why didn't they check on it? And what about all the buzzers and alarms? Didn't they go off?"

"Once again, I must express my deepest condolences on your loss. But I've given you all the information that the hospital's legal team will allow me to divulge at this time. Our internal review team is currently looking into the incident."

I sank to the floor, the phone slipping from my fingers and falling to the carpet. My dad was dead. He was gone forever, and I hadn't even been there to say goodbye—all because I was stuck two thousand years in the past. Why had this happened to him? Why hadn't anyone noticed? Why hadn't they heard the alarms?

The hairs on the back of my neck pricked up, and with horrible certainty, I knew why Dad's respirator had "stopped working."

Victor.

It's all my fault.

I covered my face with my hands as tears flowed down my cheeks. Victor had warned me not to cross him, but I time-jumped anyway, stupidly thinking he'd never find out. But he had—either through his spies or from Cenacus—and now Dad was gone. The one constant in my life: the man I looked up to, and who made me who I was.

My world had been destroyed.

"What's wrong?" Sam stood in the doorway wearing a fresh change of clothes, her hair dripping.

"Victor killed my dad," I sobbed.

Sam rushed to my side and put her arms around me. She didn't say anything, just held me tight. I buried my face in her shoulder and cried as I remembered all the good times I'd spent with him, camping, sparring, going to museums, hanging out and watching movies. Each memory was another stab of pain that brought fresh tears. My dad and I would never be together again. I was truly alone now.

I let all the sadness, fear, and pain flow out of me and into Sam's shoulder until I was out of tears and the only emotion left was a cold, simmering hate.

I wiped my eyes with the palm of my hand and stood up. I couldn't stay here any longer. Victor needed to pay for what he'd done. He needed to suffer and hurt like I did.

"I have to get home," I said to Sam. "Do you have any money I can borrow?"

Quietly she closed her door and tiptoed over to the bookshelf. She took down a book of poetry from the top shelf and flipped it open to the middle, revealing a white envelope stuck between two pages. "There's four hundred bucks in there," she whispered, as she handed me the envelope. "And one other thing ..." She crouched next to her bed and reached her arm in between the mattresses. After fishing around for a few seconds, she pulled out a jump rod. "Our last spare."

She dropped it into my hands.

"Thanks. I don't know what I'd do without you." Outside her bed-room window it was beginning to get dark. "You don't know when the next train leaves, do you?"

"Yeah, I do," she said, her voice quiet. She sat down on the bed and caressed one of her unicorns. "This crappy little town is too small to have its own station, but there's one in Clifton Forge, about half an hour away. There's only one train, and it passes through just after noon. If you grab that one, you can get a connection home." She pointed to her floor. "You can sleep here tonight."

"Won't your mom and stepdad mind?"

"Probably," Sam sighed. "But that's nothing new. When it comes to me, there isn't much they *do* like."

I had money, a new jump rod, a place to stay for the night, and a way to get home. Now to get Victor. I couldn't wait to see his stupid condescending face grimace in shock and pain as I plunged my sword slowly into his chest, just like he'd done to Dad.

Sam grabbed my hands and stared into my eyes. "Don't be like this, Dan."

"Like what?" I snapped.

"I've seen that look too many times in my mirror. I know what you're thinking—you want revenge. But you can't just rush off and attack Victor. You'll get yourself killed." She glanced sadly at the picture of her father and brother. "I don't want another picture on my dresser."

I wrenched my hands away from her. "I've faced Normans, Batavians, and Romans, and I'm still standing. I can take Victor."

"Think, Dan. You don't even have shoes, but you want to rush across the country and kill a congressman, with bodyguards and police escorts? You won't get anywhere near him."

"I'll figure out a way," I replied defiantly.

"Really?" Sam raised an eyebrow. "Do you think you're the only one who's wanted him dead?"

"Well … no … but—"

"So why do you think you're going to magically succeed where everyone else has failed?"

My fists clenched at my sides as I struggled for a response. Every fiber of my being wanted to make Victor suffer for what he'd done to me. But Sam was right. I'd be a fool to attack Victor.

"So what am I supposed to do?" I pleaded. "Let him win?"

Sam put a hand on my shoulder. "We've both suffered, and one day Victor will pay. But only if you're smart. Do you think your dad would want you confronting Victor head on?"

Dad had always preached restraint, to think things through from all possible angles. Even picking out a campsite would take him forever. He had to make sure it had good drainage, not too many rocks or roots, and good sunlight. No, he wouldn't want me going straight after Victor. He'd agree with Sam. I could almost hear his voice chiding me for trying to rush into things without planning everything first.

The anger fizzled out of me like a deflating balloon. "All right," I sighed. "I'll do this your way."

Sam kissed me on the cheek. "There might be some hope for you after all."

"Whatever," I grumbled. "So what do we do now?"

"Well, first of all, you stink, so I'd recommend a shower. And we still need to eat." She tilted her head at me. "I seem to remember you inviting me out on a non-date."

"How can you think of eating now? My dad's dead."

"I know," Sam said softly. "The week after my dad died, I barely left my room. But—you know what? Sitting in my room didn't solve anything. He was still dead. I realize you don't feel like doing much of anything right now, but we both still need some food." She put both her hands on my shoulders and gazed at me with her beautiful green eyes. "Why don't we follow the Celtic example and celebrate that we're alive? We can go out, grab some food, remember our dads—and maybe even figure out the proper way to get that bastard Victor."

"You make it hard for a guy to say no."

Sam leaned closer so that her lips were next to my ear. "So don't."

CHAPTER 24

I t took me a full day to get home. A full day of staring out the train
window, watching forests and farms zip by—the monotony broken
only when I switched trains or we stopped to take on passengers. I
slept as much as I could: it was the only thing that took me away from
my pain. But there's only so much sleeping a person can do. The rest
of the time I spent thinking—alternating between sadness and rage. I
imagined all sorts of deaths for Victor, but my imagination only made
me more upset as I realized that Sam was right: Victor was too smart,
too protected, to let a simple kid like me get to him.

By the time the bus from the train station pulled up at the stop
near my condo, I was an empty shell of a person. I should have been
excited about getting home, but the familiar sight of my building only
reminded me I'd never see Dad again. He'd never be there to offer me
advice or help me out of a jam. I'd have to fend for myself.

Since my keys were still sitting on the kitchen counter, I had to
ask the building superintendent to let me in. The place looked exactly
as I had left it. No creeps hiding in the kitchen, and nothing had been
trashed. I guess Victor had run out of surprises for me. I grabbed my

phone from the bottom of my trash can, plugged it in, then turned it on. Three texts from Sam flashed across the screen, all asking if I'd made it home okay. I fired off a quick reply, then collapsed on the couch to listen to my messages.

The first was an automated message from my school, informing me that I hadn't been in on Monday. *Delete.*

I skipped to the next one. *Hi, Daniel, this is Henry Morris. I'm so sorry to hear about your father. It truly is a tragedy. Please give me a call back at your earliest convenience.*

Mr. Morris had been a great friend of my dad and my legal guardian since Dad had been in a coma. Whenever I needed something, he was always there to point me in the right direction or sign whatever needed signing. Outside of Dad and Sam, Mr. Morris was the only person I trusted.

I punched in his number and waited while his secretary patched me through. "Daniel?"

"Hi," I said, my voice a monotone.

"I am so truly sorry, Dan," Mr. Morris said. "Your father was a good man, and a great friend. I'll miss him."

"Thanks," I mumbled.

"Now, I know that you are grieving, and my timing may not be the best, but we need to talk about your father's will. Would you be able to come to my office?"

"I thought we already sorted things out a few months ago."

"Those were legal arrangements your father had set up in case he became incapacitated for any reason. But now that he has passed away, his will comes into effect. Primarily it concerns his funeral arrangements. Most of the details were prearranged with a funeral home."

I hadn't even considered planning a funeral. "Uh, okay. Do you need me to do anything?"

"Not really, unless you want to. I've submitted an obituary to the papers and informed his friends and colleagues of the time and location—Saturday at noon, at Oakmeadow Cemetery. Do you know where that is?"

"Yeah." Of course he would be buried there, with my mom. We used to visit her grave at least once a month when I was younger. "Thanks for calling me, Mr. Morris. I'll be there."

"Very good. Now, there are some other details in your father's will that are pertinent to you. In particular, there's the matter of life insurance. The policy has a benefit of two million dollars."

The phone nearly tumbled out of my grasp. "Two *million?*"

"Yes. I have some papers that need your signature. And I would like to suggest some financial advisors who might be of interest to you. They can help you manage your money so you'll be able to live comfortably for the rest of your life."

Two million dollars.

That was Dad, always looking out for me, even in death. I was rich now—I could do anything. I should have been thrilled. But the wealth had come at too huge a cost. "Thanks, Mr. Morris," I said half-heartedly. "I'll be there soon."

I switched the phone off and tossed it on the table, then pounded the couch pillow, my fist shaking with pent-up rage. I was angry at Victor for robbing me of my dad and making me an orphan. I was mad as hell at Cenacus for leaving me to rot there in Wales. But, most of all, I was pissed at Dad for dying. If only he had told me he was a time jumper. If only he had told me about Victor's plot. What was the point of all those years of training I had to endure if he wouldn't let me help him?

I slammed my fist into the cushion again and again, but no matter how many times I punched, it couldn't take away the pain of Dad's death.

My phone vibrated on the table, jarring me with its rattle.

Another message from Sam: RU OK?

I was alone in my house and beating up my couch—I was nowhere near okay. My first thought was to ignore her message, but I changed my mind. I really needed to hear a friendly voice, to help me take my mind off things. I hit her number.

"Dan?" Sam answered.

"Yeah. I finally made it home."

"Is everything all right?"

"No," I snorted. "Everything sucks."

"Is there anything I can do to help?"

You can kill Victor for me. You can hold me in your arms and not let go. "No."

An awkward silence hung between us. I shouldn't have called her, not when I felt like this. She didn't deserve my crap.

"Well," Sam continued, "I just wanted to make sure you got home safe. We don't have to talk right now."

"Wait … Don't go," I said. I didn't want her to hang up. I'd only been home a few minutes, and already the place felt like a pharaoh's tomb, piled with the memories of a man but empty of all life. I felt like an intruder in my own home, and Sam was the only thing keeping me from facing the death-like silence pervading my apartment. "Doing anything exciting this weekend?"

"I have an English project due Monday. Why?"

"Feel like coming up for a funeral?" I ventured. "I'll pay for your airfare."

Another long silence. I didn't know if she was ignoring me or just thinking of a nice way to turn me down. Either way the answer was no, and I should have known that.

"Forget it," I sighed. "I just thought it might be better if I didn't have to face it alone. But I'll be fine."

"Don't be stupid. You need a friend. I'll try to be there, but I can't guarantee anything."

"Sure. I'll send you the money and the funeral details."

"Sorry, Dan, but I have to get ready for work now. I'll talk to you soon, okay?"

"Okay," I mumbled. I hung up and texted her the funeral details, then I Venmo'd her ten times what she'd loaned me, so she could get a plane ticket for Saturday and whatever else she needed. Then I grabbed my coat and headed out. Time to cross the t's and dot the i's on the paperwork of my dad's life.

CHAPTER 25

A chill autumn rain drizzled down, dotting the coffin lid with beads of water and drumming off the umbrellas of the mourners. I stood beside the grave, my rain-soaked hair plastered to my head and trickles of water running down my neck. Mr. Morris had offered me an umbrella, but I had waved it away. This was it. After all the time Dad and I had spent together, this cold fall morning would be our last.

Other people were present at the funeral, but they were just a blur of teary-eyed faces and black clothing. They had come up to me during the visitation on Friday night, shaking my hand or hugging me, telling me how they knew my dad. They were all just names and faces that I quickly forgot. Their words were the same: meaningless, empty. To everyone, I had mumbled the same words of thanks, over and over.

They stood now in little groups next to the grave. Work friends in one spot, old school friends in another, and the time jumpers in two small but separate cliques. Not that anyone there actually admitted to time-jumping. But I could tell they were jumpers by the way they stood, calm yet wary.

The smaller group, five men, stood quietly like sheep in the rain, listless, eyes down, as if not daring to draw attention to themselves. If this group was the sheep, the larger group was the wolves. They stood proud and upright, chatting with each other as if they were at a family barbecue, not a funeral. And in the middle of them stood Victor Stahl, four burly men clustered around him to keep everyone else a healthy distance away. Drake hovered slightly behind him, obediently holding a large black umbrella over Victor's head.

I couldn't stop glaring at Victor. His presence was an insult to my father and to me. For the first time in days, I felt something other than numb, as sheer rage trembled within me, clawing to get out. I wanted to scream at Victor, to punch his face in, to stab him. Not now, though. My dad deserved a funeral worthy of the peaceful man he had been. So I stood there quietly with my fists clenched and teeth gritted, keeping my anger at bay.

Victor seemed oblivious to my hatred. He remained nearly motionless, with his head bowed and his gloved hands clasped in front of him. If I hadn't known better, I'd have said he was actually sad. But I did know better: he was a murderer, and his grief was just another despicable act.

The priest walked to the head of the grave, his black robes skimming the top of the wet grass. Silently, people turned to face the casket as he began the service. I didn't pay attention to his words, just stared at the lid of the coffin, listening to the rain patter like a thousand marching feet on its glossy brown wood.

The clicking of heels on the pavement brought a momentary interruption as a black-haired woman rushed along the walkway toward the grave. She seemed somewhat clumsy in her shoes, wobbling a few times as she ran, as if she wasn't used to wearing heels. She wore a thick winter coat with the collar pulled up, a winter hat, and overly large sunglasses. Nothing about her looked familiar. Probably another of my dad's coworkers. She nudged her way through the crowd to my side, leaning in close to shelter me with her umbrella.

I prepared myself to listen to meaningless words of condolences, and to mumble my thanks again—like I had done countless times already.

"Sorry I'm late," she whispered.

The voice startled me. "Sam?" I peered at her through tear-filled eyes.

She nodded. "I couldn't leave you here alone."

"Thanks." That single word couldn't begin to convey the happiness I felt having her there. I grabbed her hand and clung to it like an anchor to keep from being swept away on a tide of grief.

We stood silently together for the rest of the service, until the priest said his last words and the coffin sank slowly into the cold ground.

That was it. Done. My dad was officially gone.

People filed past the grave to pay their final respects. Some shook my hand or gave me a comforting pat on the shoulder. Others told me their own fond memories of Dad. And then, one by one, they filtered away to continue with their own lives. Even Mr. Morris and his wife, after reminding me once again that they were always there for me, bowed their heads over the grave one last time and left. Eventually only Sam and I and a few others remained at the cemetery—including Victor and his bodyguards.

Victor caught me looking at him. He nodded once toward me, then strode over, leaving his bodyguards behind. "Daniel," he said. "My condolences for your loss." He offered me a gloved hand to shake.

I ignored it. No way I was going to pretend to be nice to him. I wasn't stabbing him in the chest right now, so he should be happy with that.

He withdrew his hand and instead gestured to the grave. "Your father was a fine man. You may not believe this, but in our younger days we were the best of friends, and we shared many an adventure together. I wish events could have unfolded differently. He will be sorely missed."

My head snapped back as if I had been smacked. "You wish things could have unfolded differently?" I yelled. "You're the one who killed him, you psycho!"

Victor shook his head slowly. "Please, Daniel, show some decorum. There is no need for outbursts. We *are* at a funeral."

The remaining mourners hastened to leave, casting pitiful glances my way as if I was some dumb teenager who didn't know how to control himself.

Screw them.

Screw Victor!

How dare this jackass come to my dad's funeral and then try to school me on what was proper? "Just get the hell out of here," I growled.

"I will leave in a moment, after I have paid my proper respects," Victor replied. "By the way, I had an interesting meeting with our mutual friend William—or should I say Cenacus?" He said it as if we were having a casual conversation. "He told me a fascinating story about druids and Romans, and he also happened to mention you and a female time jumper." He gave Sam a curt nod. "So tell me, Daniel, where did you manage to find another time-travelling device?"

"I bought it at a garage sale," I snapped.

"Really, Daniel?" He tsked. "Despite your impertinent attitude, I am willing to forget your deceit and instead offer you and your companion both a simple choice. You can either swear allegiance to me or hand over all your time-traveling devices."

"Why don't you go jump off a bridge instead?"

"Do not try my patience, Daniel!" Victor's voice dropped to a menacing hiss. "Otherwise, things will become quite *difficult* for you."

The last few mourners had left the cemetery, leaving me and Sam completely alone with Victor and his bodyguards. My simmering rage was suddenly replaced by the icy chill of fear. "You can't threaten us," I said, trying to put on a brave face.

"Threaten?" Victor raised an eyebrow. "I do not threaten. I merely state the consequences of your choices. Both of you have so much life ahead of you. It is therefore in your best interests to choose wisely. Your father is a prime example of what happens when you make the wrong choice." He turned to Sam and bowed slightly. "But how rude of me, I have yet to properly introduce myself. I am Victor Stahl, and you are?"

Sam bit her lip but said nothing.

"No matter," Victor said, waving a hand dismissively. "Our dear friend William told me all about you. A female time jumper? I never thought I would live to see one. How whimsical ... like a monkey playing a piano." He reached over and stroked her hair with the tip of his gloved fingers. "Do not fear me, child." Victor gave her a reassuring smile that only made him seem even creepier. "I mean you no harm."

As Sam jerked her head away from his touch, her black wig shifted to one side, revealing a flash of red hair. Victor yanked his hand away and an odd expression passed over his face. "Your hair ..." His voice had this strange tone to it, as if he was startled or maybe even confused. "William failed to tell me it was red." He leaned in closer to Sam and peered intently at her face for a few seconds. "No ..." He motioned to Sam. "Please remove your sunglasses."

Sam's one hand still trembled in mine, but with the other hand she slowly removed her sunglasses.

Victor inhaled sharply and his eyes widened. "Samantha!" he said in an awed whisper. He looked back and forth between me and Sam a few times, as if mentally trying to piece together a puzzle. Finally he settled again on Sam. "You have your father's device." He wasn't accusing her, but actually seemed happy that she had it.

"And I'm not giving it to you," Sam said defiantly.

Victor shook his head as if to clear it. "Of course not. You must keep it. That is what Robert would have wanted."

I blinked a few times as I tried to make sense of what I'd just heard. Had Victor really told Sam she could keep her jump device? Why would he do that? Did Sam have some sort of connection with him? Was I going crazy?

Victor turned quickly to Drake and the rest of his bodyguards. "We are done here now. The time has come for us to depart and leave Master Renfrew here in his grief."

"You're leaving?" I asked incredulously.

"Yes," Victor said. "I have finished paying my respects to my old friend."

"And what about your ultimatum?"

Victor raised the collar of his coat against the rain. "You may keep that device for now. Just make sure you use it to keep Samantha safe— and keep yourself safe as well." He reached into his pocket and pulled out a business card, which he tucked in my coat pocket. "And if you or Samantha ever need anything, please do not hesitate to call me." He began walking away, his guards still in a tight circle around him.

Sam and I said nothing as we watched them all head down the walkway and climb into three large black cars with tinted windows. Victor and Drake got into the middle one, while two bodyguards took the lead car and the other two took the trailing car.

Only when Victor and his men were out of sight did I finally get my thoughts organized enough to speak. "What's going on, Sam? Victor came on like he was going to kill us both, then he sees you and suddenly he's our best friend?" I looked her straight in the eye. "How does he know you?"

"I—I've never met him," Sam replied, her brow furrowed.

I let go of her hand. "Then how do you explain what just happened?" There was no hiding the accusation in my tone.

"Please, Dan, believe me," Sam begged. "I've never met the guy. He clearly knew my dad, but that shouldn't mean anything." She motioned to the open grave. "We can see how Victor treats his friends."

I stared at Sam long and hard, suddenly doubting everything I'd ever known about her. Was she hiding something from me? Was she allied with Victor? Was she—

You're an idiot, Dan.

This was Sam. She had saved my life countless times. There was no way she was in league with Victor. "Sorry, I'm getting paranoid," I said, embarrassed by how quick I'd been to suspect her. "The attitude shift just threw me. I've never seen him act like that."

Sam shuddered as if she had just met the devil himself. "Well, I hope to never see him again."

"That makes two of us," said a familiar voice from somewhere behind me.

I spun around. Stepping out from behind a mausoleum was a face I thought I'd seen the last of—Cenacus, the backstabbing snake who had drugged me and left me to die in Celtic times. The boot-licking scumbag who had told Victor about me and Sam. The bastard who'd caused my father's death.

I raced across the slick grass toward him.

"Wait! Stop!" Cenacus raised his arms defensively as his eyes went wide.

I threw a wild punch at his face. He turned at the last second, saving his nose from shattering, but my fist connected with his jaw and knocked him to the wet grass. As he lay there helpless, I knelt over him and began raining down punches. He raised both his hands to cover his face, and bobbed his head back and forth, trying to dodge the blows. I pounded his chest, his head, and his shoulders, my anger building like a volcano threatening to erupt.

"Stop!" he cried, but I ignored him. I had been kind to him before, and he had repaid me with treachery.

A second later, someone grabbed me by the arm and hauled me away from him. I whirled around to face my new attacker.

Sam?

"He's had enough," she said.

"But—"

"No." Sam stared me down and I lowered my fists.

Cenacus edged slowly away from me, then staggered to his feet. He leaned against the mausoleum and wiped the blood off his lip with his sleeve. "Okay, I deserved that," he wheezed through gritted teeth. "But hear me out. I want to make it up to you for what I did. So please give me two minutes."

I didn't want anything to do with this guy. He had betrayed me and left me for dead. Because of him I'd spent the most miserable week of my life as a slave of the Romans. I could have been stuck in Celtic times for the rest of my life.

I was ready to walk away from him, but his appearance gave me pause. In Celtic times he had stood tall and proud, his hair and beard neatly groomed, with an almost kingly appearance. Now, even if I ignored the blood dripping from his nose, he still looked like crap. His pants were stained, he wore a dirty coat a few sizes too big, and his hair looked greasy, as if it hadn't been washed in days.

Cenacus bowed his head in shame. "Yup. Look at me. Only one week back and I've got nothing. No home. No money. But I guess it serves me right." He looked hesitantly at me and Sam. "I did you wrong, and I want to set things right. Can we go and talk somewhere?"

I crossed my arms over my chest and glared at him. "We're talking now."

"I understand your anger with me," he said quietly. "But can we just get out of this rain?" He pointed to a shopping center in the near distance. "You pick the spot. It can have tons of witnesses, so you know nothing's going to happen."

Sam and I exchanged glances. Her lips curled into a scowl, but she nodded slightly. "All right," I said. "We'll give you five minutes."

"Where do you want to go?" Cenacus asked.

I pointed down the street. "That coffee shop is fine. But you lead. I don't trust you walking behind me."

As Cenacus began limping ahead, Sam and I followed, leaving a good space between us and him so he couldn't hear our conversation. I held the umbrella to shelter us both from the rain.

"Do you trust him?" Sam asked.

"Not for a second."

"Good."

CHAPTER 26

The coffee shop was quiet in the middle of the afternoon, with only a few people seated near the big windows at the front. We found a spot in the back, and I bought a round of hot drinks. Sam and I sat next to each other, facing Cenacus across the table. He huddled over his cup of coffee, grasping it in both hands as if this was the only warmth he'd experienced in days.

"So why are we here?" I asked.

Cenacus leaned forward so his voice wouldn't carry beyond our table. Indoors, with no wind or rain to dissipate it, the reek of booze rolled off his breath, mixing with the stench of his clothes. "I've been in hell since I got back. I lost everything. My house is gone, seized for mortgage default. Two and a half years passed in our time, but I aged seventeen years in Celtic times, so I can't get the bank or the government to believe who I am. Which means I can't get access to any of my accounts or even get on welfare. For all intents and purposes, I've disappeared. And I can't get a job because of my leg." He stared into his coffee cup. "I've been living at a shelter since I got back. I had no choice but to call Victor. I hoped that if I pledged my allegiance to him, he'd take care of me. But apparently his plans don't include one washed-up old man with a bum leg. He just laughed and took my time-travel device, and left me to rot on the streets." Cenacus shook his head. "I should have stayed with the druids. But I was a coward, and now I'm paying for it." He wiped his cheek with a dirty sleeve and looked at me through bloodshot eyes. "I want to do right by you, though. I screwed you over, so I at least owe you something."

He reached into his coat pocket and removed a clear plastic lunch bag with a sheet of white paper inside it. The paper looked so clean and crisp compared to the grime that covered Cenacus. Carefully he removed it from the bag, unfolded it, and slid it across to me and Sam. There was a row of six symbols drawn on the paper, with something written under it. "That's the pattern for jumping out before the time glitch is fixed. And underneath it are the words you need to say to activate it. I didn't tell you about it when we were there because I was worried you'd jump out without me."

"That's it?" I scoffed. "One setting? You think this is supposed to make things right between us?"

"I'm sorry, but that's all I can remember," Cenacus said, a pained look on his face. "I was stuck there for so long that I forgot most of my previous life."

Sam's lips pressed together, and she shook her head. "That's what you said the last time you lied to us."

"I'm telling the truth!" Cenacus yelled, spittle flying from his lips. "I know there are tons of possible settings on these things, but even when I was younger I only knew about four or five of them. Most time jumpers only know that many. The rest have been lost to the ages."

"Well, thanks for the *one* setting," I said sarcastically, pocketing the sketch. "I hope it's worth my week of slavery."

"Wait! Don't go!" Cenacus pleaded. "I need your help."

"What could possibly make you think that we'd *ever* help you?"

Sam asked.

Cenacus glanced around us to make sure no one was listening. "I want to kill Victor," he said in a hushed voice.

"Do you even have a plan?" Sam asked.

"Nothing yet. But I'm working on something."

Not a single day went by without me thinking about killing Victor. Today alone I'd fantasized about it at least twenty times. But coming out of Cenacus's mouth, the idea sounded ridiculous. Victor was too well guarded and too intelligent. A pair of teenagers and a treacherous bum would have no hope of succeeding. "Uh-uh. Pass. I already fell for one of your schemes. I'm not doing it again."

"You don't get it." Cenacus leaned forward across the table and I pulled away. "Victor's going to become the next president. When that happens, it's all over. No one will be safe. We can't just stand around doing nothing like all those weak-willed ex-jumpers at your dad's funeral. Wishing they had done something, but instead staring at their shoes whenever Victor comes around." Cenacus slammed his hand on the table, rattling our cups and bringing a look of concern from the lady behind the counter. "This ain't the Boy Scouts; you're not going to stop Victor by walking a bunch of old ladies across the street. We need to do something now!"

I knew he was right, but I'd be insane to trust him again. "I listened to you once, and you left me to die. Whatever you plan on doing, do it without me."

Sam pushed her cup of tea away. "And don't even think of asking me. I'm done here." She stood up to go.

"Don't go!" Cenacus wailed. "Please! We need to stop him!"

I followed Sam out the door and took a deep breath of fresh air, trying to clear the stench of Cenacus from my nostrils.

Sam opened her umbrella and held it over both of us. "That was almost as bad as meeting Victor," she muttered.

"The smell was definitely worse."

As she began walking down the street, I fell in step beside her. "Do you think he was telling the truth about the settings?"

"Yeah, I do."

"So do I." With one hand she yanked off her black wig and tossed it in a nearby trash can, then shook out her red hair. "At least that one he showed us will come in handy. I wonder what other ones were 'lost to the ages.'"

Lost to the ages. I thought again of the city I'd seen floating in the emptiness of the time stream. Was it linked to the jump rods, or was it there for some other reason? And if it was linked to the jump rods, then how? So many questions. Now I just had to figure whether that place was real or a figment of my imagination.

"What do you want to do now?" Sam asked, breaking my thoughts.

"I don't know. When's your flight home?"

"Tomorrow morning."

"Do you have a place to stay?"

"I kind of figured I'd be staying with you. Since you got to see the wonders of my unicorn collection, it's only fair that I get a chance to see how you decorate." She tapped her lips with a finger. "Let me guess. Posters of swimsuit models on the wall? Clothes lying everywhere?"

"You're right about one of those," I chuckled. It was the first time in days that I'd felt anything other than anger or sadness. "I'm so glad you came."

"How could I have passed up the chance to meet Victor and see Cenacus again?" she said with mock excitement.

"No, really. Seeing you is the only good thing that's happened to me all week. Did you have any trouble getting away from home?"

Sam stopped walking. "No. You sent me way too much money! My mom was in my room bitching about something when your text popped up on my phone. And of course she saw it. She couldn't believe the shoeless bum she nearly didn't allow into the house had that much cash. Her eyes just lit up as she thought of all the things she could buy. She even drove me to the airport so I could catch my plane. Know what she said? 'Try to get yourself knocked up, girl. That boy's a keeper.' Nice, right?" She shook her head sadly. "Why'd you send me so much?"

I shrugged. "I didn't know how much a last-minute ticket costs. Then there's cab fares and whatever else you might need."

"Well, my mom took most of it. She demanded back rent and food money, and a whole bunch of other stuff." Sam cast her eyes downward. "It was really nice of you but … please don't send me money again."

I nodded.

We continued walking again in no particular direction, both of us silent. The rain dribbled on Sam's umbrella and her heels clacked along the pavement.

"I know this hasn't been the best day," I began hesitantly, "but do you wanna grab some dinner out and then maybe watch some movies back at my place? You know … another non-date between two friends."

"I don't know," Sam replied, trying to sound serious, but her eyes glinted mischievously. "That makes two non-dates in the same month. I'm not used to being swept off my feet like this."

"I'll even let you pick the movies."

Sam gave me a huge smile. "Who could say no to that?"

EPILOGUE

As I strolled through the terminal at JFK, I wondered for the thousandth time if I was doing the right thing. In the two months since my dad's death, I'd felt perpetually lost. I went through the motions of going to school and talking to other people, but inside I was empty. I had no goals, no purpose. I was existing, just barely. Christmas had come and gone, and I realized that I couldn't keep living like this—I had to move on with my life. The big question was: Which direction should I go? Hopefully this trip would provide the answers that I so desperately needed. But first, I needed to find out if Sam would show.

The not-knowing was the worst part of getting ready for this trip. I'd texted her countless times since I'd sent her the ticket, and she never gave me an answer either way. Even when I texted her to tell her I was at the airport and asked if she was coming, she'd ignored my message. I knew she wasn't interested in me romantically and, as much as it hurt, I could deal with that. But right now I really needed her—as a friend and as my time-jumping partner.

I found an empty seat at her gate. The screen showed her flight arriving on time. The next hour would be brutal. To pass the time I scrolled through CNN again. *Congressman Stahl Cheats Death*, the home page headline screamed. Every time I read it, it pissed me off. He hadn't come anywhere close to death—at worst he broke a fingernail or maybe got his hair mussed. But *Congressman Stahl Breaks Fingernail* doesn't get page views, so I guess the editors pumped up the headline. I read through the article again, even though I had pretty much memorized it by now. An "unidentified homeless man" had stolen a car and floored it right at Victor and his entourage as they were leaving a fundraiser. Cenacus never even got close. Victor's bodyguards shot out the tires of the car, and it sailed harmlessly past them and into a wall. Victor walked away without a scratch, and with a crap ton of free publicity for his upcoming presidential run. He had shown the voters how cool and calm he would be under pressure. As for Cenacus, after seventeen years in Celtic times, he must have forgotten about seat belts, because his wasn't fastened. He crashed through the windshield and was pronounced dead on the scene. I was willing to bet that he'd left it unbuckled on purpose, just so he wouldn't have to deal with Victor anymore. At least he died trying to set things right.

After a torturous hour of watching the minutes slowly tick past, the display finally showed that Sam's plane had landed. I tensed and held my breath as the door opened and passengers began to disembark. But as stranger after stranger came walking out, my excitement faded, and the certainty that Sam had stayed home crept in.

For about the hundredth time I checked my phone. It had been at least five minutes since the last person came off the plane, then the flight crew, and still no sign of her, and no response to any of my texts. If I didn't leave soon, I'd miss my own flight.

I'm such an idiot.

I should have known she wouldn't come. With the heavy weight of rejection settling on my shoulders, I picked up my carry-on bag. She could have at least told me she wasn't coming. Did I really mean so little to her that she couldn't even respond to my messages?

"Dan?"

And just like that, she was standing right in front of me in a yellow puffy jacket and gray sweatpants, her hair pulled back in a ponytail.

"Sam!" I wrapped her in a huge hug. "You came, I thought for sure you'd stayed home."

"I almost did." Sam stood at arm's length. "It kind of defeats my entire don't-get-emotionally-involved thing if I go on vacation with you."

"What made you change your mind?"

"Manchester?" She gave me a knowing smirk. "If you'd been trying to impress me, my Christmas gift would have been a ticket to Paris or Rome." Her eyes narrowed and her face grew serious. "We're going back to Wales, aren't we?"

I nodded. "I want to see it again."

Sam punched me playfully on the shoulder. "I knew it! Why didn't you just tell me?"

"I ... I don't know." I thought of all the texts I'd written and then deleted, half-filled with different explanations of why I wanted to go there, and why I thought she should join me. None of them had been good enough to send. I couldn't get into words the two reasons why I wanted to go there. She'd probably laugh at the first reason and, the second ... ? How could I have possibly explained it to her in a text?

"What about you?" I asked. "Why didn't you answer any of my texts?"

She shrugged. "I didn't know *how* to answer them. I wasn't even sure I was coming until I actually got on the plane. And then I thought it would be nice to surprise you. And then ..." She rolled her eyes and shook her head. "The flight attendant spilled an entire cup of water right on my phone. I didn't want to risk turning it on until it had a chance to completely dry out. Anyway, we had to fill out an incident report after we landed, and that took freakin' forever." She raised her hands in mock triumph. "But yay! I'm here now. I'm so excited about this trip! I've never been to Europe before"—she lowered her voice—"at least not in our time."

With a soft jolt, the plane touched down on the runway, the cabin rattling and the engines whining as the aircraft decelerated. The captain's English accent came over the intercom. "Welcome to Manchester International Airport. The local time is 6:25 a.m. and the temperature is a chilly four degrees, with a bit of our customary British rain. Please remain seated until the Fasten Seatbelts sign is turned off. From myself and the crew, we would like to thank you for flying British Airways."

As the plane taxied to its gate, I looked out through the small window at the soggy English countryside. What would Sam think about my reasons for coming here? On the long plane ride she'd asked why a few times, but I still hadn't figured out how to tell her. She'd find out soon enough.

It took about an hour to clear customs and get our bags. After that we hopped on a train heading west across the English lowlands to Chester, the old Roman military town. There we switched trains and crossed over into the Welsh highlands. The train wound through the hills, staying to the forested valleys.

Sam pressed her fingers to the window, watching tree-covered hills zip by. "It looks just like when we jumped here."

"It hasn't changed much," I agreed. Every valley we passed looked familiar, but I didn't know if this was just my mind playing tricks on me. My memories of this part of Wales would forever be hazy, clouded by fever. Could this really be the path the Roman slave caravan had taken on leaving the island?

After a while the hills flattened toward the coastal plain facing across to the island. As the train pulled into Bangor station, I grabbed our backpacks from the overhead rack. "This is our stop."

Outside the train station, the rain drizzled down, making the sidewalk slick. Sam glanced up at the gray sky, and one corner of her mouth turned down in distaste. "The weather clearly hasn't changed in two thousand years," she muttered as she pulled up her hood.

I beckoned toward one of the many cabs lined up outside the main door. A small black car pulled up next to us and an older man with short-cut gray hair and ruddy cheeks jumped out. "Where you headed, my young friends?" he asked in his thick Welsh accent as he placed our backpacks into the trunk of his cab.

"Anglesey," I said. "The Inn on the Hill, please."

"A fine establishment," the driver replied. "A great place from which to see all the wonders that northern Wales has to offer."

"Do you know any good historical sites around here?" I asked.

"But, of course, young sir. You can't take a step here in Wales without stubbing your toe on some piece of history." As our car nosed out onto the main road, he pointed north. "In that direction is Beaumaris Castle. King Edward Longshanks started construction in 1295 as one of the many hulking slabs of rock that he built to subdue the Welsh. He never got to finish it, but even still, it is probably the most beautiful castle you'll ever see."

He steered the cab on to the bridge between Wales and the island of Anglesey, with the dark turbulent waters of the Menai Strait rushing below us. "Just to the south is Caernarfon Castle. Longshanks did manage to finish that one, although you wouldn't know it now."

"How about Roman and Celtic stuff?" I asked.

Keeping one hand on the wheel, the driver scratched the side of his head. "Now you're really going far back. Not too much survives from those times. Just some overgrown bumps in the ground that were once forts, and a few fields with bloody names that most people have forgotten."

"Could you take us to those?"

"You sure, lad? They're a bit out of the way."

"Just the places near the strait. I don't mind if we have to drive around a bit."

The cabbie looked in his rearview mirror and locked eyes with Sam. "What about you, my fair lass? Surely you don't want to be bored driving around the countryside, listening to an old man prattling on about people long gone?"

"I love that stuff," Sam replied, completely serious.

"Kids these days," the driver muttered in mock disapproval. "Well, I'll give you a bit of history as well," he began in a louder voice. "The Romans invaded this island twice. They wanted to crush the druids because they saw them as the biggest troublemakers in the ancient world—always spreading foolish ideas about disobeying unfair Roman laws and such. Their first invasion was in 60 AD. It was brutal and bloody, but the Romans stopped mid-conquest because Queen Boudicca of the Iceni had thought that, with a good chunk of the legions here in Anglesey, it would be a fine time to start a rebellion of her own against the Romans." He pumped his fist in the air. "That's a proper queen for you. She raised a mighty army and burned the Roman towns of Camulodunum and Londinium—what we now call Colchester and London. So the Romans left Anglesey half-conquered and rushed all across England to fight Boudicca's forces—eventually beating them. Legend has it that Boudicca killed herself rather than become enslaved. Her death ended the last big Celtic rebellion against Roman rule. The Romans came here again in 78 AD, and that time they finished their conquest, wiping out the druids forever."

After a few minutes, he stopped the car near the shore, rolled the window down, and pointed to a grassy plain rising above the beach. "That area is called Maes-hir-gad in Welsh, which means 'the long army's field.' That's most likely where the Roman army set up during one of their two invasions. You can just imagine what it would look like: the Roman legions standing on the plain, all in perfect order, while thousands of Celts pounded their shields and screamed their war cries."

I inhaled the salty air, memories of this beach and the grassy rise above it flooding back to me. The clashing armies. The mass slaughter. The screams of the dying. "It was horrible," I said quietly.

"Pardon?" the driver asked.

"It must have been horrible," I said loudly.

"You have that right, young sir." He pointed to the channel. "A while back a diver even found an ancient anchor resting on the channel floor. They think it came from one of the Roman boats."

"Did they find anything Celtic around here?"

The driver shook his head. "Not so's I can recall. There are some nice burial mounds up in the north and deeper inland, but other than some place names, nothing Celtic remains on this part of the island."

I sagged back in my seat.

"What's wrong?" Sam whispered to me.

"Nothing," I whispered back. "Just tired." I could tell she didn't believe me, but she didn't press further.

The cabbie passed another field. "And this area is called Cae-oer-waedd, which translates to 'field of bitter lamentation.' No doubt this is where the biggest battle happened. And, judging by the name, it didn't have a good outcome for the Celts."

Farm plots and fences had sectioned the area into a jumble of squares dotted with the occasional house. In Celtic times this had been one large open grassy area, and I remembered riding madly around it on my poor horse, trying in vain to muster some sort of defense.

"And if you look just to the west a bit, you can see a rise in the distance. Locally, that is known as Bryn Beddau, the 'hill of graves.' According to legend, the surviving Celts buried their dead there once the Romans withdrew."

The cabbie steered down a narrow dirt road. "That's it, then, for the Celtic history of this part of the island. Did you want me to show you any other sights?"

"No, that's great," I said. "Can you take us to the inn now, please?"

"Sure thing." In a few minutes, he pulled up in front of a small two-story farmhouse that looked out over the channel. "Well, here we are, then. I hope you enjoyed your tour of our island."

"It was great, thanks." I said, and handed him the cab fare and a generous tip.

With a touch of his hat to me and Sam, he deposited our bags on the front porch and then drove off.

A bell tinkled above the door as Sam and I walked into a sitting area furnished with a pair of antique chairs and a coffee table strewn with old magazines. Lace curtains framed two large windows, and a counter stretched along the back wall. A short woman wearing a light-gray dress and an apron emerged from the main part of the house. "Welcome, friends," she said warmly. "I am Mrs. Llewellyn. How may I be of service?"

"We have a reservation," I said. "We're Dan Renfrew and Samantha Cahill."

"Oh ..." She blinked a few times in surprise. "You're Mr. Renfrew? I didn't expect someone quite so ... young."

"Will that be a problem?"

"Heavens, no!" she waved her hands dismissively. "I was just taken aback for a second. Most young people like to stay at the youth hostel."

From her apron pocket she pulled a worn leather-bound notebook and flipped it open to the middle, her finger sliding slowly down the page. "There you are. Two rooms for one week, departing fourth of January."

"Just one room," Sam said. "As long as there are two beds."

One room?

I glanced at Sam, but all her attention was focused on our hostess. Mrs. Llewellyn snapped the book shut and grabbed a key from a row of them hanging on the wall behind the front desk. "You can have room three. It's the biggest one here, then. We don't get many visitors just after Christmas, so the place is fairly empty." She pointed to a narrow wooden staircase. "It's just up the stairs. If you don't find it to your fancy, please let me know."

"I'm sure everything will be wonderful," Sam said. She took the keys from Mrs. Llewellyn and went bounding up the stairs.

I jogged up after her, finding her already halfway down the hall, standing in front of the third door. As I skidded to a halt beside her, she turned the key in the lock and the door swung open.

Our room matched the decor of the reception area downstairs. Antique furniture. Lace curtains. Flowery quilts on the bed. Old people would call it "quaint."

"What made you pick this place?" Sam asked.

"Well … it got good reviews." I picked up an embroidered pillow with two fingers and held it far away from me, as if it was toxic waste. "I just didn't realize all those reviews were written by grannies. You want to find another place?"

"Are you kidding? I love it!" She tossed her backpack on the bed farthest from the door. "I call window!"

I smiled and dumped my backpack on the nearer bed. "Are you sure you're okay with one room?"

Sam rolled her eyes. "Seriously? How many tents have we shared? And did you forget about the healing hut? We've always slept in the same spot. Don't start making things weird now."

"I was just trying to be a gentleman."

"Don't. Just be my friend."

I stood next to Sam at the window and looked out with her. The sky had cleared a bit and the rain had stopped. "Feel like checking out the neighborhood before the rain starts up again?"

"Sure. Where do you want to go?"

"I was thinking of the beach."

"Oooh! A Welsh beach in December!" Sam said with mock excitement. "Which bathing suit should I wear?" She smiled at me and shook her head. "You're about as mysterious as a glass of water, Dan. Why don't you just admit that the entire purpose of this trip is so that you can go back to the siege hill and see if Atto left you something there?"

"Because it sounds dumb," I said. "You heard the driver: there's nothing Celtic left around here."

"But you still want to check it out, don't you?"

"You don't think I'm being lame?"

"Maybe a little. But I also know you won't think of anything else until you've visited that hill."

"You're the best, Sam! Just give me maybe an hour to look around, and then I swear for the rest of the week we'll do nothing but fun stuff."

"Take all the time you need. And, when you're done, how about we grab some lunch? My treat. I'll give you my Christmas present then."

"You didn't have to get me anything."

"I can't let you bring me all the way to Europe without getting you a gift. Don't worry, it didn't cost much, but you'll love it." She turned and headed for the door. "Come on. The sooner we get you to that hill, the sooner I can get some food. I'm starving."

The siege hill had changed drastically in two thousand years. Most of the trees had been cleared for farmland, and the rocks had been carted away. On the slope leading to the beach, houses now stood, with a dirt road cutting between them. No giant statues. No triumphant columns. Not even a pile of stones. For about half an hour I wandered over the hillside, flipping over rocks, examining the few remaining tree trunks, and padding through the wet grass, looking everywhere for even the smallest sign that Atto had once been here.

"Dan," Sam finally said, "there's nothing here."

I raised my head skyward and sighed. "You're right," I replied glumly. "I knew it was dumb to expect anything, but I still kind of hoped ..."

"Why does it matter so much to you?"

I kicked half-heartedly at the dirt and looked out over the channel. Covered with whitecaps, the waves looked black and cold in the winter wind. "You're probably going to think this is stupid, but I was just hoping for some sort of sign that what we're doing might actually succeed. If Atto managed to leave something behind, it would prove to me that we have a chance of doing the impossible. Victor is smarter than us, has tons of people helping him, and has almost unlimited funds. Not to mention that his plan has been in place for years, and we still don't have a clue of what his plan actually is, or how to stop him. That amounts to one heaping load of impossible, if you ask me." I tossed a pebble down the hillside and watched it disappear into the grass. "Everyone who isn't allied with Victor has either been killed or given up. We barely even know what we're doing. What chance do we have?"

"I try not to think of our chances."

Now for my other reason behind bringing Sam to Wales. I took a deep breath to psych myself up. "I ... I wanted to ask you something really important."

Her back stiffened and she took a step backward. "I'm just going to warn you right now that if I even begin to see you drop down on one knee or pull out a ring, I *will* slug you."

"No. Not that. Something bigger."

That stopped her in her tracks. Her mouth hung half open and she looked at me quizzically.

An awkward silence hung between us. I had rehearsed this speech so many times at home, but now, when it really mattered, I couldn't remember any of it. "Victor scares the hell out of me," I began, struggling for words. "Every night since I got home, I wake up in cold sweats, worried that he and his men are inside my house. And my dad must have been scared, too, because he didn't want me to fight them. He took out a huge insurance policy on himself so I could have loads of cash and run as far away as possible. So here I am, with two million dollars in my bank account, trying to figure out what to do."

"Are you quitting?" Sam asked, her eyes wide. "You can't!"

I held up my hand. "I'm not finished," I said, the words coming out easier now. "Like I said, Victor scares the hell out of me—but I also hate him. He ruined my life, and he wants to end the lives of billions of others. So I figure I have two options. I can either do what my dad wanted, and find a nice remote island to live on, free from the threat of Victor, or I can spend the money figuring out a way to stop Victor. I've given this a lot of thought, and I think we need to do more than just time jumps. We're not getting information quick enough."

"I'm guessing you already have a plan?"

"I do. We need to start tracking down other jumpers in our own time. People who still have fight left in them and want to take Victor down. There have to be more people out there than just us two. And maybe they can help us discover ways to beat him."

One of Sam's eyebrows rose. "So what's your question?"

"I can't do this without you, Sam. We've been through too much together. So I'm giving you the option. Do you think it's time to throw in the towel? Should we just find some nice island where we can get away from Victor and you can get away from your mom and creepy stepdad? Or do we keep fighting even though our chances are next to impossible, and we'll probably both end up getting killed? I know it's kind of a heavy question," I added. "You don't need to answer now. Just—"

"I'm fighting," Sam broke in without hesitation.

"Are you sure?"

"Positive. I've had this kind of doubt before, and there were even times when I actually quit—sometimes for days, sometimes for weeks. But it's impossible to lead a normal life when I'm constantly reminded that my brother and dad both died fighting Victor." Sam put a gloved hand on my chest. "And you say you're scared? I've been living in fear for almost two years now, worried that I'm next on his hit list. The funny thing is you get used to fear. But you'll never get used to letting Victor win. So the island thing sounds awesome, but I'd rather die fighting for something I believe in than live knowing I gave up."

I'd kind of known she was going to choose fighting; I'd never seen her back down from anything. And I realized that, deep down, I wanted to keep fighting also. I stepped back and took her in. Standing there tall and determined, with the ends of her red hair poking out from underneath her hood and whipping across her face, she had never looked more beautiful. "You know, part of me was really hoping you'd choose the island option," I joked. "I'd love to see what you look like in a bikini."

"Keep dreaming. Wales in the dead of winter was your bright idea, so you're getting all parka, all the time." She rested her hand on my arm. "Well? Did you find the answers you were looking for?"

"I did. So why don't we grab lunch, and then we can start hitting the sights?"

Sam brushed the stray hair from her eyes with her fingers. "Sounds good. And I saw the perfect place when we drove in." She pointed to a cluster of buildings in the distance.

I followed her along the road, passing gray stone houses and shops. None of them looked familiar. "Are you sure we actually came this way?"

"Trust me," Sam said, an enigmatic smile on her face. She stopped in front of a small pub with a gold-lettered sign: *The Angry Celt*.

I laughed. "Not a bad name. Though the Drunken Celt might make more sense."

She pulled open the front door, revealing a dimly lit room with a large bar at the rear, a few booths along the walls, and a scattering of tables in the middle. Age and history clung to the place like a cozy blanket. Old pictures, swords, and maps hung all around the walls, and thousands of feet over the ages had worn a depression in the wood floorboards next to the doorway. Only a few locals were in the pub, and they all looked up as Sam and I entered.

"*Prynhawn da,*" the barman greeted us from behind the bar.

My jump rod was currently stored in a safety deposit box at my bank, so I had no clue what he was saying.

"Good afternoon." He switched from Welsh to English. "Grab any seat that pleases you."

We took a seat by the window, sitting across from each other in a wood-paneled booth.

"Now this is more like it," I said as I flipped through the menu.

Sam tossed her coat onto the bench next to her. "I still have to give you my Christmas present."

"You being here with me is enough."

Her eyes sparkled with excitement. "Trust me. You're really going to like this." She turned and waved to the barman.

He shambled over, his large belly covered by a thick wool sweater. He wiped his hands on a rag tucked into one side of his belt. "Welcome to the Angry Celt. What can I get you fine people?"

"Are you the owner?" Sam asked.

"Glyndwr Rees at your service," he said, bobbing his head.

"Do you know how this place got its name?"

"But of course! This pub has been in my family for over three hundred years," the barman replied, a note of pride in his voice. "And for even longer than that we have owned land in this area. The name comes from a giant hill carving that used to be on one of my family's fields."

I sat up straighter in my seat. "A hill carving?"

"Aye. The primitive inhabitants used to carve pictures into the hills. Massive things, hundreds of feet long. The one on my family's fields looked like an angry Celt, so that's where the pub got its name."

The hair on the back of my neck stood up. Could Atto have made the hill carving? Did he really survive? "Is it still around?" I asked, my voice cracking with excitement.

The barman shook his head sadly. "No, it's long gone. People on this island have always tried to honor their Celtic past. But that was one right monstrosity of a carving, and situated on good farmland too. So a few hundred years back one of my ancestors decided that feeding the present was more important than honoring the past, and he plowed it under."

My shoulders slumped as the excitement fizzled out of me. "Where was it?" I asked.

"Just to the south of the village, stretching from the little hill all the way down to the beach."

Right by my siege hill. "I wish I could have seen it," I muttered.

"But you can. Whoever decided to plow it under was at least smart enough to draw a picture of what it looked like." He glanced toward the ceiling. "Oh ... if only that carving was still on my land—just *think* of all the tourists!" He waved his hands dismissively. "Pay no mind to me; just an old man ruing what's not to be. Now, where was I? Ah yes!

The original sketch is fragile with age, and I don't bring it out anymore. But I've traced the design so many times, I can remember every detail." He pulled out a napkin and a pen and began drawing, the only sound being his pen moving across the wooden tabletop. "You can see that the figure is naked, and clearly male. And, no, that isn't a slip of the pen; the original drawing really did have the man's *equipment* that large. My ancestors should have called this place the Boastful Celt." The barman sketched a bit more, then pulled his pen away. "Not sure why they left the right arm off," he said as he slid the napkin across the table. "But that's it: the Angry Celt of Anglesey."

His drawing was barely more than an outline—something simple enough to be carved into the soil. It showed a naked left-handed warrior raising a sword in triumph over his head, while his foot rested on a stack of ovals that could only be heads or skulls. His right arm ended just above his elbow.

Atto!

I knew I had the world's goofiest grin on my face, but I didn't care. Somehow that crazy drunken braggart had actually survived his attack on the Roman fort. How long had it taken him to dig out that hill carving? What had happened to Senna, Vata, and Cario? So many questions—but all I could do was look at the napkin and chuckle.

"Would you care to order now?" the barman asked, interrupting my musing.

"I'll have fish and chips and a tea," Sam said.

"I'll have the same," I muttered, too stunned to even contemplate food.

The barman left, leaving us alone in our booth. I held the napkin in my hand, inspecting every line, every poorly drawn detail, and imagined it carved into the hillside. "How did you know?" I asked Sam.

"Like I said, Dan, you're as mysterious as a glass of water. As soon as I saw we were going to Manchester, I knew what you had in mind.

So I typed 'Celt monument Anglesey' into a search engine and eventually ended up on this pub's website. I had a feeling this place had something to do with Atto." She tapped the picture. "Now I'm positive."

"I can't believe he actually survived ..." How had he done it? The Romans numbered in the hundreds, while he just had a group of ten men with him. I shook my head. Through dumb luck and sheer stubbornness, Atto had done the impossible.

"You said you were looking for some sort of sign that what we're doing isn't impossible. Is that good enough?" Sam teased. "Or do you need more two-thousand-year-old messages?"

"Nope, that'll do," I chuckled. "If one-armed, drunken Atto can take on the Romans and win, we sure as hell have a chance of taking on Victor."

This was turning into the best vacation ever. I was here with Sam, alone for a week, without having to save history or run from people trying to kill me. And for the first time in a long time, I felt hope. It would take a lot of work, a lot of luck, and a lot of jumping through time, but somehow, we might figure out a way to stop Victor.

"Are you two kin?" the barman asked as he dropped off our drinks at the table.

"Kin?" Sam asked.

"Aye, kin. You know, brother-sister, uncle-niece, father-daughter?"

Sam shook her head. "No. Just friends."

"Then are you trying to bring bad luck to my pub?"

The look of confusion on Sam's face was priceless. I'd have laughed if I wasn't feeling so confused as well.

"Are we doing something wrong?" Sam asked.

The barman tapped the light fixture suspended above our booth. Nestling in between its arms was a sprig of greenery with white berries. "We take our Celtic past seriously here. And you two have picked the only booth with some mistletoe left from Christmas. As you may know, mistletoe was one of the plants sacred to the druids. So you two better have a kiss, or you'll risk bringing the wrath of the druids down on my establishment. And we wouldn't want that now, would we?"

"But kissing under the mistletoe has nothing to do with Celts!" Sam protested. "It was invented much later."

"I don't know, Sam," I said, trying to sound serious. "Mistletoe was very important to the druids. You should probably kiss me just to be on the safe side." I pointed to the mistletoe. "Or do you need any more two-thousand-year-old messages?"

Sam smiled and shook her head—she knew she was beat. With an exaggerated flourish, she slid out of her side of the booth and into mine, then leaned into me so that our lips met. I expected her to cheap out and give me a quick peck. But her kiss lingered, making every hair on my arms stand on end.

She pulled back, breaking off the kiss. Slowly she exhaled, her face flushed. Turning to the barman, she tossed back her hair. "That good enough to save your pub?" she asked.

"Aye. Probably for the next few years." He grinned and gave me a thumbs-up, then turned and left us alone in our booth.

"I don't know which present I liked more," I said, "Atto's picture or the kiss. Maybe you should give me that second one again, just so I can compare them better."

"Nice try, but that's not happening," Sam replied, but without her usual conviction. She didn't return to her side of the booth either.

I sat back in my seat, a warm feeling of satisfaction spreading through me. Another item had just been added to my list of impossibilities that now seemed slightly less impossible.

I looked out the window, with the coast of the Welsh mainland just visible through the gaps between the buildings and the trees. Somewhere out there, Atto had lived. He had fought the Romans, won, and hopefully spent the rest of his life in peace with his family.

I raised my cup in salute.

Here's to you Atto, my friend. And to doing the impossible.

HISTORICAL NOTES

The Romans originally attacked Britain under Julius Caesar in 55 and 54 BCE. The legions crossed the English Channel from modern-day France and fought a few small skirmishes against local tribes. The legions eventually pulled back from England and, over the next ninety years, left the Celts alone. A few invasions were planned during this period, but more important matters in the empire always delayed such invasions. Finally, in 43 CE, Emperor Claudius sent four legions to invade England. This time, the Romans planned to stay.

Over the next seventeen years, the Romans expanded their presence throughout England, bringing more and more Celtic tribes under their control. Some tribes willingly joined them, seeing the advantages of the civilizing effect that Rome brought, while other tribes strongly resisted Roman imperialism.

The Roman invasion of Anglesey occurred in 60 or 61 CE; the exact date is not known because of a lack of clarity in the original texts. Anglesey (known as Mona by the Romans) is a large island off the coast of modern Wales. In Celtic times, the island was home to the druids, as well as to large copper deposits—both very attractive targets to the Romans. The druids were the wise men and women of Celtic society. They preserved Celtic history, acted as judges, and provided guidance to the Celtic people. They were also strong opponents of Roman rule, wisely understanding that Celtic culture and autonomy wouldn't survive Roman domination. By wiping out the druids, the Romans hoped to destroy any potential leaders of a Celtic rebellion.

Gaius Suetonius Paulinus, the governor of Britain at the time, and a man much hated by the Celts in Britain, led the invasion, bringing with him multiple legions as well as Batavian auxiliary troops. When the Romans attacked, the island would have been full of Celtic refugees who had fled there to avoid Roman rule. But despite their advantage in numbers, the Celts were no match for the Romans. When it came to fighting, the biggest drawback for the Celts was that they could not fight effectively as a group. Individually they were fantastically brave, but this bravery did them little good against the Romans, who were well armored and fought as a unit, easily fending off any brave individual attacks. Despite their resistance, thousands of Celts were killed and a large number sold into slavery.

Paulinus, however, could not complete the initial conquest of Anglesey. The Celtic queen Boudicca, ruler of a tribe called the Iceni, saw that the Roman legions were occupied elsewhere and began an uprising against Roman rule. This forced Paulinus to rush his legions back to the east of England where, after many large battles, they eventually crushed Boudicca's rebellion.

The island of Anglesey was fully conquered in 77 CE, after the Romans came and wiped out the last pockets of Celtic existence on the island. Over the next three hundred years of Roman occupation, there were some further rebellions by the Celts against Roman rule, but for the most part the Celts had become "Romanized"—their culture and traditions absorbed into the Roman way of life.

There are no accurate numbers of how many Celts died at the

hands of Roman aggression, as the large Celtic population centers in Spain, France, along the Danube, and in Britain were conquered by the Romans during a gradual war of expansion that lasted hundreds of years. When Julius Caesar conquered the Celts (who were also known as Gauls) in what is now France, he is believed to have killed over five million people and led countless more off into slavery.

The only recorded history of the attack on Anglesey occurs in the *Annals* written by the Roman senator and historian Tacitus. He was born about a decade before the attack itself and was the son-in-law of Agricola, a later governor of Britain, so it isn't unreasonable to assume that, later in life when he was writing his history, he would have been able to get firsthand accounts of the battle from Roman soldiers who had actually been there.

There are no known Celtic records of either this or any of their other countless battles with the Romans. The Celts were primarily an oral people, meaning they passed their histories and laws down through memorization and the spoken word. Anything they might have written down has long been destroyed, so we can only guess what happened among the Celts leading up to the battle.

Of the characters mentioned in this book, only Boudicca, the fiery Celtic queen and Gaius Suetonius Paulinus, the Roman governor of Britain, are real. The Celtic names used in the book are actual Celtic names but, even then, they are the names recorded through history by the Romans, so the actual Celtic versions might be slightly different.

For my research on the battle of Anglesey and the Celtic people, I am heavily indebted to many modern books on the Celts and the druids, as well as various online resources such as archaeological papers, Celtic gravestone registries, and Celtic-language sites. Without these it would have been impossible to recreate the feel of a Celtic village, the festivity at a Celtic funeral, or to bring to life the wonderful and lively history of the Celts themselves.

Regarding landscape features mentioned in this book, there never was a huge figure of a man carved into an Anglesey hillside. However, that sort of hill carving is fairly common throughout England, so I didn't think it impossible for Atto to have produced one. The various Welsh names of the different archaeological sites on Anglesey are real—as is the mention of a scuba diver finding a Roman anchor in the Menai Strait.

On a final note, when compared to ancient peoples such as the Romans and the Greeks, very little is known about the Celts. They used to be one of the widest-spread people in Europe, living all the way from Ireland to Turkey. But Roman expansion gradually crushed them as a separate people, and they fell under Roman rule. What we do know of the Celts shows them to have been an advanced society, with complex artwork, sophisticated knowledge of astronomy, and a legal system that treated women as equals of men. Unfortunately, their individuality and free outlook is what doomed them, because they could not present a consistent united front to deal with the war machine of the Romans.

ACKNOWLEDGMENTS

This book could never have been written without the countless people who helped me move it from scattered thoughts to chapters to manuscript, and finally to finished book. There are not enough pages to allow me to mention them all here, but I would like to specifically call out a few.

First and foremost, I would like to thank my wife, Pam. She's always there for me to bounce ideas off, butt heads over word choices or terms, or point out ways to make the text better. And although she likes to think of herself as Sam, she was definitely the inspiration for Senna.

Next I'd like to thank my children, Leah, Arawn, and Calvin. I wouldn't have written the first two books of this series if it hadn't been for them. After all the great fictional stories they've read from many great authors, I wanted to show them that real history is just as incredible. And they've been the constant inspiration for me to write more.

This book definitely wouldn't be possible without all the previous and current members of my critique group, particularly Cryssa Bazos, Tom Taylor, and Gwen Tuinman. I don't know how many times a scene was tweaked or the story expanded because of their feedback. Not to mention that they continually push me to make my writing stronger.

Special mention has to go out to my two amazing editors, Peter Lavery and Maya Myers. They took my rough, uncut stone of a manuscript and then cut and polished it into the shining work it is now. Maya especially helped shape the text through her constant suggestions, questions, and feedback.

Mark and Megan at Imbrifex Books deserve immense thanks for all their help in taking the book from finished manuscript to published book. Imbrifex has been an incredible publisher to work with. They have listened to my concerns, solicited my feedback, and kept me in the loop for every step of the journey. There's been a lot of hard work along the way, but the end result is worth it.

Finally, I would like to thank all the readers who have been following Dan and Sam on their time travel adventures. I hope you'll join them on their next jump in time.

ABOUT THE AUTHOR

Ever since his mother told him he was descended from Vikings, Andrew Varga has had a fascination for history. He's read hundreds of history books, watched countless historical movies, and earned a BA from the University of Toronto with a specialist in history and a major in English.

Andrew has traveled extensively across Europe, where he toured some of the most famous castles, museums, and historical sites that Europe has to offer. During his travels he accumulated a collection of swords, shields, and other medieval weapons that now adorn his personal library. He is skilled in fencing and Kendo—the Japanese art of sword fighting. He has also used both longbows and crossbows, built a miniature working trebuchet, knit his own shirt of chain mail, and earned a black belt in karate.

Andrew currently lives in the greater Toronto area with his wife Pam, their three children, and their mini-zoo of two dogs, two cats, a turtle, and some fish. It was his children's love of reading, particularly historical and fantasy stories, that inspired Andrew to write this series. In his spare time, when he isn't writing or editing, Andrew reads history books, jams on guitar, or plays beach volleyball.

Connect with the author online:

🌐 andrewvargaauthor.com

📘 @AndrewVargaAuthor

📷 @ andrewvargaauthor